Leftover Soldiers

Life on the American Frontier

by

Bert Entwistle

blackmulepress.com

Other Books by Bert Entwistle

The Drift

Uranium Drive-In

The Black Rose Banker

The Taylor Legacy

New Mexico

Murder in the Dell

For Nancy, Jeremy and Chad.

Published in the United States by Black Mule Press
Colorado Springs, Colorado

www.blackmulepress.com

Leftover Soldiers
Copyright © 2019 Bert Entwistle

First Edition, January 2019

Library of Congress Number: 2019900281

ISBN: 978-0-9896761-8-2

Price: $16.00

Rear cover photo: courtesy of Don Kallaus

Front cover photo: Library of Congress

<u>Maps</u>

Texas panhandle buffalo hunt

Texas to Cheyenne cattle drive

Winter 1865-1866 buffalo Hunt

1867 Longhorn Drive

Cheyenne

Missouri

IOWA

Des Moines

Omaha

COLORADO

Arkansas Crossing Kansas City

KANSAS

St.

MISSO

Arkansas R.

Wilsons

PUBLIC LAND

Adobe Walls

INDIAN TER.

ARKA

Little Rock

Santa Fé

XICO TER.

Red R.

Del's Crossing

TEXAS

LO

San Antonio

Rio Grande

Mexico

Gulf of Mexico

Brownsville

Chapter 1

New Mexico Territory, November 1864

"First time you ever seen someone that lost their hair to a Comanche . . .?"

"No, I seen it twice before — just never a female."

The sergeant mounted up and looked down at the dead woman. "That's how you knows it was a Comanche, they don't care who they're killin', long as they get the hair for their lodge."

"Sergeant, you saying they did this just for a trophy?"

"Mostly horses and hair is all, 'cept maybe if they find sumpthin' good to eat. Now and again they'll take a woman though — mount up corporal."

"Sergeant, are we gonna bury these folks first?"

He shook his head. "Later — we got us some murderin' shit-devils to kill first."

For the next hour, the cavalry patrol followed the tracks of the Indian ponies. After the first mile, it was clear the Indians were careless about leaving a trail as they appeared to slow down to a walk.

Nearing a small noisy stream, the sergeant's horse curled up his nose at the faint smell of smoke. He signaled them to stop and dismount. Within seconds the troopers could smell it too. Tying off to the chaparral, they began to work their way through the scrub toward the source. Gathering the men in close he whispered to them, "as soon as we see 'em, open fire, and keep on shootin' 'till they're all dead for sure, then shoot 'em again — understand?"

When they were close enough, he gestured to the men where he wanted them to go. They all nodded their heads and made one last check of their rifles and revolvers.

Approaching the creek, they could hear the Indians talking and laughing. One held the bloody scalps of the two travelers over his head while singing and dancing in circles. Two others tended to something cooking over a small fire.

Carefully picking their way through the brush until they were in easy range, the sergeant stepped into the clearing and screamed at the top of his lungs: *"Hey you black-assed shit-devils — here's a present from the U. S. Army!"*

All six troopers opened fire at the same time. The Indian's bodies jerked and shook around like rag dolls spraying blood across the ground as round after round of .56 caliber slugs pierced their bodies with deadly accuracy. When the smoke cleared, each of them had been hit many times. The sergeant walked between the bloody corpses and shot each of them once more in the head with his revolver.

They wore little more than muddy moccasins, deerskin leggings, and a breechcloth with a belt and knife. Their long, greasy hair was pulled back in two long braids wrapped with rawhide. Red and black paint with white streaks covered much of their faces in strange patterns. The big sergeant bent down and ripped the earrings out of their ears and put them in his bags. "Nowadays, a lot of them are silver — it's probably enough to get some civilian to buy me a drink or two, that and a good story. Corporal, their hair is yours fer the takin' if you want it." said the sergeant, spitting a long stream of tobacco juice on the closest body.

The young soldier was still shaking from what just happened, nearly sick at the sight.

"Get that away from me — I don't want no stinking hair!"

"Well shit, least take their scalp locks, they'd make a mighty fine trophy for your wall."

"I ain't got no wall, and I don't want no filthy scalps."

The rest of the troopers laughed out loud. "He's just yankin' on yer chain son," said one of the older men. "He don't really want you to scalp them — he likes to do that himself."

Looking over the carnage, the sergeant shook his head. "Ain't nothin' much of value here, their rifles are just old junk muskets. Break 'em up and pitch 'em in the creek, do the same with the bows and arrows. Keep any powder and lead you find and take whatever else you want." Cutting the scalp locks from the three dead Indians, he put them with the earrings. "Corporal, grab one of those scalpin' knives for yourself, a man can't have too many knives out in this country. And put out that fire, no need sendin' a signal to the rest of them murdering bastards — then shoot their ponies."

"Sergeant? You want me to kill their horses?"

"That's what I said, one shot between the eyes."

"Can't the Army use them?"

"These are wild-ass Comanche horses. It ain't worth bringing 'em back to retrain 'em for Army use, and we can't leave 'em here for the rest of those savages to use again."

"Yessir."

The ponies, painted up much like the Indians themselves, were already tied up, and he followed orders, shooting each of them with his revolver.

Picking up the scalps of the two murdered settlers, the sergeant scraped out a shallow hole under a mesquite tree and buried them. Removing his hat, he said a short prayer. Noticing the corporal watching, he put on his hat and walked to his horse. "Don't want any of those murderin' sons-a-bitches to find those good folks hair. Now let's get goin', we got some more buryin' to do."

The scene of the murders was the worst thing the young corporal had ever seen. The bodies had been stripped, mutilated and dismembered. Everything within ten feet of the bodies was covered in blood. The wagon had been burned as well as their bodies. When they rolled the woman onto her back, they saw even worse mutilation. The corporal bolted for the bushes, getting sick before he reached them. When they finished burying the couple, the sergeant repeated the same short prayer he recited earlier. When they finished, he gathered up a few small personal items to bring back to Fort Bascomb to help identify the victims.

"Sergeant, what makes them do such terrible things?"

"They do it 'cause they ain't nothing but filthy, murderin' savages. This here ain't nothin' at all. The things I seen 'em do ain't to be believed. You should see what they do to families that travel with little ones . . ."

"I don't think I want to see that."

"When I joined up, all the old timers said you don't never want to get caught by a Comanche with an empty gun. You always have to keep the last bullet for yourself, 'cause it was better to die that way than to be tortured to death by one of 'em. Take it to heart corporal. It's damn good advice. It's the war that's causin' most of these Comanche raids," said the sergeant, as they rode back to the post.

"How's that sergeant?"

"Most of the real army is off fightin' the rebs. They call us the Western Army. That means we're the ones stuck out here in this worthless chunk of desert spending all our time chasin' down these murderin' savages. Most of the people that were here before the war are long gone — either killed by the Indians or they left on their own outta fear. As long as the rebs keep fightin', there ain't never gonna be enough of us out here to get 'em all and the Indians damn sure know that."

Chapter 2

A thin, hawkish looking Union General named Theodore Barrett sat in his office brushing the dust from his hat. At twenty-five years old, he had just recently been promoted to brevet general and ordered to Texas from Louisiana. It was already unbearably hot and sticky at Fort Brazos Santiago, the army headquarters at the southern tip of Texas. Built on a narrow barrier island just above the mouth of the Rio Grande, it stood alone without any civilian structures of any kind. Union troops were garrisoned there to keep watch at the mouth of the river for Confederate boat traffic.

The island itself was little more than a large sandbar protecting the mainland. No trees or shrubs grew anywhere on the island to provide shade, nor was there a reliable source of fresh water. The only native population on the island was the never-ending supply of sand fleas, ticks, and seabirds.

The new general had been in charge of the fort for nearly a year, commanding the 34th Indiana Volunteers, a battle-hardened regiment, and the 62nd United States Colored Troops. The majority of the colored regiment was made up of free-born men and freed slaves, and few had any real combat experience. Barrett himself had seen little action before he was promoted to general and reassigned to Brazos. A few minor skirmishes with the Indians were all he could claim in his brief military career.

Troops on both sides had already heard rumors about General Lee surrendering his army and were waiting for the formal orders to make it to Texas. They also knew the soldiers back east were already on their way home. The two Texas armies, separated by no more than a few hundred yards in some places, had been keeping an informal truce for nearly two months, just waiting for the day they could go home.

However, to Barrett, the idea of the war ending without achieving personal glory for himself was unacceptable. If he were to get the accolades he craved, he knew it had to be now. A regiment full of hardened veterans like the Indiana regiment would be exactly what most commanders would hope for, but their very presence at Brazos Santiago served only to remind him of his inexperience. He much preferred the colored troops. Despite their inexperience, to his way of thinking, his lack of leadership skills wouldn't be as obvious.

For reasons he could only justify to himself, the young general chose not to honor the cease-fire situation. Disobeying direct orders from his superiors, he decided to attack the Confederates camped along the Rio Grande. His plan was to retake Fort Brown and the town of Brownsville before the formal order of ceasefire reached him at Fort Brazos.

Tom Lee Daggart was 21 years old and in his third year with the U.S. Cavalry. At nearly six feet, he'd always been lean from the constant, backbreaking work on the farm. His time in the Army had filled him out well, packing twenty pounds of muscle onto his once thin frame. He had developed into a fine horseman and a fearless Indian fighter.

Like always, powder-fine trail dust had found its way into everything, and the recent storm had turned the dust to mud. Inside the tent by the light of a pair of candle lamps, Daggart cleaned his Colt, replacing the muddy caps with new ones and slid it back into the holster. When he finished cleaning his Spencer, he slid out the magazine one last time, checked it, and pushed it back in. Then he checked his extra one and tucked it into his waistband. Sharpening both his knives to a razor edge, he put them back in their sheaths. As he worked, his knee bounced nervously, and sweat drenched every inch of him.

"You okay corporal?" asked his sergeant, Delbert Beale, a thick giant of a man with coarse dark hair, close set black eyes, and a droopy, coal black mustache. Born to a Mexican father and a white mother, he looked just as mean and rough as the reputation that followed him wherever he went.

Daggart nodded. "Yessir Sergeant, I'm good. This is my first night battle is all."

"You'll do fine. Just keep your eyes peeled wide open and kill ever' gray-back, sons-a-bitch reb you can find, then shoot 'em again to be sure they're dead."

"Yessir, I'll do that," he said, putting his hat back on. "I'm ready to go."

They sat across the tent from each other, finishing the last of their meal. "Corporal, remember those three Comanches we killed near Fort Bascomb last year?"

"I remember."

"Well I'm here to tell ya', these reb bastards are worse than any Indian."

"How's that sergeant?"

"Those Indians killed for horses and food and hair. After killin' those settlers, they just wanted to get away so's they could celebrate and dance. These rebs though, they're killin' for a cause. The idea of givin' up their slaves and bendin' over for the North makes 'em all plumb crazy. A Comanche is smart. If he sees the odds are again' him, he'll jus' ride away and wait for a better time. We all know the damn war is over, but the gray-backs down here don't really got nowhere to go — so when we stir 'em up, they'll just' keep on fightin' like they can still win it."

Daggart nodded. "Sergeant, you know those Indian ponies I shot that day?"

Beale nodded.

"Darn sure be nice to have them right now, my feet hurt from all that marching."

The sergeant cracked a smile at the thought, showing a mouthful of crooked and missing teeth. "Mine hurt too. I signed up fer the cavalry, not the goddamn dust-eatin' infantry."

"I guess the Army must have run out of horses."

"Nah, that's bullshit. They have plenty for the officers. If you ask me, all the generals and colonels decided the war was over anyways and took 'em home for themselves. Now they call us the dismounted cavalry."

"Maybe we can get us a couple of reb horses," said Daggart, "they ain't gonna need them anyway."

"Good idea. As soon as we finish killin' all of 'em, we'll have our choice."

Until now, all the action Daggart had seen was out in the desert chasing down Indians in the daylight. "Shoot, I ain't never even seen a reb before."

"I think we're gonna see plenty of 'em pretty soon. You rather be back on the farm?"

Tom Lee shook his head. "I'll never go back to the farm." His father had moved the small family from Kansas to Texas looking for work when he was just a young boy. For twelve years they worked the flat, rocky ground together planting cotton and doing everything they could to try and scrape out a living. After several years on the farm, his mother died of smallpox. Daggart knew that the years of drought, dust, and loneliness had killed her spirit long before the pox took her body. When he buried his father three years ago, he decided it was time to move on. Stopping for a moment at their graves, he said his goodbyes, turned and rode away, never looking back. He joined the army at Fort Union in the New Mexico Territory, to get away from the hardscrabble life of a farmer and was assigned to the 2nd cavalry unit.

Army life on the Western desert wasn't easy, but he had enough to eat, good horses to ride and a job to do every day. For now, that suited him just fine. He was issued a new .56 caliber Spencer carbine capable of shooting seven times without reloading, and a hundred rounds of ammunition. They were also issued a cavalry saber, but he never really cared much for it. To him, carrying it around was more trouble than it was worth. "It just flops around and gets in the way whenever I walk or ride," he told the sergeant one day. "I'd just like to lose it on the trail somewhere."

"As long as you got those crossed swords pinned on your hat you best not let them catch you without it, you'll surely get writ up if they do," said Beale. "They'll probably charge you for it too."

The fifty troopers of the 2nd had recently been provided with 1860 Colt .44 caliber revolvers. Six shots could be fired in rapid succession. Tom Lee loved the smooth feel of the oiled wood grips, and the weight tugging at his belt made him feel a little better about tonight's raid.

The troops had set-up for the night against a thick line of chaparral brush along the river. The colored infantry, with another

250 men, was camped on the opposite side of the clearing. Lt. Colonel David Branson, nearly as inexperienced as the general, could be seen silhouetted in the lantern light of his command tent finalizing his plans to attack the Confederates.

May 13, 1865 – Palmito Ranch, Texas

It was nearly 2am when they got the order. Colonel Branson had decided to engage the Confederates on the White Ranch just outside Brownsville. Intelligence had identified about seventy Confederate soldiers at the ranch. The two armies had fought battles over Fort Brown and the small town that had grown up around it twice already. After a cold, miserable night, the recent thunderstorm had passed, and the soldiers formed up and began their march toward Brownsville. Small streams of moisture evaporated off the heavy wet uniforms as the day began to warm up.

"Goddamn it to hell," said Beale, peeling off his trousers and shaking them wildly. "I'd like to have ol' general what's his name here right now. I'd give him a little taste of what it's like to soldier out in the swamp and sleep with a bunch of chiggers chewin' on his nuts."

Tom Lee nodded, "Yeah, I got a few down there too, and a couple under my arms."

"Well be sure and complain to the general when you get back," said Beale, pulling his pants back on. "He can put it in the official report, that's as close to the action as he'll ever get."

The troops advanced through the early morning haze to the spot on the White Ranch that intelligence had identified as a rebel campsite. As soon as they got close, they charged in with sabers flashing only to find it abandoned. All the buildings and corrals were empty. With no enemy in sight, the colonel realized that the intelligence report was bad and the rebels had moved up the river to the Palmito Ranch. Taking this opportunity to rest the exhausted troops, he led them back into the chaparral near the river for the night. It had been a long, exhausting day, and the men needed to eat and rest before the sun came up.

Daggart and Beale lay on the ground with their heads on their packs. "Some kinda big screw-up tonight, warn't a goddammed reb in sight."

Daggart shrugged. "Maybe they all went back home."

"Not likely. Like I told ya, they ain't got nowhere else to be right now. They're out there, jus' waitin' fer a chance to put a ball in us."

The camp was awakened just before sunup by people yelling and shooting from the Mexican side of the river. They were attempting to warn the rebels. Branson and other soldiers ran through the camp, waking up everyone. "Everybody up — now — get moving !"

Leading the soldiers on a slow, steady march to the Confederate camp on the neighboring Palmito Ranch, Branson kept the column out of sight as much as possible and was able to move quietly through the wet chaparral. Just before they reached the ranch, they began to take fire. Rebel skirmishers were firing from every direction out of the tall grass. Several balls whizzed by Daggart's head, and two soldiers in front of him went down hard, one bleeding badly from a bullet in his belly. The Confederates proved to be tough and aggressive fighters. They kept up a withering fire, filling the tall grass with smoke making it difficult for the Union troops to spot them.

"Keep yer head down boy or one of those reb balls is gonna take it clean off." yelled Beale. Screaming like a madman, he pulled his sword, waved it wildly and charged straight into the enemy camp.

After nearly five hours of intense fighting, Branson's troops overwhelmed the Confederate camp and sent them in full retreat. The colored infantry plunged into the thick brush after them, keeping up the heavy fire. Following them to the river's edge, they kept firing as the rebels disappeared across the river and into the grass on the Mexican side.

When the shooting stopped around noon, the men tended to the wounded and took time to eat what they could from the captured rebel supplies. Most of the battle had been up close and personal. Revolvers and swords did as much damage as rifles, and the Union took several prisoners. After torching all the buildings and wagons on the ranch, Branson decided the momentum was on his side, and they would advance on Fort Brown.

When they had eaten their fill and taken everything they wanted, the remaining stockpile of supplies the Confederates had left behind were torched. It looked like a clear battle victory for Branson, and his troops and the excitement was obvious with the men.

"You seen how fast those reb bastards hightailed it into the bushes?" said Beale. "Hell — they's half way to Georgia by now!"

"Yessir sergeant, they was moving fast for sure," said Tom Lee, filling his pockets with Confederate biscuits.

Emboldened by the rush of his recent success, Branson decided to regroup and start marching immediately. The smoke from the Palmito Ranch fires could be seen for miles. Confederate Captain William Robinson and the men he commanded were enraged at the idea that the Union Army had broken the truce. After being run out of Palmito Ranch in a surprise attack, he quickly made a plan to retaliate. The Union Army would never make it to Brownsville as long as he was in charge. Spreading out his men, he moved them quietly through the thick brush until he got close enough to the Union troops to give the command to charge.

Branson and his troops were forming up to march to Fort Brown when the man standing next to Daggart collapsed. Writhing in pain, the soldier held his hand tight against his thigh trying to stop the bleeding. Another trooper dropped down as flat as possible and tied his scarf around the wound, slowing the flow long enough to help him into the long grass.

Screaming wildly, the Confederates charged straight into Branson's men slashing and firing their pistols as fast as they could cock them. Pulling his revolver, Tom Lee tried to pick out a reb soldier through the thick smoke, shooting blindly into the bushes. The Confederates had returned in a brutal, all-out counter attack and caught them by surprise. Emptying his Colt, Daggart stood staring into the melee swirling around him.

A large hand grabbed his arm and began dragging him away from the fight. "Come on soldier — it's time to go," said a raspy, unfamiliar voice, while the hand continued to pull him into the brush. Shocked back to the reality of the situation, he followed the colored sergeant into the brush as fast as his legs would carry him.

Branson's elation instantly turned to fear, and he ordered a full retreat. The Union troops now charged headfirst into the same thick chaparral the Confederates used when they were routed earlier in the day. The Confederates had gathered up more troops from different details and now fielded 200 men. Still under-manned, they managed to drive the Union troops all the way back to White's Ranch. Both sides settled in for the night, and both immediately sent riders for re-enforcements.

At Fort Brazos, Barrett, enraged by the new information and seeing his career glory slipping through his fingers, ordered 200 troops from the Indiana volunteers into the battle. He thought it impossible for the Union to lose to a bunch of half-starved misfits that called themselves an Army. When the troops reached the mainland, they endured a long wait for Colonel Barrett to arrive. When he finally arrived in his freshly brushed uniform and clean boots, they marched straight to White's Ranch, reaching Branson's camp at daylight.

Colonel John "Rip" Ford, commanding officer of the 2nd Texas Confederates, arrived at the site with another 200 soldiers to reinforce Robinson's brigade. Ford had been a professional soldier for nearly twenty-five years and was highly respected by all his men. Both Confederate leaders were highly trained and very experienced.

The Mexican town of Matamoros was largely controlled by France, and Ford borrowed six cannons from them in preparation for the fight. At daybreak, Barrett started moving west sending skirmishers and scouts in advance. Colonel Ford set up along a bend in the river, positioning his artillery against the main body of Northern troops. The cannons did their job well, raking the Union lines with grapeshot and shrapnel. The Confederate troops continued charging straight into Barrett's camp, and the Union soldiers continued to retreat. They fought off the last of the skirmishers for another day before they made it back to the fort. In the confusion of the retreat, more than a hundred men from the U.S. companies were left behind and captured by the Confederates.

Chapter 3

"Lay still corporal, you're just gonna make it hurt even more."

"I got a reb bullet in my butt — how can it hurt any more than that?" said Daggart.

"I told you, there ain't no bullet in your ass," said Beale, probing around with a large pair of tweezers.

"Something's been bleeding, it's all over my trousers — and it hurts!"

"Lay still, I almost got it — here's one of them," he said dropping it on the table.

"One of them? One of what?"

"You been bit by the devil boy — looks like more than once."

"Bit by the devil? What in heck you talking about?"

Beale held up a long stiff thorn, nearly three inches long with a needle-sharp point. "It's a thorn from a devil tree! Don't you know what a devil tree is?"

"Yes, I know what a devil tree is, we had them on the farm. My father cut them all down and burned them in the fireplace. But I don't know how I coulda got them in my butt."

Beale broke out in a loud burst of laughter. "Shit boy, you was standing in the middle of that clearing like a statue made of stone. If it hadn't been for Sergeant Parker jerkin' you outta there, you'd be dead for sure. You musta met up with a devil-tree when you started running."

Looking up, he saw a stout black man, wearing a thick beard streaked with gray. His was the shiniest bald head and the darkest skin he'd ever seen. "Sylvie Parker pleased to make your acquaintance corporal."

"Likewise Sergeant, I thank you for pulling me out of there."

"Any time soldier. Just call me Sylvie, everyone else does."

"I'm Tom Lee Daggart. They always call me Tom Lee."

"Keep still — there's still a little more of the devil in you that's gotta come out."

"Yessir Sergeant."

"Just as well call me by my name too, it's Del, short for Delbert," he said as he pulled out the next thorn. After the third one, he splashed some ointment he got from the quartermaster on the wound and a put on a makeshift bandage. "Okay soldier, you're ready to ride."

Tom Lee stood up and got dressed. "I thought there weren't no horses?"

"Gonna have extra ones pretty soon. The Rebs won't be needin' 'em."

"I ain't in no big hurry for them horses right at the moment," said Daggart, slipping on his trousers.

The official report of the Battle of Palmito Ranch listed 115 Union casualties including 1 killed, 9 wounded, and 105 captured. 21-year-old private John J. Williams, from the 34th Indiana Volunteers, was the dead Union soldier and would be listed as the last official death of the Civil War.

The Confederates recorded five wounded and none killed. The fight at Palmito Ranch was recorded as a Confederate Victory and the last official battle of the Civil War. Two weeks after the fight, on May 26, the surrender in Texas was made formal, and the victors of the Battle of Palmito Ranch surrendered their weapons to the losers.

The three Confederate soldiers captured by the Union had been held in a makeshift cell in the corner of the quartermaster's storeroom. They were allowed to move around as long as they didn't leave the confines of the fort. When the surrender was finally official, many of the troops had already left on their own. Some of the ones along the Rio Grande went to Mexico, and others melted back into the Texas countryside. Those that were prisoners of war were released and told they had to sign a loyalty pledge to the United States. This entitled them to draw rations and keep their horses if they had one.

Two of the Confederates, both cavalry prisoners, drew their rations and horses and left the fort immediately. The third, a short, thin, red-haired infantryman with scruffy matted whiskers named Boyd Stamps, stayed at the post.

He told several men that: "I ain't really got nowhere to go. Where I come from, everyone wanted the South to win — now what we got left? Nothing but dead soldiers and bad times."

Stamps had been slightly wounded in the ankle by a Union bullet in a previous battle and still had a slight limp. All he had was what he was wearing, worn-out boots, ragged gray jacket, and kepi hat. Extremely emaciated, a piece of rope held up his trousers, now big enough for a man half-again his size.

Several days after the surrender, Del and Tom Lee were sitting with Sylvie Parker at a makeshift table outside the barracks talking about what they would do after their time in the Army. "Won't be no problem getting out," said Sylvie, "they won't need such a large Army now."

"I heard we have some muster out money coming to us," said Tom Lee, "and whatever pay we got coming."

"So, you gonna get out for sure?" asked Sylvie.

Tom Lee nodded. "I don't see any future in the army. There's gotta be something better out there in the real world."

"Well," said Beale. "We're gonna have to get our outfit together first. I've been put in charge of inventorying all the horses and weapons that we've been collecting from the rebs. We got hundreds of rifles and sidearms, and a small mountain of tack. There's maybe three hundred horses in the big pen right now."

"Well damn Del, we could surely find us a couple of good mounts in there somewhere," said Parker, "even if they are reb horses."

Del nodded. "I'll bet you're right. Maybe even a good rifle and revolver too, what do you think Tom Lee?"

"I think I'm mighty tired of walking and I don't want to be in the dismounted cavalry anymore."

As they talked about their plans, Del saw Boyd Stamps walk by and called him over. "Hey reb, what are you gonna do now that ol' General Lee gave it up?"

He shrugged and looked at him. "Don't call me a reb. I wore a gray uniform because I was a conscript, not because I supported the cause."

Sylvie stared quietly at the ragged looking soldier with his hand resting on his Colt. "Were you a goddamn slave owner? I ain't got no use for any slave-owning reb stinking up this camp."

"Hell no! I just told you not to call me a reb, and I mean it. My two brothers and I farmed a small cotton operation for a rich old white guy west of Charlottesville. I can guarantee you, the only slaves on that farm were us. We worked our hearts out for that old man. Then one day a bunch of gray coat's rode into the field we were working, pointed their pistols at us and handed us a piece of paper. It said all three of us were going into the army for three years whether we liked it or not."

"Shit Boyd, that's some kinda crap there," said Del.

"It is for sure. A lot of soldiers in the Confederate Army were just conscripts like me and my brothers. Some were enlisted, and a few came from smaller farms that had slaves. I never met a rich slave owner or one of their sons carrying a rifle and marching in the ranks. The only ones I saw were sittin' on big fancy horses givin' us orders from behind the lines."

"You and your brothers never had anything to do with working slaves?" asked Sylvie, his hand still firmly on the pistol.

Boyd shrugged. "Pretty much everyone in the south had some kind of connection to slavery. But most of us had no reason to own slaves. The truth of it is that more people than you or I could ever count died in this miserable war, just so a bunch of fat, rich white men could keep their cheap labor and way of life."

"Where are your brothers now?" asked Tom Lee.

"One was killed at Gettysburg on the first day, and one went missing in the fight at the Wilderness."

"Ain't any other family you can be with?"

He shook his head. "All we had was each other."

"Boyd Stamps, good to meet you," said Sylvie, relaxing his grip on the pistol and pointing to a spot across from him. "Have a seat."

Stamps took his hand and shook it firmly. "Thank you sir, good to meet you too."

"No need to call anyone here sir, we're all free men. Ain't none of us here got anyone neither," said Sylvie. "We're just sittin' and talkin' about what we're gonna do now that the war is over."

"And what did you come up with?" asked Stamps. "Ya'll stayin' in the Army?"

"I ain't," said Del. "All I'd be doin' is chasin' a bunch of naked-ass Comanches across the desert, and I already got a belly full of that. Sylvie, what are you thinkin'?"

"Don't really know, but it's for sure if we stay in the army, it'll just be more of the same."

"One thing I know," said Stamps. "Unless you got someone or something waiting for you back east, I wouldn't consider heading back there. I think the next couple of years are gonna be hell for all those that supported old Jeff Davis."

"Tom Lee, what about you?" asked Del.

Daggart shrugged. "Well I ain't got nobody back east or nobody around here either, so I guess I don't really know."

"You said you were from Texas, how'd you end up wearing blue?" asked Sylvie.

"My father had a small farm near El Paso — it hardly grew enough to keep us fed. When he died, I could see that the gray-backs were fighting for a losing cause. So I left the farm and went to Fort Union in the New Mexico Territory and signed up. I've done nothing but chase Indians ever since."

After the Confederate soldiers had been processed and all of their arms stacked, they were told the terms of the surrender and given the loyalty pledge to sign. Most of the defeated Confederates had already started their long trip home.

Many of the Union soldiers found themselves at or past the end of their enlistment. Discharges were offered to those that qualified. Del and Sylvie were already over the limit, and Tom Lee was only weeks away. All three decided to take their muster papers and leave the Army. Sergeants Beale and Parker each received $54 in muster out pay and back wages, and Tom Lee received $32. From that amount, the Army took out for the clothes and boots they had been issued, the same clothes they had been wearing for months.

"Tom Lee, go ahead and pick out a horse you like from the big pen, when you're done, grab a saddle and bridle," said Del. "Boyd and Sylvie already have theirs."

"I can have any horse I want?"

"That's what I'm sayin', long as it's a reb horse. When you're done, put it in that long pen over on the west side of the camp."

"Yessir, I'll find me a good one." Climbing over the fence, he walked slowly through the groups of horses with a rope in his hand. Some of the horses were nearly as emaciated looking as the troops that just surrendered. Some had only two or three shoes, some didn't have any. Most were in sad condition, and more than a few needed to be put down. When he walked up to a tall bay gelding standing alone, it held perfectly still and watched him as he gently slipped the rope around his neck. After walking it around the pen a few times, he decided this was the one.

Del watched as he brought the horse over. "Looks like a pretty good mount, he could use a little fattening up though. Shoot, Tom Lee, he ain't all that old neither," said Del, looking him over closely. "Take him over to the wrangler and tell him I sent you. Then stop by the quartermaster and get you whatever saddle and bridle you want — just the reb stuff. I made a deal with him to re-set the shoes, fatten them up, and have them ready for us in a couple of weeks."

Once the horse was in the pen, he picked out his saddle and tack. Most of them were badly worn McClellan's, Grimsley's and dozens of broken and poorly repaired units. Finding a decent McClellan, he picked out the rest of the tack he needed. Beale led him and the other two men through a large field tent containing rows and rows of stacked rifles and piles of side arms. "Find yourself a good rifle first, there's plenty to pick from," said Beale. "They'll likely destroy or give away all the old muzzleloaders, but there's plenty of others. There's a good bunch of revolvers and belt holsters too. Plenty of swords too, if you want one."

"Look here, I found me a Spencer carbine!" said Sylvie, holding up his prize. "Musta come from a Union soldier somewhere."

Tom Lee also found a Spencer and held it up, "here's another one, but it's not a carbine, it's the long one."

"Shoots just as good," said Sylvie, "but it's a little heavy on the muzzle. You can't carry it on the horse all that well, I'd see if there's another carbine. Boyd, what are you finding?"

"I found a good-looking Colt and a Spencer. The stock's a little scarred up, but it's solid."

"That's good; the Spencers will handle anything you want to kill."

"Yep, I'm gonna be a buffalo hunter — I just now decided," said Stamps.

"Buffalo hunter?" laughed Sylvie. "Boy, you ever even seen a buffalo?"

"Nope — but I aim to pretty soon. What about you, what did you decide?"

"I don't know, ain't really give it much thought yet." After a few minutes, he looked at Boyd and shrugged. "You got room for another buffalo hunter? I reckon I could hit one of those big hairy bastards if I had too."

"Now ain't that somethin'," said Del. "A black, ex-slave, a farmer, a Union sergeant and a skinny little red-headed reb all ridin' together . . . I think I seen it all now."

"I told you not to call me a reb — don't do it again," said Stamps.

Beale laughed out loud, making Stamps even madder. "I ain't messing around here Del, don't call me a reb."

"Okay boy, what would you like me to call you from now on?"

"Boyd — my name is Boyd — is that some kind of problem for you?"

Del shook his head. "We're good re — I mean Boyd. How is it you know where to find all them buffalos you plan to kill?"

"Read it on this paper that was hanging on the quartermaster's wall," said Stamps, handing the crumpled poster to him.

Hunters Wanted

Sturdy young men for adventuresome work as buffalo runners. Must have own horse and saddle and pistol. Good pay for hunters, skinners, cooks, wranglers, teamsters and blacksmiths.

Report to Fort Dodge, Kansas by 30 September.

Del looked it over for a minute and handed it back. Read it for me. "It's probably some kinda nasty ol' dirty work; I don't think it's for me. Probably don't pay fer shit anyways."

"It says right here that it pays good," said Stamps, pointing to the poster. He looked at Beale's face while he was pointing. "Shit Del, can't you read?"

He shook his head. "Never did learn a lot of readin'. I can write my name though, that's good enough."

"Now that you know about the buffalo, you coming with us?" asked Stamps.

"Don't know yet. Tom Lee, you going buffalo huntin' too?"

"I think it's better than sittin' around here doin' nothing. The horses are ready, and we're gonna muster out pretty soon. I guess I'll go along 'till something else comes up."

Del looked it over for a minute and handed it back. Read it for me. "It's probably some kinda nasty ol' dirty work; I don't think it's for me. Probably don't pay fer shit anyways."

"It says right here that it pays good," said Stamps, pointing to the poster. He looked at Beale's face while he was pointing. "Shit Del, can't you read?"

He shook his head. "Never did learn a lot of readin'. I can write my name though, that's good enough."

"Now that you know about the buffalo, you coming with us?" asked Stamps.

"Don't know yet. Tom Lee, you going buffalo huntin' too?"

"I think it's better than sittin' around here doin' nothing. The horses are ready, and we're gonna muster out pretty soon. I guess I'll go along 'till something else comes up."

Del looked at the three men across from him, trying to decide if he wanted to throw his lot in with them. He knew that Texas had all these recently discharged Union veterans, and ex-Confederates that were facing the same thing they were. Right now, he figured maybe having any job would be a good idea.

"Fort Dodge is a long way up north, maybe seven or eight hundred miles," said Sylvie.

"You got someplace more important you gotta be?" asked Del.

"I guess not. Then we'll be going through San Antonio?"

"As good a way as any, you got somethin' to do there?"

"I do." Del looked at the three men across from him, trying to decide.

29

if he wanted to throw his lot in with them. He knew that Texas had all these recently discharged Union veterans, and ex-Confederates that were facing the same thing they were. Right now, he figured maybe having any job would be a good idea.

"Fort Dodge is a long way up north, maybe seven or eight hundred miles," said Sylvie.

"You got someplace more important you gotta be?" asked Del.

"I guess not. Then we'll be going through San Antonio?"

"As good a way as any, you got somethin' to do there?"

"I do."

"You gonna tell us what it is?" asked Del.

"You'll see when we get there."

The horses all had been re-set and looked to be in good shape. "How'd you get him to do all this work Del?" asked Tom Lee.

"One Spencer carbine, one Colt and two Confederate swords, it worked out for both of us. Boyd, I got somethin' for you too."

"What's that?"

Del tossed him a good coat, pants, and shirt he found at the quartermasters and a beat-up flop hat with a high crown. "Pitch that gray coat and hat in the fire; they're all wore out anyway."

Boyd didn't hesitate to toss his uniform coat, pants, and kepi in the fire, and put on the new clothes and hat. "Glad to see those go away, that's for sure."

Del dropped a pair of used cavalry boots next to him. "Hope these fit you, they're the only ones I could come up with."

"Thank you Del, I will pay you back for these."

Del shook his head. "No need. The U.S. Army was happy to help you out." That night the four men slept in an army tent for the last time.

Chapter 4

The future buffalo hunters packed up their horses just after sunrise and headed for San Antonio, 250 miles to the northwest. The long trip was mostly uneventful. Two brief encounters with the Comanches proved to be little more than an attempt to scare them with a lot of whooping and hollering and fast riding just out of rifle range.

The first three days they made good progress, with two short rainstorms to help cool them down. By the third day, there were no clouds anywhere in sight. The days became scorching hot without the slightest sign of a breeze. On some days, more time was spent searching for water for the horses than making progress to San Antonio. Many of the springs and water holes were dried up or had been fouled by hundreds of buffalo passing through.

Late in the afternoon, they came across a lone buffalo calf standing helplessly belly deep in the edge of a muddy wallow. Del killed her with a close-up shot to the head, and they made meat for the trip.

By the time they reached San Antonio, they had crossed paths with dozens of Confederates on horseback, but many more were on foot. When Del asked several of them where they were going, some said home, and others said nothing and kept walking. Confederate jackets and hats were scattered along the trail.

"Christ, Boyd, they all look to be near dead," said Sylvie. "They're never going to make it all the way back east."

"What else they got?" said Boyd. "The thought of home is the only thing that keeps them moving."

Sylvie shook his head. "They don't even know if they still have homes. All of this because the South wanted to keep their slaves."

Boyd shrugged. "Like I said before, a bunch of fat, rich white farmers didn't want their way of life and their big profits to change," said Boyd, as they rode by several ragged, hollow-eyed men sitting alongside the trail. "Sylvie, I need to thank you for your and Dell's help; otherwise I'd likely be one of these guys. Del is right you know, a black Yankee soldier riding with a white Confederate soldier is sure to raise a few eyebrows."

"You don't care nothing about any raised eyebrows do you Boyd?"

"Don't care nothing about 'em, Sylvie, nothing at all."

Reaching San Antonio, they tied up on the main square and looked for somewhere to get a meal. A strong smell of chilies led them into a tiny, rough looking cantina on an alley behind the main street, where they had tamales, beans, and tortillas. All but Sylvie had several pieces of dark bread smeared with a large helping of a strong-smelling, white cheese with black specks in it.

Sylvie had a second helping of everything but the cheese. Declaring himself full, he dropped a few coins on the table and walked outside.

Buying another dozen tortillas, Boyd wrapped them in paper and put them in his pocket. "That was some good chuck," said Boyd. "But I sure never tasted cheese like that before."

"It was good, but I wonder what the little black specks were?" said Tom Lee.

"Probably just pepper," said Boyd.

"It ain't pepper," said Sylvie, laughing out loud.

"Well just what is it if it ain't pepper?" asked Tom Lee.

"Moscas," said Sylvie, still laughing. "You been eatin' moscas. You know what a mosca is?"

"Something the Mexicans cook with?" asked Boyd.

"A mosca is a fly. You all been eating the flies that get stuck in the milk when they make it!"

"Awww . . . heck, that's just nasty," said Tom Lee.

Del just shrugged. "I guess I ate worse than that one time or another."

"Why didn't you say something before I ate it?" asked Tom Lee, draining his canteen.

"You never asked."

From the boardwalk in front of a dry-goods store, they watched the frenzied activity of the city all around them. San Antonio, already an old city, had grown to several thousand people. Since the surrender, hundreds of men were looking for work.

The main street was choked with the greatest assortment of people Tom Lee had ever seen. People of every color, shape, and size moved through the road as though they were all late for something important. U.S. Cavalry men rode through the streets, mixed in with Mexican vaqueros, many riding beautiful mounts dressed out in silver-trimmed tack like he'd never seen before.

Men on horses and mules threaded their way through the wagon traffic, and dozens of dogs barked as they ran through the legs of all of them. Giant work horses pulling heavily loaded freight wagons pushed through the congestion at the crack of the teamster's whip, hauling everything from lumber to coal. Swirling, billowing clouds of gritty road dirt engulfed everything. People on foot darted through all the chaos to places unknown.

Several brightly dressed women with colorful hats brushed by them. Mexicans with straw sombreros, groups of Chinese men with impossibly long pigtails and small, close-fitting caps mingled in front of the stores and saloons. Two men in Confederate uniforms could be seen leaning against a wall in a spirited argument with several union soldiers.

"There's sure a hell a lot of those Chinamen here, where do they all come from?" asked Del.

"If I was to guess, I'd say China," said Sylvie, with a straight face.

"Then they oughta put them all on a boat back to China," said Del.

"I gotta say Del, that would be one big boat for sure," said Tom Lee.

"Shit Del, I'll bet you don't even know where China is," said Boyd.

"I do so know where it's at."

Boyd looked surprised. "Then tell us, exactly where is it?"

"It's exactly where all these people outta be right now," said Del, now laughing at the conversation.

"Well, I guess you can't argue with that," said Sylvie.

"Holy crap, it looks like some kind of human dust storm," said Tom Lee. "What the heck could all these people be doin' here?"

"Same as us I'd guess," said Boyd, watching the flow of people coming and going. "Just trying to find their way."

"I think there's too many people here for me," said Tom Lee. "I want outta here."

Riding out of town, they went by the old Alamo mission. "This here is where David Crockett and Colonel Travis got their asses shot off by old Santy Anny," said Del, pointing at the old run-down mission.

"Don't look all that impressive," said Tom Lee. "I thought it was really big, like a fort or something." The men settled in for the night along the north bank of the San Antonio River. "Del, you got any of that ointment left? My backside is hurting something awful from so much saddle time."

Del reached into his bag and found the tin. "Here, you're gonna have to rub it on by yourself, I ain't about to touch your sorry ass no more," said Del, tossing it to him. "It may be that you need a better saddle, that old one looks to be in pretty bad shape."

"Maybe so, but that devil bite still hurts too much to be sure."

"You're gonna have to toughen up if you plan on being a buffalo runner boy," said Sylvie.

Buttoning up his trousers, he tossed the tin back to Del. "Why do they call it buffalo running? You gotta run to catch up with them or what exactly?"

"They say that the Indians used to ride into the herd and kill them with their arrows while they were running," said Del. "But I never seen them do it."

Sylvie shook his head. "No — it's because the Mexicans and the Indians used a spear to kill 'em from horseback."

"A spear? I ain't ever heard of anything like that before," said Tom Lee. "You ever see them do that Sylvie?"

"You calling me a liar boy?"

"No . . . I'm just saying I ain't never heard of anything like that before is all."

"I seen 'em do it lots of times down by the border, you got it boy?"

Tom Lee glanced at Del who was listening carefully. "Yessir Sylvie, if you saw it then it has to be so."

Sylvie laid back and pulled his hat down over his eyes. "Just don't never call me a liar . . ."

After talking over everything they'd seen in the last few days, they eventually drifted off. In the morning, Boyd made coffee and pulled out the tortillas and some jerky from his bag. The smell of strong, fresh coffee brought them all around quickly.

Sitting around the fire they waited for the coffee to cool off enough to drink. "Ya'll feel that?" asked Boyd.

"I don't feel nothin', what in hell you talkin' about?" said Del.

The ground started to vibrate even worse as they talked. "Yeah, I do feel something," said Sylvie.

Across the river, they saw an enormous, ghostlike, twisting swirl of dust rolling their way. "What the holy hell is that?" said Boyd.

Through the cloud, they began see the tips of horns and could hear cattle bawling and men hollering in Spanish as they went. When the herd reached the river's south bank, hundreds of cattle plunged into the water and began to drink. The herd strung out along the river, and the cloud momentarily engulfed the cattle then rolled across the river, blanketing all four men.

When it settled, they could see that the river was completely filled with rangy looking long horned cattle. A dozen Mexican vaqueros moved slowly around the herd waving their riatas and keeping them together.

"Damn Sylvie, those things sure got some horns on 'em," said Boyd. "You ever seen any of them this close up before?"

"Bunches of them, and I don't want to see them any closer than this, thank you."

Del stared at the spectacle for another minute. "I know what you mean. I seen lots of those snorty bastards, but not so many all together at one time though. When you're ridin' through the tall brush thinkin' about injuns or somethin' else, those nasty bastards will charge you. They're hell on horses with those big horns. I knew a fellow that was killed by one of them — a damn good soldier too."

"I killed one of 'em once, when we was real hungry," said Sylvie, "tasted like putrefied buffalo shit — couldn't even chew 'em they were so tough."

"How is it you know what putrefied buffalo shit tastes like Sylvie?" asked Boyd. "You been sampling a lot of shit lately?"

All four men burst out laughing at the same time, including Sylvie. "You can kiss my fat black ass boy. If I say it was tougher than putrefied buffalo shit — then you'd do damn well to believe it."

"Well I don't know for the life of me why anybody would want a whole herd of these wild ass critters," said Del, "but I do know that if we don't start killin' some buffalo pretty soon, I'll be broke soon enough."

"So, we all headed to Fort Dodge today?" asked Tom Lee.

"Not yet," said Sylvie. "I got me a little business in town first. Won't take but a few minutes, then we can get on the road."

"Exactly what is this mysterious business of yours anyway?" asked Del.

"You're gonna see soon enough, quick as we can get movin' here."

"Well we better get packed up and goin' then, I wanna get to killin' them buffalos."

Riding back into the busy street, they passed through all the activity and rode to the edge of town, stopping in front of a group of small, squat adobe houses. Sylvie dismounted and told the rest of them to wait. Taking a small package out of his bag, he walked up to the door of one of the houses, took off his hat and knocked. An elderly Mexican woman let him in and then closed the door behind him. A few minutes later he walked out hand in hand with a pretty, olive-skinned Mexican girl with large dark eyes, about fifteen or sixteen years old. Wearing her thick black hair pulled back in a braid, a long thin scar was obvious on the side of her chin.

The riders took off their hats and nodded at the young girl. "Hola, Señorita."

"I want you all to meet my beautiful daughter, Sancha." He walked up to the others with the girl at his side. "Sweetheart," said Sylvie in fluent Spanish, "these are my friends that I work with."

She looked at the men on the horses, and nodded her head slightly, "Hola, Señors."

"Ain't she the most beautiful child you ever seen?" said Sylvie.

"She's a pretty one for sure," said Boyd. "Sylvie, you said you didn't have no people, like the rest of us. Why don't you just stay and take care of her?"

"Her grandmother will take care of her just fine. Let's get to riding — there's buffalo to be killed."

Tom Lee, obviously taken with the girl, couldn't take his eyes off of her. "Sylvie, don't she have no mama?" he asked as they turned back toward town.

Sylvie didn't answer.

"She sure is pretty, how'd she get that scar on her chin?"

Del poked him on the shoulder. "Tom Lee, it's time to stop talkin' now."

"I was just wonderin' is all."

By the time the soldiers had been on the trail for a day or two, they had settled into a comfortable routine. Tom Lee cared for the horses and Boyd took over the cooking duties. "Damn, boy," said Sylvie, with a mouth stuffed full of beans. "Those rebs sure taught you how to cook some mighty fine chuck. I believe these is the best beans I ever ate."

"Sylvie, I told you before, don't you ever call me a reb," said Boyd, pointing the spoon in his direction, "and I ain't gonna keep tellin' you that."

Sylvie laughed at the little redhead shaking his spoon. "Calm down boy, I didn't call you a reb. I jus figured one of them musta taught you to cook this good is all."

"My Mama taught me to cook, and don't you dare say no bad about her — understand?"

"Weren't no offence meant," said Sylvie. "Can I have some more of those beans now?"

Boyd had fried up a pile of backstrap steaks from a doe that Del had killed earlier in the day. Rolling them in their meager supply of flour, he put in a good dose of salt and pepper and another pinch of something that looked like pepper.

"What's that you're putting on there now?" asked Tom Lee.

"It's my secret cookin' powder. I put it on most all my meat and beans."

"Well what is it?" asked Tom Lee again.

"Tom Lee, you just heard me say it was a secret. If I tell you, then it wouldn't be no secret, now would it?"

"I suppose not. I was just wonderin' what made those beans so good. They got a little special spark to 'em or something."

Boyd spooned some more beans on his plate. "It's just beans, pork fat, molasses, and my secret stuff. I like to put a little bacon in too when I can get it."

"Well, whatever it is you're doin', keep on doin' it," said Del. "This chuck is so good that I might even get fat on it."

"Shoot Del," said Tom Lee, "you're already fat!" They all laughed but kept on eating until every bite was gone.

Del proved to be an expert at finding game, keeping them in fresh meat for the whole trip. A variety of deer, pronghorn, and turkeys made for good eating. Sylvie took care of the butchering and making meat for the group. He also found edible greens as well as different roots and nuts to add to their larder.

"You sure about eatin' all this stuff?" asked Del. "It looks like a bunch of weeds."

"So, don't eat it — it don't make me no matter," said Sylvie. "But when you're somebody's nigger, you don't get a lot of food, so you learn pretty fast to how find more to eat."

On the third day out, they spotted a band of Comanches watching them from a distant ridge. "Everyone pay close attention," said Del. "We're being followed by a bunch of them murdering red-asses. They're probably lookin' for the best place to attack us."

For the next hour, the Indians followed their every move, keeping just out of rifle range. By late afternoon they had disappeared. "I think two of us need to keep guard all night, we'll do two-hour shifts," said Del. "Me and Tom Lee will take the first one."

When daylight started to show, the men grabbed a few quick bites of cold jerky, quietly saddled their horses and started to move out. Boyd scanned the country around them. "Del, it looks like they might have give up on us."

"Don't you believe that," said Del, "they're out there, just waitin' for the right time."

"We ain't got much worth stealing," said Boyd, "don't hardly seem like they'd go to all that trouble."

"We got horses, food, and hair," said Del, "three of their four favorite things. They're out there, just waiting for their chance."

"You said three out of four, what's the other one?" asked Tom Lee.

"Women. If we had any women with us, we'd likely be dead already."

Moving cautiously, they reached a stream running through a narrow section of rocky ground. An enormous dead cottonwood lay on one bank, its branches stretching across the creek forming several small pools. The burned remains of a settler's cabin and a corral sat back a hundred yards from the pools. Tying off to the branches, they scanned the country for the Indians. "Looks about as good as it's gonna get," said Del. "What do you think Sylvie?"

Sylvie nodded. "Too risky to have a fire, and we'll have to keep a good guard, but it could be worse."

After a meal of hard biscuits and cold jerky, Del and Tom Lee settled in for the first shift on night guard. Things in the makeshift camp had been quiet all night. As the horizon started to lighten up, Del heard something thump against the tree branch next to him. Turning to see what had caused the noise, another arrow hit the branch several inches from the first one.

"Indians — Indians!" screamed Del — "Indians . . .!"

Everyone dropped down and scrambled for what little protection the creek and tree branches offered. Del and Tom Lee were already firing by the time Sylvie and Boyd got their rifles to their shoulders. Comanche balls tore off chunks of the tree branches and ricocheted off the rocks.

The battle-hardened soldiers kept their composure and chose their targets carefully. Sylvie killed one rider in the first charge and shot the horse out from under another one. Two rifle shots killed the second Indian as he tried to get to his feet. With loud, terrifying shrieks, the Comanches charged again, riding straight at them along both sides of the creek. All four rifles opened fire, and two horses went down, one pinning its rider in the creek bed. Two more were shot off their horses. Three more Comanches on foot came close enough to use their bows, and two of them fell dead in their tracks. The third one took a bullet in the hip from Del's Spencer and went down in the creek screaming in pain.

Riding out of range, they regrouped, screamed and attacked the men again. Dropping down low behind their horse's heads they charged at full gallop, this time straight at the soldier's position.

Musket balls splashed into the creek and buzzed past their heads, splintering more branches. The soldiers kept up a steady fire, and several horses and Indians fell into the path of the others causing even more carnage. Now on foot, the Indians kept coming, and somehow a few reached the men through the steady rifle fire.

The soldiers, running low on rifle cartridges pulled their Colts and kept firing. When three Indians reached the cottonwood at the same time, they lunged onto the soldiers with knives in hand, shrieking at the top of their lungs. Tom Lee's Colt went off against the neck of the first Indian, and he crashed down on him, momentarily pinning him against the trunk of the tree.

Boyd raised his left hand against another one and fired into his chest. The Indian bounced off and landed on his left arm. Boyd shot him twice more while he was still moving. Another Indian came down hard on him with his knife raised. Before he could react, a deafening explosion went off alongside his right ear, and the Indian's blood sprayed all over him. Sylvie had fired at the Indian at the last second with the muzzle of his pistol just inches from his head.

The scene went eerily quiet after Sylvie's shot, the rest of the Comanche braves were nowhere in sight. Still crouched down in the fallen tree, the men waited quietly to see what would happen next. "Sound off," said Del. "who's hurt?"

"I'm good," said Sylvie, "never got touched."

"I think I'm okay," said Boyd, "But someone needs to get these dead Indians off of me."

"Tom Lee, you still with us?" asked Del, starting to pull himself out of the tangle of branches and bodies. "Tom Lee?"

"I'm here, but I'm not so good."

Dragging the bodies off Boyd, he saw Tom Lee waist deep in the water. "You hit?" asked Del.

Tom Lee reached for Del's hand. "I'm hurting in the back pretty bad, I think I got an arrow in me."

Sylvie and Del lifted him up to dry ground and laid him on the grass. "Watch him, Sylvie. I'm gonna make sure all these murderin' sons-a-bitches are fer sure dead. At the edge of the creek, one Indian was still pinned under his dead horse and unable to move. Del locked eyes with him, and the Indian began to chant something he didn't understand. Del stared at him for a moment, cocked the Colt and pushed it firmly against the Indian's forehead. Staring up at Del, he never blinked or stopped chanting. Del pulled the trigger, and the fight was over.

Boyd and Del rolled Tom Lee onto his belly and pulled up his shirt. A short piece of arrow shaft stuck out of the left side of his back just above his waist. "Tom Lee, it looks like they got you pretty good here," said Boyd. "Want us to pull it out?"

"Yes, I want you to pull it out! You think I want to have that thing sticking outta me everywhere I go?"

Sylvie looked at the bloody wound. "Okay, don't get all excited, we'll get it out of there. Del, you ever do this before?"

Del nodded, "sure, lots of times, let's take a look." Grabbing the shaft, he wiggled it side to side and pulled hard. On the third pull the shaft came out cleanly, but the arrow point stayed in place. "Tom Lee, it looks like I'll have to sharpen up the old greenriver and start diggin' for it."

"No! You ain't doing no cutting on me — I'll wait till I find a real doctor!"

"Well, if that's how you feel, I'll just rub on a little ointment and bandage it the best I can."

"That's how I feel about it."

"Here, pour a little of this on it," said Sylvie, holding out a bottle of whiskey. "Then take a few swallows too, it'll help kill the pain."

"Didn't know you had any whiskey," said Del.

"That's the last of it. You just as well finish it off Tom Lee, we got a lot of hard riding ahead of us.

Did anyone check on the horses?" asked Sylvie.

Del nodded. "They're all good. They were picketed just far enough away that they missed the worst of it. The Indians would've avoided killing them if they could. There's some damage to a couple of saddles that were across the tree branch is all."

Del walked through the bodies taking the scalp locks and anything else he thought might be of value. A lone Indian pony stood next to the dead body of an Indian, still clutching the reins firmly in his hand. Del killed it and pulled off the bridle, a simple rope affair with two feathers attached to it. Collecting a few more feathers and knives, he put the spoils of the battle in his bag and finished saddling up his horse. Destroying the Indian rifles, he collected the remaining bows and arrows and knives, throwing everything in the creek under the cottonwood branches.

"Can you believe what just happened?" asked Boyd, looking back over the bloody scene.

"Hell of a fight, that's for sure," said Sylvie. "We ain't gonna forget this one for a good long while. Thirteen dead Comanche braves is a hell of a thing."

"I hereby name this place Tom Lee Creek," said Del, "in honor of him takin' a Comanche arrow in the back and killin' a pile of them no-good murderin' red-asses. From now on this day will be called the Battle of Tom Lee Creek day!"

Tom Lee wrapped his extra shirt around his ribcage and pulled it tightly together, taking one last look back at the dead Indians and horses. "I seen all I want of this place. Let's get moving. I gotta find someone to take this thing out of my back."

Chapter 5

Reaching Fort Chadbourne without further Indian trouble, they found the doctor attached to the small garrison of soldiers and told him about the arrowhead.

The doctor, a grizzled looking, gray-haired veteran of the Western Army, nodded. "Bring him in, and we'll take a look, I can probably get it out. I've done more than a few of these over the years."

Tom Lee lay on a wooden mess table face down in the back of the commissary. Giving him an injection of morphine, the doctor washed off the wound. "I don't have any ether, so each of you will need to take an arm, and one of you sit on his legs and hold him as still as you can. Even with the morphine, he ain't gonna like this very much. You ready son?"

Tom Lee grabbed for the sides of the table. "Let's get this over with."

Del and Sylvie each grabbed an arm and Boyd pinned down his legs as the doctor started to work on the wound. After several minutes of probing and pulling on the arrowhead, he stopped, wiped off the blood and smeared on some kind of salve, stretching a bandage over it. "What's his name again?" asked the Doctor.

"It's Tom Lee," said Del.

"Tom Lee, you hear me okay"

"Yeah, I hear you, did you get it out?"

"Son, I can't get it out the way things are now. It's a long, iron point. It's wedged tight between two of your short ribs. I think the tip is a little bent or something, if I dig too deep, I'm afraid I'll mess you up even worse."

"So now what, I'm just gonna go around hurting forever?"

"You need a real surgeon in a real hospital, probably someplace like Galveston. I heard they have two good surgeons there. I'll give you some morphine pills to take with you for now, but you really need to rest up for a couple of weeks before you do anything too physical."

"I ain't got no time to go to Galveston, nor to rest up," said Tom Lee. "And I sure ain't got no money for a fancy doctor — just pull it out so I can get going."

"I'm sorry son, but if I do it here, you'll still be laid up for a long while. Your only choice is to get to a surgeon or live with it."

"Then I guess I just have to live with it — we got buffalo to kill."

The men laid-up just outside the walls. Fort Chadbourne had been abandoned by the Union early in the war and taken over by the Confederates. Most of the buildings were still standing, all of them in bad need of repair. Just a few dozen cavalry troops were officially posted there. Another hundred or so hunters, teamsters, immigrants with wagons full of families and rough looking men of all kinds were also camped in and around the old buildings. Most were just passing through, spending a few nights for protection from the Indians while they rested their stock.

After two days, Sylvie made a trip to the commissary for a few supplies. The next morning he wasn't back in camp, so Del and Boyd rode into the fort to find him.

Checking every building in town, they finally found him sprawled out on his back in a muddy ditch behind the post headquarters. Boyd walked up to him and poked him with his boot. "Damn it Sylvie, get on up, we got a lot of miles to go," he said, poking him again. "We're fixing to leave you where you lie, you hear me? Shit Del, I think maybe he's dead."

"Well, that ain't all bad Boyd, if he's dead then there's gonna be more buffalo for the rest of us. Let's see if we can find his horse so we can get movin'."

Walking around the perimeter, they found his horse in a shallow gully a quarter mile from the fort with the reins tangled in a deadfall. "He looks all right Del, probably needs a little water is all."

"Let's get him back to camp and go check Sylvie once more before we leave," said Del.

Boyd squatted over the muddy figure and shook his shoulder. "Seems dead to me Del, I think we just as well get goin'," said

Boyd, shaking him one last time. Pulling the canteen off his horse, he uncorked it and poured it on Sylvie's face. "The reaction was immediate and loud. "I ain't dead goddamnit!" said Sylvie, sitting straight up. Spitting and cussing, he shook the water off his head and started to repeat it, "I ain't de . . ." then passed out again, pitching backward in the mud.

It was several minutes before they could stop laughing at what they'd just witnessed. Del laughed so hard he had to turn away from the scene so he could regain his composure. Boyd emptied the rest of the canteen on Sylvie's face, and he sat straight up again, spitting out the water, still proclaiming loudly that he wasn't dead. This time he stayed upright.

Still laughing hysterically, they looked at the filthy mess that used to be a soldier. "Just what the hell you find so funny?" Looking around, Sylvie suddenly realized where he was. "What the holy hell did you do to me? Why am I here? My boots are gone — where the hell are my boots?"

"Well, you dumbass, you didn't come back to camp last night, so we came looking for you," said Del. "It's you that needs to tell us what happened."

It took Sylvie three tries to stand upright. "Well ain't ya even gonna give me a hand?" The sad looking figure standing in front of them asking for help caused them to break into spasms of laughter again. "Screw both of you," said Sylvie, "if you ain't gonna help, then just get the hell outta my way." Taking a step out of the ditch, his bare foot slipped and he hit face first in the mud, splashing it onto Del's boots.

Boyd offered Sylvie his bandanna. Wiping off his head and face he looked at them. "Did I get it all off?"

Del couldn't contain himself, and the laughter started all over again.

Sylvie looked at his partners wondering what was making them laugh so hard. "What's so goddamn funny that you'd laugh so hard at a man in his moment of need?"

"Shit Sylvie, how can we tell if you got it all? You and the mud are the same color!"

Sylvie stomped off toward camp without saying anything else. When he got there, he rinsed off in the creek, added wood to the fire and stripped to his skivvies to dry off.

In camp, Boyd and Del recalled the details of the story for Tom Lee, adding in a few extra touches of their own, and he joined in the laughter. "So Sylvie, we still ain't heard the story of how you come to be sprawled out in the mud all passed out and half dead," said Boyd.

Warmed up by the fire with a belly full of chuck and mostly sobered up, Sylvie told them the story. "I was pissin' out behind the commissary, minding my own business, and when I turned around to leave, two men were walkin' my way. We talked for a minute and well, they had a jug and some dice. That's pretty much all I remember right now."

"What did they look like?" asked Tom Lee.

"Like a couple a thievin', goddamn assholes, what do you think? One had overalls, and both had ragged looking coats and hats. Oh, they both had whiskers too. They got my money and my boots, and I got this big knot on my head," said Sylvie. "Gonna kill 'em when I catch 'em, that's for damn sure."

"They got all your muster money?" asked Boyd.

Sylvie nodded and finished off his coffee. "Ever last cent, and I guess they musta got my Colt too."

"Least they didn't get your horse and saddle," said Boyd.

"It's sure gonna be interesting watching him ride without any boots though," said Del, unable to contain himself.

Sylvie couldn't take it any longer and finally began to laugh at himself. "Okay, okay, laugh all you want, but I ain't got no boots and no money to get me some."

Not ready to give up their fun, they continued to poke at him. "Shit — my boots are gone!" said Boyd. "Where the hell are my boots?"

"Probably on the feet of some drunken teamster that's halfway to New Mexico Territory by now," said Del with a grin.

"Piss on all of you," said Sylvie.

"Ain't that what got you into trouble to start with? I mean the pissing part?" said Boyd.

When they tired of having fun at Sylvie's expense, they let him off the hook. "Don't worry Sylvie, we'll spot you enough cash to get a pair of boots. I saw some Army made ones in the commissary."

"Thank you Del. I would sure appreciate that. I'll pay you back soon as we start killin' them buffalos."

"I know you will. I ain't concerned about that. There's jus' one thing though . . ."

"What's that Del?"

"Try not to lose them."

Standing in the commissary, Sylvie picked a new pair of Army boots from the shelf. "Shit almighty Del, ten dollars for these things? They ain't hardly worth half that."

"So yer gonna go hunt those buffalos in your bare feet are you?" asked Del, pulling out his muster pay.

"I ain't got no socks neither," said Sylvie.

"Fine," said Del. "Get you some socks too." Dropping a ten dollar gold piece and three silver dollars on the counter, he pushed it toward the clerk. "Just put the things on, we gotta get movin'."

"You boys buffalo hunters, are you?" said a strange voice from behind them.

"Fixin' to be," said Sylvie, turning to see who was talking. The man was tall, with a full black beard and thick dark hair down past his shoulders. Intense blue eyes peered out from under a flat-top black hat with a wide brim.

"Name's Case, what's yours?"

"I'm Sylvie and this here is Del. We're headed for Fort Dodge to join a buffalo outfit up there."

"Fort Dodge? It's one long ride to get there, especially with the Indians and all. My outfit's leaving from here tomorrow morning, and we'll be into buffalo in a few days. I need a couple of more hands, can you shoot?"

"Hell yes we can shoot," said Sylvie. "We could shoot the eye out of a buff at five hundred yards easy enough."

The stranger looked at him for a minute then shook his head. "Friend, I got no use for bullshit, and I don't need no trick shooting. Just runnin' a bullet through the lungs is plenty good enough."

"There are four of us," said Del, "can you take all us on?"

He shook his head. "No way I can use all of you, least not as shooters."

"We all need work. What else would we be doing if we're not shooting?" asked Sylvie.

"A buffalo camp has plenty to do. I need skinners, wranglers, and teamsters. They're just as important as a shooter."

"How about a cook, you got a good cook?"

"We got a cook," said Case. "I doubt you'd hear anyone call him good though. It ain't all that easy to find a good one that wants to be out there for such long stretches."

"Well Mister Case, it jus' so happens that we got one of the best cooks in the whole damn frontier with us," said Sylvie. "His beans are so good that men have fought over the last spoonful more than once."

He looked over the two men standing in front of him. "Tell you what I'll do. We're camped out back of the livery. You tell him we want to try those beans tonight. If they're that good, I can find a place for two of you, one shooter and one cook."

Sylvie shook his head. "Like I said, we all need the work — it's all of us or none of us."

"Okay, we're all tired of what we've been eating for sure. If those beans are as good as you say, I'll hire the four of you, but if they're not, there's no job for any of you, we clear?"

"Yessir Mister Case, we're clear. You're in for a special treat here."

"It's just Case. Tell him to get on those beans and bring 'em over by dark."

Walking back to camp, they talked about their good fortune to find work so close. After they told Boyd and Tom Lee about the offer from the stranger, they quickly agreed. Fort Dodge was a long ride through some wild country if you didn't have to do it.

"Better make them beans extra good," said Del. "Cause if Case don't like 'em, we ain't got no jobs."

"All my beans are extra good. Just stay the hell out of my way while I'm working — got it?"

"We all got it," said Sylvie. "Just let us know when they're ready to eat is all."

"Tom Lee, how you feeling?" asked Del. "Let me look at your battle wound, we probably should put on a fresh bandage."

Peeling off the bloody rag that passed for a bandage, Del was surprised how good it looked. "It don't seem all that bad Tom Lee. It's kinda starting heal over I guess." Smearing on a healthy dose of the doctor's ointment, he pressed a clean piece of linen against it and wrapped a long piece of cloth twice around his chest and pulled it tight. "That's the last of the clean bandages. This'll at least keep it from rubbing against your clothes all day. How bad is it hurtin' right now?"

"It ain't bad right now, but I got those pills. I don't know what'll happen when they run out."

"We'll just have to wait and see. If we gotta get you to a fancy surgeon in the big city, we can do it."

Sitting at the fire with a bunch of seasoned buffalo hunters made them realize that this must be some really dirty work. "Jesus Sylvie," said Del, "every one of these boys smells like they've been livin' inside a buffalo's ass for the last few months."

Sylvie nodded. "They do stink some, but as long as they got work for us, I'll take the smell."

Case took a second spoonful of beans and savored them for a moment. "Well damn almighty boy, old Del warn't spinnin' tales about your chuck, these are the best beans I ever ate. I can't hardly get enough of yer biscuits neither," said Case. "I'll hire all of you. Tomorrow, Boyd and me will go to the commissary before we head out and get whatever supplies he needs for the hunt."

"Will all of us be shooting?" asked Tom Lee.

"Can't all of us be shooters. I only got four rifles, that's good for two shooters."

"We all got rifles with us."

Case shook his head. "We only use my rifles and the cartridges I supply. That way I know everything's right when we find the buffs."

"What kind of rifles you talking about?"

"Boy, you sure do ask a lot of questions. My partner got me four trapdoor Springfields a few days ago, right outta the factory. The ones I got have been converted to the new .50 - 70 center fire cartridge. They're faster and easier to load, and that big bullet will go clean through a bull buff."

"So, what will I be doing out there?"

"Whatever I tell you. Could be skinnin' and butchering buffs or peggin' them out. Maybe wrangling the horses and mules too, you got a problem with that?"

"No sir, no problem," said Tom Lee, "I was just wondering is all."

"Once more, just so you all understand, there ain't no towns, railroads, white men, maps or any kind of civilization from here on out. I doubt we'll even see any other hunters out here," said Case, lighting a fresh smoke. "What we will see are Indians, buffalos, coyotes, prairie dogs, and pronghorns. Until it gets cold, you'll run into rattlesnakes and every kind of stinging, biting bug known to man. Are all of you good with that? If not, now would be a good time change your mind."

"You can't scare us off, we've all been livin' on the prairie for years," said Del.

"Then be ready to leave in the morning, soon as we get out of the commissary."

Chapter 6

The company pulled out of the fort at first light. They had two large Studebaker freight wagons recently purchased from the army and a well-used but solid camp wagon. Creaking and bouncing between the breaks and over the grassy hills, the harsh pop of the teamster's whip drove the mules hard. The mounted riders kept the extra horses and mules gathered close behind. Boyd rode up front with Tom Lee in the camp wagon and Case and one of the Mexican skinners scouted ahead of them for the first campsite.

After several days travel, the company stopped just before sunset at a small creek below a scattered string of beaver ponds. Long grass surrounded the water for a hundred yards in every direction and ancient cottonwoods towered along both sides of the creek making a natural windbreak. To the south was a long, flat field of grass.

"I like this spot, it's far enough north of the Colorado River and east of the Llano that maybe the Indians ain't so thick," said Case. "Back the wagons out of the wind and get a fire started."

"What's the Llano?" asked Tom Lee.

"Hell on earth," said Del. "The Llano Estacada, a land of nothing but more Indians than you ever saw."

"Are there buffalo there?"

Del nodded. "There are plenty of buffs there and lots of game, but I ain't goin' in there to get 'em, nobody who wants to keep their hair would ever go there."

Boyd pulled the picket pins and ropes out of the wagon, as the teamsters unhitched the mules. After they had been watered, he staked them and the extra stock out in the grass at the edge of the creek. Everyone was responsible for their own saddle horses and did the same. When he finished with the mules and horses, he helped set the sleeping tents.

With that done, he walked knee-deep into the first pond, splashed into the water face down and stayed submerged for a few seconds. Trying to beat the relentless sun and rinse off the miles of trail dirt, ticks and other bugs off himself, he came up shaking his head and running his fingers through his hair. Filling his hat, he poured water over his head again and again. "God almighty, this feels so fine I might never come out of here," he said to no one in particular.

Case watched each man closely as they took care of the night's business. "Boyd, plan on setting up here for a spell. We're headin' out at first light to find some buffs."

"Will do. Chuck for tonight is jerky and hard biscuits with some tortillas and coffee. In the morning there'll be fresh biscuits and bacon and eggs."

Case looked surprised. "Eggs? Where did you find eggs around here?"

"A couple of old Kiowa women camped out back of the barracks had a basket of fresh duck eggs. They didn't really want to sell them, but I was able to make a trade."

"What did you trade them for?"

"Eight Spencer cartridges."

"Two old Indian women had a Spencer rifle?"

Boyd shrugged. "I didn't see one. I think they just took them as trading stock."

"Sounds like a fair trade to me," said Case.

"Don't want get used to it though, the eggs will be gone tomorrow and you won't be eatin' bacon much longer either."

"We find the buffs, you can figure on cooking up some tongue tomorrow." Case looked at his new redheaded cook. "I like you boy, you are one fine cook, and I never thought I'd say that to a reb."

Boyd turned and instantly stepped up to confront him. Case looked down at the smaller man with surprise. "I ain't no reb — I was a conscript in the war, I didn't have any choice. Don't ever call me a reb again — you got that?"

"Relax little man. I won't call you nothin' but Boyd from now on, that okay with you?"

"Just don't never call me reb again . . ."

By the time the hunters lined up for morning chuck, it was already hot and the sun hadn't yet cleared the horizon. The two men, who stood watch with their rifles for the last shift, ate first. Boyd served everyone a pair of giant, golden biscuits, then covered them with several long, thick strips of bacon. Fishing two runny eggs out of the hot grease, he dropped them on the bacon and finished each plate with a fresh tortilla over top of everything. All the hunters took a cup of steaming-hot, black coffee and made their way to the fire. When they finished the coffee, they knocked the grounds into the fire, several asked for more.

"This time without a pound of Arbuckle's in the bottom." cracked Sylvie.

"If you don't like it, you can go drink pond water," said Boyd. Holding up the lard can that served as his coffee boiler, he tapped the spoon on the side. "Who else wants more?" He watched them from the wagon as they devoured the food without a sound between them. The white hunters gathered together on one side of the fire and the Mexicans directly across from them. Sylvie sat in between.

When Case gave the order to get moving, the Mexicans asked about extra food to take on the hunt. Boyd handed everyone two biscuits and several chunks of jerky wrapped in a fresh tortilla. "Muchas Gracias, Señor."

Boyd nodded. "De nada."

The rest of the hunters took theirs without speaking.

"Yeah, and you're welcome too," said Boyd, after they filed past.

Tom Lee's horse was still tied to the picket pin.

"Tom Lee, for now, I need you as camp rustler with Boyd, and to watch over the stock," said Case. "Take a good look at their feet, if they need some work, everything's in the wagon."

"Yessir, I'll take care of it, no problem."

"And check all the wheels and grease the axles if they need it. Then dig a cache hole to hide the cartridges and extra knives and cover it good. I don't want none of those thievin' red bastards to find it."

"I'll take care of it."

"When you finish that, you and Boyd grab the hatchets and start makin' pegs for the hides."

"Yessir, how many are we going to need?"

"We're gonna kill tons of buffs, and each one takes a bunch of pegs. Tom Lee, you gonna be able to do this with your back hurtin' and all?"

"I can do it, no problem."

"Okay. You say you can do it, I believe you. Both of you, one more thing, double-check your guns," said Case, as he mounted up. "Keep your pistols strapped on and your rifles close. The Comanches and Kiowas are runnin' wild all over this country. Boyd, keep the cook fire as small as you can and be sure to keep the water barrels and the possum full, just in case we gotta move outta here fast."

Boyd and Tom Lee watched as the hunters disappeared into the grassy hills. "Well heck Boyd, I was hoping to shoot me a couple of those buffalos too."

"We're gonna be here a while, so I'm sure you'll get your chance. Let's have another cup of coffee and a biscuit and visit a bit."

"Sure. Boyd, what is he talking about a possum?"

"It's that big stiff buff hide strapped to the underside of the wagon, they call it a possum belly. It's a place to keep a dry supply of chips and kindling and extra pegs when there ain't none around. Oh, I almost forgot, I got a treat hid away for us."

"What kind of treat would that be?"

He grinned and tossed him a green apple. "What they don't know ain't gonna hurt them none. I got some raisins, and a few taters hid away too."

"Where did you get apples and taters out here?"

"Well, when you and Del were off looking for Sylvie, I found an old Mexican couple that just got a visit from their son. He brings them supplies from his cellar to sell at the post, so I traded them for an old Indian knife I had. The raisins come from the commissary."

"Boyd, you're a pretty handy man to have around."

He nodded. "It's kinda like what Sylvie said, when you ain't got a lot, you learn how to scrounge up what you need."

The camp wagon was ten-feet long and five-feet wide. It had been refitted and set-up with three-foot sideboards and a new chuck box. There was room for the food stores and space for the crew's bedrolls and personal gear and could easily be pulled by a single span of horses or mules. Under the seat was a small box for tools. It held the butcher knives, sharpening steels, and a grindstone. Two large, wooden boxes contained the supply of cartridges. Everything was tightly covered with well-greased buffalo hide.

At night Boyd draped the canvas across the sideboards and slept under it. When they were traveling, he threw it over the bows to keep everything covered. As he saw it, not sharing a tent with a bunch of filthy, stinking hunters caked with buffalo blood and dirt was the best part of his job. By late afternoon, the biscuits and beans, this time with bacon, were ready for chuck. Tom Lee had been working steadily chopping a pile of pegs for the skinners.

Shortly after the sun dropped over the ridge, the hunting party rode silently back into camp. After caring for their horses, each man grabbed his bedroll and threw it into a tent. A few cleaned up in the creek then joined the others already standing in line for the food. The smell of Boyd's beans was obvious when they rode in, but when the lid came off the oven, they all began to crowd around for their share, nearly knocking Boyd into the coals. "Get the hell back right now, or I'll dump them in the fire, and you'll have nothing to eat but ashes."

"We're just hungry is all," said Sylvie. "And the smell is makin' us even more hungry."

Finishing up the meal, Boyd sat down next to Del at the fire. "What happened out there? I ain't heard a single word about a buffalo since you got back."

"Just spent the whole day lookin' is all. We finally run into some just 'fore dark. We're gonna go after 'em in the morning. We're takin' one of the hide wagons with us so we'll be ready to load 'em up."

"You see a lot of them?" asked Tom Lee.

"Jus two small bunches and a few strung out in the gullies right before dark. Case says that's common this early. The big herds move north in the spring and leave a lot of small bunches scattered around. When it starts to get cold up there, they begin to herd back up and head south. He says the colder it is, the better the hides are, and more money for us."

"Might be a while before they head back down here, hot as it is," said Tom Lee.

"Case says when it starts getting' cold up there, they'll start movin' in, and he wants to be ready when they get here," said Del. "The ones we get now ain't worth near as much, but they'll pay the bills 'till the big herds show up. When it gets cold enough, we might start taking some of the meat for jerky. If we can find a market for it, we could even make a little extra money."

The hunters lined up in the morning with their plates in hand. Biscuits, leftover beans, bacon, and tortillas filled the plates. Boyd filled their cups from the lard can. When Sylvie held his cup out, Boyd stopped pouring and looked up at him. "You want coffee with extra Arbuckle's or pond water, what's it gonna be?"

"Well I damn sure ain't drinking no pond water!"

"Well then, you ought to know by now, don't never insult the cook, and that goes double for his coffee — you got that clear?"

The rest of the hunters erupted in laughter at the conversation. "Yeah little man, I got it clear," said Sylvie, still holding out his cup. "Just pour me some coffee." The hunters were still chuckling as Boyd filled his cup.

"How's the coffee Sylvie?" asked Del, "strong enough for you this morning?"

Finishing his meal, Sylvie dumped his grounds in the fire and walked toward the tent.

"Kinda the sensitive type ain't you Sylvie?" said Del.

Case finished the last of his coffee and stood up. "Okay, everyone listen up. When we get a full wagonload of hides ready, two men will take them to Adobe Walls to meet my partner and his men. They'll take them from there to the market. We're just a small outfit right now, but we're early enough to get a jump on most of the other outfits that are starting to form up. If we get a big batch of quality hides to market early enough, the buyers will know we can be trusted."

"When do we gotta meet up with your partner?" asked Sylvie.

"The first load has gotta be to the Walls the first day of November. If everything is going good, we'll deliver every two weeks until I call it a season. That means we might be out here the best part of four months or more depending on the buffs and the weather. Is anyone here not up for that?"

Nobody spoke up. "Well, them buffs ain't gonna wait around all day. Roly, get the mules hitched and make sure that you got everything we need for a long day."

"Yessir Case, we'll be ready quick enough." Roly Gant had been a teamster since he was fifteen years old. At five foot-eight inches tall and nearly as wide, he never seemed able to get enough to eat and weighed at least three-hundred and fifty pounds. His father called him Roly-Poly when he was a child, and he's been called Roly ever since. In his early fifties, he still moved like a much younger and lighter man and could whip any three men in a fight. His love for cheap whiskey and Bible verse gave him many opportunities for confrontations and bar fights.

All the men he worked with liked him, but nobody wanted to ride with him for very long. His nonstop postulating on God and the good book was more than most could take. He was known to stop his wagon and challenge a rider to a fight if they didn't agree with him.

Case had worked with him before and knew what he was like. He also knew he was a brute for work, which is what he wanted. Roly could hitch a mule-team faster than anyone in camp had ever seen and could maneuver a wagon into a tight space better than anybody thought possible. Alcohol was forbidden on the hunt and Roly dearly missed his whiskey but needed the job worse. Case decided his work was good enough that as long as he wasn't drinking, he could put up with his never-ending Bible thumping.

The sun was already scorching hot as the buffalo hunters pulled out of camp with Roly bringing up the rear. After an hour on the trail, Case called a stop near two natural water tanks tucked up against a long strip of rimrock. They held more than enough stock water for several days if they needed it. A string of long-dead cottonwoods curled around one end of the waterholes.

"This is our spike camp for today. We'll start with two shooting teams," said Case. "Me and Del are heading northwest to try and catch up with the larger group we saw yesterday. Sylvie and Sergio will go north up the wash and look for those little bunches. One skinner will go with each team. Arturo, you understand?"

"Si Señor."

Case pulled the rifles and two heavy belts full of thumb-sized cartridges from the wagon. The leather belts were made with suspenders attached to support the heavy weight of two rows of .50-70 centerfire cartridges. A skinning knife and a steel hung from one side of the belt. He handed them to Sylvie and Del. "You two will shoot first. I want to see if you can hit anything, and no trail huntin' neither. Keep 'em all together in one spot so the skinners ain't running all over the country. You got one chance to show me you can shoot. If you miss and spook the herd, they'll be gone, and you'll be done shooting. The skinners will have the water and food and everything else we need with them. As soon as we get some down, they will get Roly, and he'll bring up the wagon. Let's get moving."

Both teams saddled up and headed out. Roly and one skinner stayed at the spike camp with the wagon and waited for the call. Reaching the rolling grass plain, Case and Del dismounted, checked the breeze then walked partway up the first hill, stopping just short of the crest. The skinner hobbled the horses and sat down to wait.

Dropping flat, they began a slow belly crawl. Reaching the top, they parted the grass with the rifle barrel and Case scanned the horizon with his binoculars. "Nothing. This is where we found the first ones yesterday," said Case, still scanning the next hill. "They can't be all that far away" Signaling to the skinner they moved to the next hill and repeated the process. "Still nothing, let's keep moving." Reaching the third hill, they parted the grass and were looking directly at the tail end of a young cow grazing fifty yards away. "Del, you comfortable there?"

He nodded. "I'm good."

"Okay, when she turns sideways, put one right through both lungs. Don't shoot if you can't hit her perfect."

Del waited with the Springfield tight against his shoulder, the hammer cocked and the barrel resting across the matted grass. His heart raced as he squinted down the barrel placing the sights on her chest. With sweat running down his face, he pulled his hat a little lower trying to block out the sun. After several minutes the cow swung broadside to the hunters, took several steps, stopped and put her head down to graze. Touching the trigger, the big .50 went off in a thick swirl of acrid smoke. Hitting the buffalo behind the front leg, she humped up and spun around in a complete circle with blood spraying from her nose. They could see a pink boil of air and blood blowing out of both sides of her chest. Before they could say anything, the buffalo gave a deep, growling bellow and collapsed in her tracks.

"Get reloaded — there's surely a few more around here, they should be coming around to see what's going on."

Del ejected the empty, put in a fresh cartridge and waited as the smoke drifted away. Several animals that had been lying in the long grass stood up and walked toward the dead cow. The first one to reach her milled around repeatedly, sniffing and bumping her nose against the carcass.

"All right Del, there's five more animals, kill every one of them. Shoot the ones that look like they might be the leaders or the ones that are getting' nervous and ready to run first. Remember, one bullet clean through both lungs."

"Got it," said Del, watching as another animal began to turn to the side. "The others won't run when I shoot this one?"

"Not if you shoot him clean like you did the first one. Buffalos are just big dumb lumps of meat and hair. If you don't spook 'em, you could shoot every single one 'till you run outta shells."

"What happens if I don't hit them clean?"

"If it ain't a killin' shot, they're likely to run. If one runs, they'll all take off."

When the next one turned sideways, Del touched off the Springfield again, and the buffalo lurched forward shaking her head hard, blowing blood from side to side. Before she could turn around, she fell over dead. The rest of the herd milled around the dead one for a minute then went back to grazing.

"Goddamnit, reload — now," said Case, "They ain't gonna stand still forever."

Del reloaded as quickly as he could and put the sights on a young bull. Waiting until it moved clear of the others, he saw the bull look his direction for a moment then drop his head and go back to grazing. When the smoke cleared, they saw the bull piled up on the ground.

Del already had the rifle loaded and had the hammer back as the two remaining cows milled around the dead bull. "Take the one on the right, she's more likely to run at the next shot."

Putting the sights on the chest of the cow, he touched the trigger, and the buffalo didn't flinch. "I can't believe I coulda missed her," said Del, stuffing in a new cartridge.

"You didn't miss, take the other one before she bolts."

"You sure I didn't miss that one?" Almost before he finished talking, the buffalo dropped straight to the ground without a sound.

"Get on the other one — she's about to run."

Del fired again just as the last one began to take a step forward. Running several yards, she hit the ground hard and slid nose first into the dirt. Case stood up and signaled for the skinner to get Roly.

"How could you tell the other buff was hit?" asked Del.

"You never know for sure how they'll react when they're hit the first time. I knew it was a good shot because she froze up like she did. If you hit them right, they won't go far. If you'd missed her or wounded her, she'd still be running."

Walking up to the dead buffalo, he reloaded and laid the rifle across one of the carcasses. "Case, I seen a lot of these critters before, but I didn't understand how big they really are 'till now. It must be tough skinnin' one of these things."

"Not so bad as you might think, least when they're warm like this. Leave them lay 'till the next day though, and you'll for sure have a sore back from all that skinning."

"All these years I heard that when you find them, there would be so many that they would fill the prairie as far as you could see in any direction, but we didn't see all that many today."

"Sometimes you find larger herds, but usually just the smaller groups. It's better for us if they are in little groups, makes it easier on the whole outfit," said Case. "You got your pistol on?"

"I do."

"This would be a good time to keep your ears and eyes open. If there's any of those red bastards around, they know we're here." Both men pulled out their Colts and checked them one more time.

The squeak and rattle of the wagon could be heard as it started around the last hill. Roly cracked the whip, and the team pulled up close to the first carcass. Pulling out a long chain he hooked one end to the back of the wagon. The Mexican skinner pulled out a leather bag with several skinning knives and a steel, dropping it next to the first buffalo. He started working on the first animal without talking. Cutting through the hide just below the skull he ran his knife all the way around the neck. His next cut slit the thick hide down the throat and the brisket and down the middle of the chest. Continuing down the enormous belly, he cut it all the way to the end of the tail. Making a slit in the hide from the knee joint and down the inside of each leg to the first cut, the buffalo was ready to peel.

Driving a long iron picket pin through the cow's nostrils, Roly pounded it deep into the dirt, pinning the head firmly to the ground. Skinning back the hide at the top of the neck, he twisted it into a large lump, tied a rope around it and hooked the chain to it. Releasing the brake, Roly cracked his whip, and the mules lurched forward, peeling the hide cleanly off the carcass.

"When they're fresh like this they come off good," said Roly. "They're still plenty warm, and the tallow is soft. You gotta be careful though. You can tear them if you don't do it right."

Roly and the skinner worked steadily, peeling all six carcasses in less than an hour. Case instructed them to take all the tongues and the hump meat of the three youngest animals. Cutting down the flat of the hump ribs on either side and across the backbone, they took two large slabs of prime meat away from the carcass. Wrapping the cuts and the tongues in canvas, they put them in the wagon along with a half-full bucket of tallow. "Fresh tongue steaks," said Roly to his partner. "Ain't nothin' in God's world that tastes any better than that."

The remains of the six huge animals were left where they fell on the prairie. Ravens and magpies already floated above the killing field, diving down and fighting over the scraps. A pair of wolves claimed the first buffalo while several coyotes circled cautiously around the far edges of the scene, all waiting for their turn at the free feast.

"You want me to shoot the wolves?" asked Del.

Case shook his head. "It's way too warm, the fur won't be any good. When it gets cold, we'll start killing the wolves and coyotes."

As they finished loading the hides on the wagon, they heard a rifle shot, then several more in succession about fifteen seconds apart. "Let's get going," said Roly, climbing onto the wagon. "We got us some more buffs to skin."

They saw the skinner on top of a hill pointing off to one side. Maneuvering the wagon around the side of the rise, they saw at least a dozen or more dead buffs scattered across the backside.

Roly pulled the wagon up to the bloody scene and backed up close to the first carcass. The skinner had already made the necessary cuts.

"How many?" asked Case, jumping down from the wagon.

"Fourteen," said Sylvie. "One wounded cow ran off, and the rest ran. Me and Sergio are gonna go get her."

Case shook his head. "Goddamn it, get to finding her before she spooks every buff for ten miles."

"Still a lot of daytime left Boss, should we head back out?" asked Del.

"Yeah. We'll move out another mile or two north and see if we can pick up a few more. We'll take Arturo with us as a skinner. When we get some down, we'll start splitting hides until the wagon gets there."

"Sylvie, you and Sergio get on that cow then head west another mile or so and see what else you can find," said Case.

For the rest of the afternoon, the two teams of hunters walked and crawled over every hill and wash for several miles in every direction. By dark they had nine more hides in the wagon.

Chapter 7

Tom Lee and Boyd could hear the hunters talking before they rode into camp. Several minutes later, the rattle of the wagon and the crack of Roly's whip could be heard getting closer. They were all laughing excitedly, telling stories about the buffalo they had killed and how good their shots were. After stripping their horses and setting them out for the night, the hunters walked over to the fire, standing for a minute to let the warmth of the fire, and the smell of wood smoke and beans wash over them.

The night was noticeably cooler, and the sky was clear. "I think we might be gettin' a little change in the weather 'fore too long," said Del.

"Why's that Del?" asked Tom Lee.

"Don't you never run outta questions? It's getting' colder and the year is gettin' later, any damn fool can see that."

"One more question Del . . ."

"Now what?"

"What stinks so bad?"

The hunters all burst out laughing at the same time. "Jesus boy, don't you know nothin'? That's the smell of money," said Del.

"Money? What in heck you talking about?"

"Blood, Tom Lee, they're talking about buffalo blood. When the fire's hot, and they're standing close to it, the blood on their boots and clothes heats up and starts to stink, it smells like money — understand?"

"Uh . . . yeah, I guess so."

The conversation was interrupted by Boyd banging the spoon on the lard can. "Come on and get some food before you stink up the whole damn prairie."

After the men had eaten their fill, they settled in around the fire and recalled the day's adventures. Several pulled out the makings and others lit their pipes. Del stuffed a fat chaw in his cheek and sat down between two of the Mexicans. "Hola, mi amigos."

"Buenos tardes Señor," said the man to his right. "You shoot many buffalo today?"

Del leaned back, spit a long stream of tobacco juice into the fire and nodded his head. "Si, mi amigos, muchos buffalo. What is your... uh... nombre?"

"I am Arturo. We can speak English if you like, I speak both."

"I'm Del. These are my friends Tom Lee, Sylvie, and Boyd," he said, pointing them out as he named them.

After Arturo introduced Sergio, he explained that Angel and Juan spoke very little English. "They are Mexicans, Señor Del, from far below the river. Sergio and I are Americans, from San Antonio. They are good men just looking for work but have not learned the language yet."

Del spit another stream of juice into the fire. "So Arturo, how many buffalo can you and your men skin in one day?"

"Señor, we can skin all the buffalo you can shoot in one day," said Arturo, looking up at him with a grin.

"Arturo, you're my kind of greaser. I say you can't skin all the buffs I'm fixin' to shoot. You up for a little contest amigo?"

After explaining to the others what had been said, they nodded and agreed. "Si, we will have the contest, but we need to wait a while until it is cooler and there are more animals here. It would be easy for us with so few here, as you saw today," said Arturo. "Maybe in a few more weeks?"

"A few weeks it is." said Del. "If I win, what do I get?

"If you win, we will make you very special food for a week of hunting. If we win, when we finish skinning the animals you kill, there will be one left for you to do. You will have to skin and butcher the biggest one and load it by yourself."

"You got a bet there amigo. Soon as the big herds show up, I'll be shootin'."

"Si and we will be skinning them right behind you."

"Just hold on one goll-danged minute, we gotta get something outta this too," said Roly, lighting his pipe. "Ain't nobody gonna win nothing without me and old Luther driving those wagons and peelin' those hides — right Luther?"

The old mule man had been riding with Roly all day as his helper. A fixture on the prairies for more than forty years, he lit his pipe and ran his fingers through his long white beard. "That's the truth of it Roly, they ain't no good without us."

"Si Señor Roly, we will make some special food for you and Luther too, even if we don't win the contest," said Arturo.

Roly's face lit up. "Extra food? I'm ready! Bring on them buffs!"

Case sat quietly, smoking his pipe, listening to the stories and soaking up the warmth from the fire.

"Mister Case, how did you get that scar across your cheek?" asked Tom Lee.

"It's just Case, nothing else — just Case. Me and my partners were hunting buffs up in the Powder River country a couple years back. We were supplying meat to the mines and the new settlements. Them no-good Sioux and Crow were always harassing us. They killed several hunters that year, this came from one of their arrows," said Case, rubbing the scar. "It glanced off the back wheel of a wagon and did this." Pulling back his hair he showed Tom Lee his ear. "Took off a little slice of my ear too. If it hadn't a hit the wheel it would likely have stuck me in the chest, so I guess it ain't all that bad, considering."

"A lot of buffalo up there Case?" asked Tom Lee.

"There were plenty up there and you never had to spend too long lookin' for 'em. I remember one time, we got a good stand going, and before we realized it, we were surrounded by herds as far as a man could see in every direction and they were closing in on us fast."

"What happened then?" asked Tom Lee. "When you got surrounded by the herd like that?"

By now the whole outfit was listening intently to the story. "What do you think happened Tom Lee?"

"I don't know, how did you escape all those buffalo?"

"We didn't escape Tom Lee — can't you see what happened?"

"No, what happened?"

"Well Tom Lee — we was all killed! Every one of us was stomped flatter than a puddle of piss by thousands of buffalos!"

The camp exploded in laughter, even Angel and Juan got the joke. Tom Lee sat looking at the rest of them laughing for a few seconds before he got the joke. Playing along with the moment, he looked right at Case with a straight face. "Well shoot Case, if you were all killed, who was left to bury you?"

When the laughter died down, the hunters started to head for the tents. "Tom Lee don't let those buffs get you surrounded tonight," said Case as he headed for the tent.

Sylvie leaned against the camp wagon as Boyd climbed in for the night. Pulling a bottle from inside his vest he held it out to Boyd. "A little nip?"

"Get that away from me — If Case catches you drinking, he'll run you off — what the hell you thinking?"

"Who gives a shit what he thinks? A man can drink a little whiskey if he wants, it ain't hurting nobody."

"Sylvie, those are the rules of outfit. You better get rid of that and get a little sleep. It's a long ride back to civilization through Indian country if you get run off."

"He can go to hell. I had all the rules in the Army that I can stand — piss on his rules. Aw horseshit!" Turning the bottle upside down the last drops fell on his boots. "I'm all out anyway," said Sylvie, tossing it into the pond. "So goodnight to you."

When Boyd got up the next morning, heavy frost covered everything in camp. After building the fire, he warmed himself for a few extra minutes before he started on chuck. Before he served it up, he made an announcement that he had something special for them. Opening up a large can of cherries, he dropped a heaping spoonful on everyone's plate. "There's just enough left to have some tonight too."

"Not if I get to them first," said Sylvie, cleaning up his plate with his fingers.

"I catch anyone messin' in the food, and they'll have to outrun a bullet from my Spencer," said Boyd.

"Shit Boyd," said Sylvie. "You ain't never gonna shoot anybody, and you know it."

Boyd shrugged. "I guess it's up to you to find out for sure, ain't it?"

Before the hunters mounted up, Case gathered them around the fire. "I saw some smoke yesterday, just before we headed back to camp. You all know what that means."

"It means there's a bunch of them heathen savages hanging around here," said Roly.

"Couldn't it be from another hunter's camp?" asked Tom Lee.

Case shook his head. "There ain't no other hunters here. I saw tracks of unshod horses too. It's likely a bunch of Comanches lookin' for buffalo for themselves. I just want everyone to keep an eye peeled. Nobody goes anywhere alone for any reason. Everybody carries their rifle and revolver all the time, any questions? Luther is gonna work in camp till we need the second wagon. He'll get Boyd and Tom Lee started on peggin' the hides."

Emptying his pipe in the fire, Roly nodded his head. "If things go good, I'll change the mules every day, we don't want to sore 'em up if we don't have to."

"Just keep 'em close in," said Case. "Those thievin' red bastards would rather steal horses than they would eat."

"Got it Boss. I'll take good care of them, no problem."

Roly pulled out the canvas covered meat and dropped it in the camp wagon. "Tongue steak tonight?" he said, looking at Boyd.

"You bring me some hump too?"

"There's a couple of 'em in there."

"What about tallow?"

"Plenty in the can," said Roly.

"I'll see what I can come up with, but it'll cost you a big pile of buffs every day to keep eating this good."

Roly nodded. "Blessed are those who hunger and thirst for rightness, for they will be filled."

"Won't be no trouble getting hides," said Del, "least not while I'm doing the shootin'."

"Enough bullshit, we're burning daylight, move out," ordered Case.

Sylvie looked at Boyd and shook his head. "See what I mean, more goddamn orders. I just about had my belly full." Sylvie mounted up and fell in line with the others.

As the hunters rode out in the early light, Luther stood up and threw his grounds in the fire. "Let's get to pegging them hides. The sooner we get them done, the sooner we can sit a spell."

After scattering the hides around the grassy meadow, Tom Lee dropped an armload of pegs next to each one. "You ever done this before boy?" asked Luther.

Tom Lee shook his head. "A few deer hides, but nothing like this."

"Well pay attention then, I ain't gonna show you just the one time," said Luther. Unfolding the hide, he stretched it out hair-side down to its full length and width. With a short pointed knife, he put a small cut near the end of the front leg and drove a peg through it deep into the ground. "Make the cut small, so the peg is tight. Then put one just like it straight across to the leg on the other side. Pull it tight before you drive it in, then stretch out the back legs and do the same thing. Do the head and all around the rest of the hide the same way, just keep it good and tight. You got it?"

"Yessir, I got it."

Twenty-nine hides pegged out flat in the meadow looked impressive to Tom Lee, and Luther saw him admiring their work. "Shit boy, twenty-nine hides ain't nothin'. I done a hundred or more a day by myself two years ago up along the Arkansas."

"A hundred buffs a day? You think we'll ever get that many?"

"We're gonna have to kill a whole lot more than this piddlin' little pile before we'll ever make any money. Twenty-nine ain't even a good start, 'sides, we ain't done with these yet."

"Not done — what else is there left to do?"

"Gotta scrape all the chunks of meat and fat off of them, if you don't, they rot." Luther handed him a curved metal scraper with a wood handle on either end. Dropping to his knees, he began to scrape the remaining flesh off the first hide. "Well, you gonna just stand there boy, or you gonna get to work?"

Tom Lee pulled his bandage tighter and took another morphine pill. "Be right there, gotta do one thing first." Pulling off his boots, he walked to the edge of the water, rolled up his trouser legs, scooped up a handful of mud and spread a thick layer on his legs from his feet to his knees. Pulling his boots back on he walked back to the hides.

"Chiggers?" asked Luther.

Tom Lee nodded and rubbed his legs. "They've been chewing on me pretty good."

"Yeah, they've been working on me too. It's starting to get cold now, that's about the only thing that'll slow 'em down," said

Luther. "Every damn thing in Texas will bite you, sting you or stick you. You ever got bit by a redhead?"

"Once, when I was back on the farm, but I got him off quick. I seen one kill a lizard one time though. Wrapped his long old body around and squeezed it with all them legs and hung on till it died. Then he drug it under a rock and ate it. They are nasty little devils for sure."

"One time, down along the Colorado, I had one crawl up my trousers while I was sleeping in the wagon. Bit me right on my bag — swelled my balls up like a couple of shiny red apples. I thought I was gonna lose my business before it was all over. Sat on a stack of buffalo hides at least a month or more 'fore things got to feeling right again."

"Sounds pretty awful. I just got bit the one time," said Tom Lee, "that was plenty bad enough."

Boyd dropped the three tongues in a large copper pot full of boiling water hung just above the fire. Turning back to the hump meat, he skinned off the fascia and sinew and cut the pieces into strips a foot long. Holding back one slab for tonight, he split the rest of them lengthwise nearly to the end, and then hung them to dry over a rough lattice he'd made from cottonwood branches. They would be good camp jerky in a few days. Cutting the steaks to size, he put them in a bowl of water for a few minutes to clean off any trail dirt or bugs then dropped them in cornmeal and spices he'd already mixed up.

When they were done, he sliced one up thin and threw it in with the steaks.

"How's chuck coming along?" asked Tom Lee, looking into the bowl full of steaks.

"Everything is fine, and no, there's nothing for you to eat — go away."

"We having beans too?"

"No!" said Boyd, shaking his knife at him for emphasis. "And if you don't leave me alone, you won't get no steak neither."

"How about biscuits then?"

Before he could answer, Luther stepped in between them and led Tom Lee away. "Son, everyone knows to leave the cook alone when he's working. None of us want to miss out on his cooking — you hear what I'm sayin' boy?"

"I was just wondering is all . . ."

"Lets you and me start getting' some more pegs ready for tomorrow and leave ol' cookie to his business."

Case and Del started to belly their way up to the top of a gentle, grassy slope topped with a cluster of broken rocks and a string of scraggly mesquite bushes on top. "Feel that?" said Case.

Del felt a gentle but steady vibration. As he laid there, it turned into a strong rumble, shaking the ground under him. "What the hell is that?"

"Buffs — a lot of buffs from the feel of it."

"Now what?" asked Del.

"I think they're slowing down, let's give them a few minutes." After the ground stopped shaking, they finished crawling to the top. Peering down the other side, they saw a large bunch of buffalo grazing a hundred-fifty yards below them. A stiff breeze blew from the buffalo to the hunters. The herd was scattered around a small waterhole, now churned into a muddy pit from hundreds of hooves. Most carried heavy coats of mud from their attempt to cool off and get rid of the hoards of insects that made their lives miserable.

"Perfect," said Case, handing Del a pair of shooting sticks. "Try these. When you can smell 'em like this, you know you're good. Crawl on over and set up with your back to that big rock and keep the bushes between you and the buffs."

Del crawled over and got into a comfortable position, resting the heavy barrel on the shooting sticks. Case pulled himself up next to Del's right shoulder and laid the second rifle between them, loaded and ready to go. Setting a canteen of water next to the rifle, he laid out a neat row of cartridges and hung his binoculars around his neck.

"Okay Del, you ready?"

"Ready as I'll ever be."

"Shoot that big old cow on the left edge of the mud hole, she looks nervous. The minute she drops, take the one that is farthest out on the left. Remember, you gotta shoot the leaders and the possible runners first, you got it?"

Del nodded and put the sights on buffalo. An explosion of acrid smelling smoke filtered back through the mesquite as the cow shuddered. Blowing and shaking her head, she collapsed where she stood. Reloading quickly, he moved to the second one and fired again. As he reloaded again, the smoke drifted away, and he saw her lying in her own tracks.

Del killed the next seven buffalo with seven shots. Case handed him the fresh shells as he dropped each one cleanly. He was well into his first 'stand' as the buffalo hunters called it when he ran a bullet through the belly of a nervous spike bull just as he turned. Running straight into the pond, the bull swung his giant head back and forth splashing through the water and then ran back out bawling in pain and confusion.

"Shoot him — now! Before he scares every one of 'em."

Del shot him again with the same reaction and the bull headed for the pond again, now with blood coming out his belly wound. Before he could shoot, Case fired his rifle, and the buffalo fell over into the pond.

Del handed him another shell. "Get back to work — there's plenty more to be killed."

After several more shots, Case traded rifles with him, and Del continued to kill buffalo without any further wounded ones. Slowly pouring water up and down the length of the barrel, Case cooled off the first rifle, cleaned it and reloaded it while watching the buffalo fall. When there were no more left standing, he motioned to the skinners to get Roly.

Del stood up and looked at the carnage all around him hardly believing what he was seeing. Thirty-four bulls, cows, and calves lay dead within 150 yards of the pond. Case was already splitting hides, getting ready for Roly. "You did damn good for your first stand."

"There's a lot of a dead buffs here," said Del. "Have you seen more than this killed in one bunch?"

"Last year up on the Platte, I killed seventy-two. They call it a stand because if you do it right, the dumb bastards will just stand around and let you keep shooting them. But there ain't no point in killing more than the skinners can handle in one day. We'll get a lot more when they start moving south. Tomorrow you and Arturo will team up. I'll be shooting with Sergio."

"What about Sylvie? Ain't he gonna shoot anymore?"

"No. He lost a cow yesterday, and she spooked off the herd. He took a lot of shots he shouldn't have, and cartridges are eleven cents apiece. He can skin and peg and take care of the mules."

"Did you tell him already?"

Case nodded. "Told him last night. He warn't none too happy about it, but that's the job, take it or leave it."

Roly pulled up to the scene and jumped down from the wagon with his rifle in his hand. "Saw a little more Indian sign on the way here. Looks like a dozen or so ponies — pretty fresh too."

Scanning the surrounding hills looking for any indication of Indians, he handed his binoculars to Del. "You keep a lookout while we get these skinned. Carry the Springfield where everyone can see it and make sure your Colt is ready. My experience is that these murderin' bastards don't like to get too close if they know we're using the .50s. They've learned the hard way, their own rifles and arrows ain't got a chance against 'em".

Sergio and Angel rode up to the site of the stand just as they were finishing up the last of the skinning. "Where's Sylvie?" asked Case.

"He's with Juan," said Sergio. "They're splitting hides, we come to get Roly."

"He's almost ready, how many you got down?"

"Seventeen," said Sergio. "Two of them are really big, dark bulls with heavy robes."

Case nodded. "That's a good sign. Skin the heads on those two and save the skulls. Big horns like that could bring a dollar apiece. It's been gettin' pretty cold. I think the herds are starting to move. It shouldn't be too long before we start seeing more good robes. Tomorrow we'll start hunting over that way. Roly, head out with Sergio and take care of them."

"On my way."

"Take a bunch of tongues and a couple more humps for Boyd too."

Roly nodded and followed Sergio and Angel across the hill.

Del looked over the remarkable scene scattered across the prairie. Thirty-four freshly peeled buffalos lay strung out around the waterhole. Bloody wagon tracks wandered randomly between the steaming carcasses as the skinners gathered the hides and loaded them up.

The Coyotes, never far from the hunters, barked and yelped and wandered through the edges of the scene, already filling their bellies. Climbing into the wagon, Del sat down next to Roly still amazed at what he had experienced today. "Roly, there ain't no end to these things, where do you suppose they all come from?"

"Same place everything comes from my friend — the good Lord almighty! Psalm 107: verse 9 says: 'For he satisfieth the longing soul, and filleth the hungry soul with goodness.' All these beasts were given to us by God to nourish our body and soul."

"And and the body and soul of a lot of coyotes, wolves, and birds too," said Del.

Chapter 8

It was well after dark when the hunters rode back into camp. Boyd and Tom Lee had a good fire and plenty of hot coffee ready to warm them up. The excitement level was not quite as high as the day before. They were all worn down by the extra work on this hunt. Sylvie stripped his horse and walked by Boyd without talking. Peeling off his shirt, he went to the pond and rinsed off. Walking back, the firelight flickered across his body, catching the long, thin scars covering his back.

"Lord almighty Sylvie, how'd you get all them scars?" asked Tom Lee.

"Tom Lee, just let it go, it's none of our business," said Del.

Sylvie pulled on his extra shirt and looked at him. "That's okay Del, I don't mind enlightening our young partner. Tom Lee, this here is what you get when you're a nigger. You know what a nigger is?"

Tom Lee nodded. "I know the word, it means slave."

"That's right, a nigger is a slave, or a whippin' boy — they's all the same thing. Those southern boys loved owning us niggers so much they went to war over it. I guess that makes niggers kinda special now, don't it?"

"Sylvie, I didn't mean to disrespect you none, I just never seen nothing like that before."

"That's okay Tom Lee, no disrespect taken. But I'm here to tell ya, them southern boys, the ones that wore the gray coats . . . they do know how to disrespect someone — ain't that right reb?" said Sylvie, looking right at Boyd. "You hearin' me reb? Does everyone know that old Boyd here carried a rifle for the rebs and killed bluecoats 'cause he loved ownin' niggers so much?"

Boyd instantly lunged across the fire, straight at him, hitting him in the chest and knocking him over a saddle, flat on his back. Sitting on top of Sylvie, he pressed a long skinning knife hard against his neck.

"Okay boy, I give up, don't do no cutting."

Boyd held the knife rock solid against his neck while he stared down at him. "Boy, I talked in favor of taking you into our group, you remember that?" said Sylvie. "People said a gray coat traveling with an escaped slave would be bad, but I didn't care. I killed that Comanche that almost got you too — you remember that?"

Boyd pressed the knife deeper into his neck, and a fine trickle of blood ran down to his shirt. "I ain't forgot nothing — that's the only reason you're still alive. But if you call me a reb, or say I owned slaves one more time, and I'll cut off your balls and stuff 'em down your gullet — then I'll kill you."

"Okay, I got it, now let me up."

Sitting up, Sylvie realized that Case was standing over him with one hand on his Colt. "Mister, I don't give a good goddamn if you're black or white, north or south, an ex-slave or the President of these United States. We got us a good outfit here, and I don't want nobody messing it up. So, you'll keep your mouth shut and do exactly what I tell you to, or you find another way of making a livin'. 'Cause you start any more crap in this outfit, and I'll bury you right here. You understand?"

Sylvie got up, threw down his cup and walked back to the tent. "Yeah, I understand everything. I understand it just fine."

An inch of buffalo tallow boiled and popped in an oversized skillet as Boyd dropped in the meat. "Plenty more hump and tongue here, you're gonna have to eat it all up before I make fresh," said Boyd.

"You got any more taters in that big pot of yours?" asked Del.

Boyd shook his head, "just hump and tongue."

"I'll take more please," said Roly, holding out his plate. "Whether therefore ye eat, or drink, or whatsoever ye do, do all to the glory of God — amen! Thank you Mister Boyd, that is some mighty good chuck. I can't remember if I ever had such good hump as this."

"Me neither," said Case, handing his plate to Boyd. The rest of the crew fell into line behind him.

With the morning fire blazing, Boyd beat his spoon on the coffee boiler, and within a few minutes the hunters were out of their tents and lined up, waiting for coffee and chuck. The first snow of the season had glazed everything with a thick icy crust, and the bitter temperature had everyone looking for a place around the fire while they waited their turn. As Boyd poured the coffee, he realized that Sylvie was missing.

"Case, I think we lost one last night," said Boyd. "Looks like Sylvie took off."

He shrugged. "He was nothing but trouble anyway. I hate runnin' short-handed, but the longer he stayed out here, the more messed up his head was gonna get. When we get the first load to the Walls, I can get someone to replace him."

As Luther unloaded the hides for the pegging work, Roly hitched the team for the days hunt. "Case, you're missing a Springfield here."

Looking into the box that held the rifles and the shells, he slammed down the lid. "That thievin' son-of-a bitch took a rifle and a bunch of cartridges with him. Damn him to hell! Stealing from your own people is worse than any murdering Indian would do! He don't want me to catch him, because if I do he'll wish it was the Comanches that got him."

"Boss, it looks like he got one of the extra horses too," said Roly. "His own is gone, and that tall spotted mare is missing."

"I planned on two rifles for each shooter. Well, there ain't nothin' I can do right now, so let's mount up and get to hunting," said Case. "I'll deal with it when I catch up to him."

Tom Lee and Luther scattered the newest batch of hides across the grass and began the backbreaking job of pegging and scraping 63 more hides. The sun came out early enough to warm them up, but the snow had turned things muddy and made the work even more miserable. "Pay attention here boy," said Luther. "We're gonna make these two big ones into robes and were gonna skin out the heads too."

"Ain't we been makin' robes outta these others?"

"Nope, still ain't cold enough to move a lot of big ones down here yet. You got yer big bulls, like these two, they'll be robe hides, that's the best money. The rest of these will likely be for small blankets or leather. When the big herds get here, we wanna kill all the large heavy bulls first. But you have to shoot a lot of the others too if it looks like they're gonna spook the rest of them."

"How much money will a big one bring?" asked Tom Lee.

"Don't know exactly. I think Case can likely get two and a half or three dollars for a good one," said Luther, driving another peg. "Maybe a dollar and a half for cows and spikes."

"And the little ones?"

"Calves and kips—maybe seventy-five cents or a dollar."

"Kips?"

"Babies and dinks and such, they're barely worth haulin' in."

"How long before they're dry enough to haul away?"

"A week or so, depending on the weather. Enough talk boy, get onto peggin' these hides."

Talk that evening was all about how many buffalo they saw and how many hides they took. Both shooters together took sixty-three hides, including five good robes. "We did fair today," said Case, stretching out on the wagon. "With two shooters, we need to be killing at least seventy or more every day from now on out. That's what it's gonna take to make any real money out here. We need to get a good load of hides to the Walls on the last day of October — that's eighteen days from now."

"How long a trip is it?" asked Tom Lee.

"It's the better part of three days. So, we need to haul out the first load in fifteen days. That'll take two hands away from camp, so we all gotta be extra careful while they're gone," said Case.

"Me and Arturo spotted six Comanches after we stopped shooting," said Del. "They just set on their ponies and watched from a good distance while we skinned 'em."

"Yeah, I been seein' a few here and there," said Case. "They won't get too close as long as they know we're shootin' the Springfields. When we get the first load to my partners, we may be able to pick up another hand to replace Sylvie, maybe even two."

After two long weeks of killing and skinning, the first load was ready to ship out. "Luther, how many are ready?" asked Case.

"Looks like something over three hundred. We got forty-six good robes and the rest are cows, spikes, and calves. Got a dozen good skulls too."

"How many more still drying?"

"Probably four hundred more, not counting yesterday's kill. That's probably another sixty or more still to be pegged. We should have another load dried by the time you get back."

"I'm not going back this trip," said Case. "I want you and Juan to take 'em back. He's a good shot, and he's good at spotting trouble."

"Then me and Tom Lee will start packing 'em up just as soon as soon as we finish up pegging these ones," said Luther.

Case nodded and took a drink of his coffee. "Tomorrow you can finish those up. You gonna use both pair of mules?"

"Yessir. Roly can use horses for the skinning work, no trouble there. I'm gonna need both pair of mules and rest them for a day or two after we unload them."

As the men rode out for the next day's hunt, Luther and Tom Lee scattered out the fresh hides. Pulling the pegs out of the dry ones, they flipped them over hair side up. Finishing with pegging and scraping yesterday's kill, Luther walked back to the dried hides. "Okay boy, I'll show you what to do and then I'll go get the wagon." Stepping on the hide with one foot, he bounced it up and down. "Hear it kinda rattle some? See how stiff it is? That's how we want it for shipping."

Tom Lee rattled it and lifted up one corner to for himself. "Stiffer than a frozen canvas, that's for sure."

"Listen boy, I know your back's hurtin' you bad, you gonna be able to keep up with these hides okay?"

"I'll keep up just fine."

"Turn around and show me where the arrow got you," said Luther.

Tom Lee took off his shirt, unwrapped the long cloth and showed him the bandage, now stuck to the wound. Luther peeled off the filthy cloth and threw it into the fire. Washing off the wound with water, he dried it, folded up his bandanna and placed it against the wound. "You're lucky boy, it don't look infected or anything. I'll wrap this long cloth back around you like it was. You need to keep it pulled tight so's no critters crawl up in there. How many of them pills you got left?"

"A few is all."

"When I get back, we'll see if we can fashion some sort of brace, maybe out of buff hide," said Luther. "That is if you make it that long."

"I'll make it just fine, don't worry none about me," said Tom Lee, pulling his shirt back on.

Completely dried, the hides were so stiff that they were hard for one man to handle. When Luther returned with the wagon, he had the bottom lined with several old worn hides. "Lay the first big one hair side up and the next one on top of it with the hair side down. Then we start a second pile and crisscross them, it makes them tighter, understand?"

"I understand — I ain't dumb you know."

Tom Lee put two four-foot long poles he carved from cottonwood branches along either side of the seat sticking straight up. They were about three inches thick and had been rubbed down with mud to darken the color. When Luther asked what they were, he explained that the Indians didn't like getting close to the Springfields, so he made up a couple sticks to look like both men had one sitting right next to them. Luther looked at the sticks for a minute, contemplating their value.

"Well boy, I think recitin' one of old Roly's prayers to the almighty would likely work just as well. I don't think they'll do much good, but I guess they surely can't hurt."

That night, the hunters came in with sixty-five hides, including twelve good robes. "Right now we're killing about sixty buffs a day," said Case, talking to the men while they ate "The herds are moving in good now, and we're seeing a lot more big bulls. We still need to get the kill up to at least seventy or more every day, and at least half of them have to be robe bulls or big cows."

"But we don't always see that many big bulls in one day," said Del.

"It's still early, the bulls are just finishing up tending the cows and they'll start to bunch up by themselves. We'll start seeing some groups with just bulls and some with nothing but cows and calves. From here on, don't shoot calves or kips unless they're keeping us from getting on the good ones. If you have to kill 'em to keep 'em from spooking the herd, that's okay, but don't shoot the little ones just for the hides."

Releasing the brake, Luther cracked his whip, and the mules jerked the wagon forward and down the slight hill. Clearing the hill, they swung the wagon north, leaving the trail they made to get there the first day. The wagon swayed slowly into the turn. "Gee — you bunch of knotheads — gee," hollered Luther, cracking the whip again as the team made the turn and headed into the early morning sun. Climbing onto the canvas covering the pile of hides, Juan laid his own rifle across his lap and one of the dummy Springfields alongside him. Pulling his sombrero down just low enough to keep out the sun, he would ride shotgun this way until they reached the Walls.

After several hours on the trail, Luther pulled up to a small depression in the rock that had filled with water from the recent snowmelt. Giving the mules a chance to rest and get a drink, he walked a few yards into the bushes looking for a comfortable spot to do his morning business. As he walked toward the bushes, he saw a trail of blood leading to the big spotted mare lying dead on the ground. A dozen arrows were sticking out of her body.

Hollering for Juan to come and help him, he checked his Colt and the rifle and started to look for Sylvie in the surrounding area. Picking up the tracks of a shod horse leading away from the rocks it looked like he had escaped the attack. Luther returned to the wagon and took one last look around.

Juan came through the bushes holding something in the air. "Señor Luther, el rifle." He handed it to him and climbed up. It was the missing Springfield with a broken butt stock.

"He must have dropped it when he was running away," said Luther. Grabbing the reigns, he got the team started back on the trail. A loud crack of the whip and he had them up to speed. "I don't want to stay around here any longer than we have to."

"Si Señor," said Juan, scanning the hillside, "con rapidez . . .!"

Reaching the site of Adobe Walls without any more Indian sign, Luther pulled alongside a weed-filled pile of adobe bricks and unhitched the team. After caring for the mules, he sat down against the bricks and pulled out a large piece of jerky. Cutting it in pieces, he handed part of it to Juan. "This spot right here is where old Kit Carson got his butt kicked by the Comanches and the Kiowas a couple of years back. You know who Kit Carson is?"

Juan just looked at him as he talked. "You hablas ingles?"

"No Señor."

"Well, that's too bad, he is a very great man — a great Indian killer. I was with him at Valverde Ford against the rebs in '62 and killed a pile of Navahos with him in '63. Carson... uh... great... uh... indio asesino . . .?"

Juan nodded and smiled. "Si, Carson, gran asesino indio — si."

"Let's get us a fire going," said Luther. "It's startin' to get cold and it looks like snow might be rolling in." Building a shelter with a sheet of canvas across the brick piles, the men finished eating, added wood to the fire and crawled inside.

By mid-morning Luther could hear the rattle of a wagon and the crack of a whip in the distance. Several inches of snow covered everything, and the wind was blowing sideways across the prairie. Within minutes a freight wagon and four men on horseback appeared through the haze and rolled up next to his wagon. "You with Case's outfit?" asked the driver, yelling to be heard over the wind.

Luther put one hand on his hat and stuck out his other one. "I'm Luther and this is Juan, but he don't speak no English. We got a full load of hides for you, some good robes too."

The stranger shook his hand. "I'm Thomas. My men will set up a tent so we can wait this out."

"That'll be good," said Luther, "I think this snow may hang around a while."

When the tent was up, they took a small tin stove from the wagon, set it up, threw in a handful of chips and lit it. "That'll warm things up fast," said Thomas. "You run into any serious Indian trouble out there?"

Luther filled him in on the disappearance of Sylvie and finding the dead horse. He also showed him the Springfield with the broken stock. "That's been the worst of it so far, but they're always around. I expect we'll see more of them before we finish. You look an awful lot like Case, you related?"

"Brothers. We've been working the herds up north selling meat to the army. A couple of good storms got them riled up, and they're starting to move down. We're gonna sell these hides and finish up some business. We should be down there in two weeks or so."

Thomas looked like Case but slightly shorter and more muscular. He had the same long hair and thick scruffy beard, and his piercing dark eyes seemed to be locked on to you whenever you looked at him. "Case wants to know if you got at least one hand to replace the one that ran off," said Luther. "We were already running short-handed before he left. He says that he'd take two if you could spare 'em."

Thomas thought about it for a moment. "Yeah, I'll send two men with you. Show me that rifle. I want to see if it can be fixed." Cutting a piece of fresh buffalo hide, he soaked it in water and wrapped it around the stock. Using a string cut from a scrap of rawhide, he laced it together with several crude stitches. "When it dries, it'll hold together good."

"How many are there in your outfit?" asked Luther.

"There were nine of us, but when we got back to civilization, three of them took their pay and left," said Thomas. "There's one more gonna catch back up with us soon, another good driver, but he had some business to attend to. The first one to go was the cook and I ain't been able to find another one."

"If you're planning on setting up with us, you won't need to concern yourself none, we got us a good one," said Luther.

"Then I won't go looking for another one. What kind of supplies are you needing?"

"I'm sure he wants more cartridges and maybe some extra powder and lead for the pistols. I think cookie can probably use things like taters and apples and anything in cans that you can come up with. We also got a man with an old arrow in his back. He's a good hand, and he's sufferin' something awful. If you can find any of those pills the doctors give out for such things, he could really use 'em."

"I got some canned goods in the wagon right now," said Thomas. "You can take them back with you. There's not much chance of finding any taters or apples though. Even if I found someone with a cellar full, it's not likely they'll want to give them up. Soon as the snow lets up, we can switch the wagons. T.C. and Baptise will go back to camp with you. They'll bring their horses with 'em too."

By dark, the wind was screaming and piercing every opening in the tent. The hunters had brought in a pile of firewood and chips and enough jerky to last at least another full day. The seven men huddled together near the stove as the wind drowned out any chance of conversation. The next morning was a repeat of the first as the men scrambled through the snow for more food and firewood.

By early morning of the third day, the wind had dropped off and they crawled out to see the damage. The snow was not as bad as they thought, but it was piled heavily against the backside of every windbreak on the prairie. The mules and horses were safe in the cottonwoods, but there was no open water for them. After chopping holes in the ice, they hitched Thomas's team to the loaded hide wagon. "All four of our Springfields are in that long box, and there's most of a case of cartridges there too. You need to take them with you. We won't be hunting again until we get down there. You planning on going back tomorrow?"

"No. Now that the sun is coming back out, I'm gonna give the mules another day of rest," said Luther. "I want them to eat all they can and drink some more before we leave. It was a long hard pull with such a heavy load."

Chapter 9

Waking up to a bitter cold morning, Luther and Juan built a fire, made coffee, and chopped the ice open for the mules. Hitching the teams, they packed up for the trip back to camp. Tying their horses to the wagon, the new men loaded their saddles and gear into the wagon, tied on their horses and climbed in for the long ride back to camp. Several old hides and a filthy piece of canvas were all they had for comfort. Juan leaned against the tailgate with an enormous old hide wrapped twice around him and his rifle across his knees. Luther wore an oversized buffalo robe coat with high collars and long, leather gauntlets. His hat was pulled down tight, held on by a rag wrapped around it and tied under his chin. Cracking his whip, the mule's ears perked up, and the wagon lurched to life.

"You been seeing big herds down there?" asked T.C.

"Getting better every day. When we left, they were seeing a lot more robe bulls than when we first got there," said Luther, cracking the whip again.

"What about the Indians? They been bothering you much?"

"Some, but so far nobody's been killed."

Several hours on the trail brought the wagon to a trickle of water coming from a spring on the sunny side of a long rimrock face. After the mules were satisfied, Luther hollered and cracked his whip, pulling onto the faint trail. Within minutes the air erupted with the shrieks of a pair of Comanche braves riding full speed straight at them.

"Injuns!" Screamed Luther. Coming right at us!" Three rifles appeared across the wagon side and opened fire from the back of the wagon without effect. "They're outta range — grab the Springfields!"

The three hunters in the wagon leveled the long rifles across the bed and fired. One bullet missed its mark to the left and the second one killed the horse out from under the rider. The third shot whizzed by the head of the Indians as they both rode away on one horse.

"Come on you bastards, try again," screamed Luther, cracking his whip as the two Comanches rode out of sight. "Keep on watching. I don't think they knew you were in the wagon, they thought I was all alone. If we seen two of 'em, then you know there's a bunch more out there lookin' to collect our hair," said Luther, cracking his whip again and again.

For the rest of the day, the Springfields were pointed out of the wagon as Luther drove the mules hard. Several times they spotted Indians on the far ridges, but none came close enough to shoot at.

After a long miserable trip, the wagon pulled into camp just as Boyd was starting evening chuck. For several days the empty wagon had bounced along the rough trail, and the men were half-frozen and more than ready for hot food and a big fire. The hide yard was covered with hundreds of fresh skins. Ricks of already dried hides were stacked around the edges, covered by canvas, ready for transportation to the market.

"Something smells good here," said Baptise, jumping off the wagon. Luther walked over to introduce the two new men to Boyd. "I am Baptise, I am from New Orleans. Good to meet you Mister Cookie, everything smells very good. You have something for a hungry hunter — oui?"

"Over there," said Boyd, pointing to the jerky drying on the cottonwood frame.

"Merci, Mister Cookie, very good," said Baptise.

"And you are?" said Boyd, looking at the second man.

"I'm T.C., from Ohio. Can I get a taste of that jerky too?"

"Help yourself," said Boyd. "You can have all the jerky you want, just don't let me catch either of you near any of the other food or I'll shoot you. Then get on those hides."

Both men looked at him with a mouth full of jerky. "Yessir," said T.C., "on my way."

Baptise looked at Tom Lee. "Monsieur, would he really shoot us?"

"He did the last guy," said Tom Lee, trying not to crack a smile.

"How's your back doin'?" asked Boyd.

"It hurts, but I'll get along just fine."

"Pull up your shirt and let me take a look at it."

"It's okay, I can handle it."

Ignoring his comment, he walked over and pulled his shirt up. "Just like I thought, it's dirty and bloody. Take off your shirt and lay down on a hide so I can get a better look." Unwrapping the dirty cloth, he found the wound filthy and caked with dried blood. "Lay still where you're at, I'll be right back."

"It's freezing cold out here," said Tom Lee, "where you goin'?"

"Just lay there and be quiet. I'm gonna wash out this cloth." After soaking the cloth and scrubbing it thoroughly with a large bar of lye soap, he rinsed it and laid it near the fire to dry.

"Shoot Boyd, it ain't bothering me all that much."

"I just wanted to get rid of the maggots is all."

"Maggots? No way, you're messing with me again — I ain't got no maggots!"

"Not anymore you don't. They done ate their fill and died, now let me get a closer look at that hole."

Tom Lee reached around to feel the wound and Boyd stopped him. "Goddamn it, lay still and let me look at it. I want to clean it off a little, to see if there's any more of them little critters left in there."

"I know you're lyin' to me Boyd — people don't get maggots! Besides, it too cold for maggots anyhow."

Boyd washed the blood off the wound, dried it and bent down for a closer look. "This is a whole lot better than I thought it would be. The maggots got all the bad stuff already. I can't see the arrow, but now that it's clean we should cauterize the hole, so it won't get infected."

"That ain't so! No maggots could get in there. I had the cloth around me!"

"A fly musta laid some eggs in there, and your body kept them warm 'till they hatched. Don't worry nothing about them — they did you a good thing. It's good and clean, and we can cauterize it proper."

"Well okay, go ahead and do it, but don't you go telling no one I had maggots — you hear me?"

Boyd motioned for Baptise and T.C. to pin him down on the hide while Boyd heated the tip of a skinning knife in the fire until it glowed red. "Ready Tom Lee?"

"Just stop talking and do it!"

Boyd pulled the knife from the fire and pressed it firmly against the wound. Acrid smelling smoke swirled from the burning skin, and Tom Lee's body stiffened. After a few seconds, he dropped the knife and bent close again to see if he had sealed the whole wound. "Let him go, he's done," said Boyd. "Lay still for another minute and let it cool off while I get the salve, and we'll finish it up."

"Boyd . . ."

"What?"

"Next time I get stuck with an arrow — just put a rifle bullet in me. I ain't never goin' through that again."

"No problem, I'll just pretend you're a buff with a good robe." Washing off the wound, Boyd and Baptise put on a fresh linen bandage, rewrapped the cloth tightly around his chest and helped him get his shirt on.

Baptise reached for Tom Lee's hand. "Mon ami, I shake your hand, you are a very strong man, not even a small sound."

When the hunters and skinners rode in after dark, they picketed their horses and headed for the fire. Roly followed them with a wagon load of fresh hides. Case called Luther over for a report. "Any problems this trip?"

Luther explained to him about finding the spotted mare and the broken rifle.

"What about the Indians that did it, you see them?"

"We saw a couple on the way back, but they didn't have the belly for a real fight. Thomas said his outfit will be down soon." He handed Case the Springfield. "He did the repair. It looks like it should shoot okay now."

"No sign of the thief?" asked Case.

Luther shook his head. "Just his tracks headin' north is all."

"Too bad the Comanches didn't get him, it woulda saved me a lot of trouble."

After chuck, Case told the men that the two new hands would work as hide men and relieve Tom Lee. "We got over ninety fresh hides today, and every man here is exhausted. Tom Lee will work with Boyd from now on. When the others get here, there'll be extra hands to feed, and he'll need more help."

"Mon ami, I was a shooter before," said Baptise. "Why can't I be a shooter here?"

"Because I said you're a hide man. When Thomas gets here, he can decide what to do with you. If you don't want the work, you can ride out."

"No, no problem — I will wait until he gets here."

"What about you, T.C.?" asked Case. "You got a problem with this?"

"No sir, no problem at all."

Del sat down at the fire next to Tom Lee. "Boyd said he cauterized your back, how's it feeling?"

"It hurts some, but I'll get along okay. Did you kill a lot of them today?"

"I killed a good pile of them, but I saw something hard to imagine when I walked over a hill though."

"What'd you see Del?"

"I saw a white valley."

"You saw a white valley? You mean a valley full of snow?"

"Not snow Tom Lee, bones. Snow white bones filling the valley as far as you can see, shining bright in the early sun."

"Bones? Del, we seen lots of bones before, are these something different?"

Del nodded his head. "The valley was covered with thousands and thousands of bleached white buffalo bones. You could hardly see the grass for all the bones. Must have been from the summer hunters. They'd been scattered all across the valley by animals I guess. It was just kinda spooky is all."

"Maybe you was seeing the ghosts of all the buffalos you killed."

"No goddamn it, they ain't no such thing as ghosts," said Del, finishing his coffee. "Just buffalo bones is all. It's a good thing there's so many of them damn things, at least they won't run out."

The next morning, Baptise and T.C. started pegging the fresh hides. The work was brutal and backbreaking, but the two men worked well together. T.C., a tall, hulking young man hardly spoke at all and Baptise, a skinny, raggy looking Frenchman, never quit talking, jabbering all day long, usually in French.

"Damn, Tom Lee," said Boyd, "old Frenchy there don't never shut up. They musta run him out of New Orleans for makin' so much noise."

"Yeah, I wish Case woulda took him, it'd be a lot quieter for sure."

"Never did like those frogs all that much," said Boyd. "Don't trust them at all. We had a couple in our regiment, they stole everything they could get their hands on, 'specially the food."

"I don't think I ever met one before this," said Tom Lee.

"I'm just saying we need to keep a sharp eye on that one is all."

One wagon was already filled with dried hides, covered, and ready to go by the time Thomas and his outfit pulled into camp. "Brother," said Case, embracing him. "Good to see you. Any trouble up north?"

"Just the usual, Indians and bad weather. Put a lot of buffs down though. The market's gettin' better every day and our company's doin' well."

"That's good to hear. You got some skinners with you?"

Thomas nodded. "Got two hands with me right now, both of them good workers. There's one more shooter still to come, he's riding guard with Dobbs, my driver. Looks like you're ready to haul a load out now?"

"Now that we have all three wagons here, we could do two loads if you think it's a good plan."

"Let's talk about it in the morning, but the sooner we get the hides out of here, the better. How you gettin' along with the Frenchman?"

"He works good," said Case, "but he never shuts up. Everyone is tired of his mouth. He bothers me every day about being a shooter, says he's being wasted in the hide yard."

"That skinny little man is a brute for hard work. He can handle anything you give him, but he's a pain in the ass to be around. I put him on the rifle to keep him away from the others, even then he wouldn't shut up. Twice already he spooked the herd when he started talking to 'em."

"He was talkin' to the buffs? What was he saying to them?"

"Don't know, it was in French."

"Then he needs to stay on the hides," said Case.

"Agreed. Is he working with T.C.?"

"Yeah, he seems to be okay with all the talking."

"T.C. don't say much, he just keeps on working" said Thomas. "Luther says you got a good cook, that right?"

"Best we ever had for sure. He's an ex-confederate soldier, from the fight down at Brownsville. He can be kinda grumpy now and then, and he don't like nobody calling him a reb, but it's worth putting up with a little guff for his cooking."

"Good to hear that. The last one I had took off as soon as he was paid. He burned nearly everything he made. Most of the hands had to quit eating his beans, or they'd spend more time in the bushes than they would hunting."

"Then you're gonna appreciate Boyd. You look a bit skinny, his beans and biscuits should fill you back out."

In the morning, the brothers walked through the yard and inventoried the hides. "Do you think we can we risk sending two wagon loads to the Walls at a time?" asked Case.

"I'd like to, but that means that four hands and two teams of mules would be on the trail at the same time. I think that's too dangerous," said Thomas. "Dobbs should be here before long with the other wagon, then we can talk about sending two at a time. As soon as he gets here, we'll have another load ready. I think we should use your guy for this load. That'll give Luther and Dobbs a break from the last trip. As soon as he says the mules are ready, he can leave."

"Good enough," said Case. "I've been killing most of the buffs straight north of here about three miles or so, the other team is farther northwest. You should probably head west and a bit south. I haven't seen any sign of other hunters down there."

"Then that's where we're heading. How are the Indians, they been bothering you much?"

"They're always around, just waiting for the opportunity to ambush you. We've seen Comanche and Kiowas both. Just don't get caught alone and keep the big rifles in plain sight."

"I heard you got a hand with an arrow in his back?"

"Yeah, Tom Lee is carrying one from just before we hooked up at Fort Chadbourne."

"Is he able to do the job okay?"

"Oh hell yes," said Case. "I think he might be one of the best hands we ever had, even with the arrow. He's definitely one of the toughest."

"I brought this tin of doctor pills, they must be for him?"

Case nodded. "Yeah, he's been run out for a long time. I'm sure he can use them."

"Monsieur Thomas, we must talk about my job."

"Goddamnit Baptise, I said no more talking. Get back on the hides or get the hell out," said Thomas.

"But monsieur, I killed many buffalo for you before, I should be shooting for you now," said Baptise. "I am a good shooter."

"That's it, you're done — get the hell out now!" said Thomas, stepping up to the little Frenchman. "You'll get your money when we finish up the winter hunt, just like the rest of us, now get out."

Baptise stared at Thomas, his face flush with anger. "Okay monsieur, I will do your hides, and I will not complain. But I will not hunt with you ever again after this."

"If you do the job and don't complain again, you can stay until we finish this hunt. When I pay you off, I don't ever want to see you or hear your voice again — you understand?"

"Oui, I understand okay."

Case watched him walk back to the hide yard. "Brother, I'm surprised you let him stay, nobody here would miss him if he was gone."

Thomas shrugged. "It's hard to find people to come out here, and ones that work as hard as he does are rare. It's not the first time he's done this — I fired him twice before. He'll be good in a couple of days."

As the teams got ready for the morning hunt, Baptise and T.C. asked for more coffee before they started to work the fresh hides. A bitter cold wind caused the hide men to pull down their hats and put on their gloves. Boyd poured them the last of the coffee and gave each one an extra biscuit. "There'll be coffee on the fire all day. If you get too cold standing out there, come in and get some." Wolfing down the biscuit, they finished the coffee and headed for the pile of hides.

"Boyd, what do you think of this buffalo hunting business?"

"What do you mean?"

"You think you want to keep on doing this? It's some cold lonely work, and I'm gettin' tired of stinking of blood all the time. In another month the ticks and chiggers will be back out, and everything will full of lice again. I think I'm gonna leave the buffalos to those that like such things."

Boyd shrugged. "It beats carrying a rifle and marching all over the country for a losing Army. At least here I have plenty of food, a place to sleep, and I can ride wherever I go. Why? You wantin' to quit?"

Tom Lee threw another stack of chips on the fire. "No, I'll finish up the winter hunt. But after I draw my pay, I think I'm gonna head back down to San Antonio and get a job closer to civilization. Maybe I can find a doctor to cut this arrow outta my back while I'm there."

"She was pretty, wasn't she?" said Boyd.

Tom Lee looked surprised at the comment. "Pretty? What in heck are you talking about?"

"You know darn well what I'm talkin' about, don't play dumb on me."

"Boyd, you ain't making no sense to me at all."

"We both know you got Sylvie's daughter on your mind."

Now red in the face, he pulled off his hat, ran his fingers through his hair and grinned. "So, what if I do? I don't see nothing wrong in that."

"It's okay. There ain't a thing wrong with that, we all think she's real pretty," said Boyd.

"Well just don't go saying nothing to the others, it ain't none of their business."

"I got no reason to say nothing to nobody. I'll keep your secret just fine."

"I think Sylvie would like it if someone checked on her, don't you think? Besides, maybe she knows what happened to him."

"I don't see as it would do any harm," said Boyd, mixing up a fresh batch of biscuits. "Grandma looks to be kinda old, she could probably use a little help around the place too."

"Okay, I'm done with this talk," said Tom Lee, "so don't bring it up again."

"Good enough," said Boyd. "Then grab me a couple more tongues and put on some more firewood."

Dropping the wood in the fire, he poked at it for a minute. "Boyd . . ."

"What?"

"How did you know?"

"Shit son, you think you're the first cowboy ever got by smitten by a pretty senorita? We all been there before, and we all know it when we see it happen to someone else."

Tom Lee's face flushed again. "She is pretty, ain't she?"

"Yeah, she's real pretty. You said you was done with this girl talk, so get back to making meat."

"I'll quit talkin' about her, but I can't quit thinking about her — that's just the way it is."

"Just don't be thinkin' so hard about pretty things that you end up cutting off any fingers," said Boyd.

Chapter 10

By the first signs of spring, the ***Thomas and Case Hide and Fur Co.*** was well established as a dependable source of good buffalo hides. Buyers had set up at Adobe Walls to serve the few outfits that were brave enough to spend the winter killing buffalo among the roaming Comanches and Kiowas.

"How much longer?" asked Case.

"We should start packing up tomorrow," said Thomas. "The buffs are already starting to shed, and we've been seein' more Indian sign lately. We're done shootin' as of now. Tell the men to finish up the hides we already got. Some of us will have to wait here for the last ones to dry while we start hauling out the rest."

The brothers sat in front of the fire going over the numbers from the winter hunt. "This has been a long season, I'm glad to finish up," said Case.

Thomas nodded. "It has been. We've been out here almost five months, that's too long. I thought we would get more good hides if we started early. Next season we will start the Texas hunt on the first day of November and finish no later than the first day of March."

"I think that will be just right," said Case. "There will be less poor-quality hides to kill and skin."

"I have it that we shipped 4,706 hides from this camp already," said Thomas. "That's nearly 240 a week, a good season for a small company like ours. With what we got up north and the ones still drying, we should have plenty of cash for next year's hunt."

"How'd we do on good robes?" asked Case.

"Good. I figure we had nearly 2,300 bulls and big cows that should be good for robes. The rest were spikes, calves, and a few others for leather," said Thomas. "We also killed seventy-six coyotes, seventeen wolves, eight foxes, and one badger."

"A badger? I don't remember that."

"Shot him on the trip down here. Went to the bushes to do my business and when I squatted down, the damn thing poked his ugly head out of a hole and started snarling and snapping his teeth at me, so I shot him."

"You shot him with your drawers down around your ankles?"

"I did, then I finished up and skinned his ass for scaring me so bad," said Thomas.

"I guess that'll teach him not to scare the shit outta people," said Case, laughing out loud.

Finishing up his biscuit and coffee, Thomas grinned. "At least that one won't."

"We still have probably two loads dryin' on the ground right now," said Case. "I'll get the men packing up. In the morning we'll send Dobbs out with the wagon that's already packed, and I'll have Roly get another load ready."

Climbing into the wagon, Dobbs, a tall, straight man with an enormous pot belly poking out between his suspenders, set his rifle next to him and started the team moving. The mules strained into the harness at the crack of the whip, and the wagon groaned under the weight of a full load. Case sent two men along as guards on this trip. Both settled into the pile of hides and laid a Springfield across their laps.

Two days later, Roly was loaded and ready to haul. Juan and Arturo were assigned to the guard jobs and climbed onto the pile. "By the time you get back, everything here will be ready to haul out," said Case. "Keep a sharp eye, the warm weather's gonna bring out more trouble makin' Indians."

Roly pulled down his hat and released the brake. "The grace of the Lord Jesus be with all — amen!" Cracking the whip over the heads of the mules, he pulled out of camp and headed for the Walls. By the end of the first day, the weather began to warm, but everyone was already wet from a light spring snow. The wagon stopped near a spring running into a shallow pond. Making camp for the night, Roly started a fire and hovered over it, trying to warm up.

"Señor Roly," said Arturo, "Perhaps a fire is not a good idea? There are many Indios in this area."

"I don't care nothing about no Indians. I'm wet and cold, and I'm gonna dry out."

"Si, I understand Señor, but quickly please, so we can put it out before they see us."

Roly shrugged. "I'll be dry when I'm dry, and that's the way it is."

When Roly had warmed up, he kicked dirt on the fire, grabbed a handful of jerky and crawled under the wagon, pulling a robe over himself. Within minutes he was snoring loudly.

Arturo leaped up at the first scream to see Roly leaning against the wagon, touching off a shot, hitting a running Indian square in the chest. The Springfield knocked him off his feet and blew right through him. Dropping the rifle, he grabbed his Colt and shot him again in the head. Arturo could see an arrow sticking out of the middle of his back. Roly spun around and fired again at another Indian running straight for him. The brave pitched face first into the dirt several steps in front of him.

Two more shrieking Indians were nearly on top of Arturo just as he fired, hitting the first one in the jaw. Before he could get another round in the chamber the second one was on top of him. Knocking his rifle away the Indian pulled out his knife, wild-eyed and screaming at the top of his lungs. Holding the knife away with one hand Arturo twisted his belt holster around, cocked the hammer on his Colt and fired through the leather, hitting the Indian in the belly. When the brave fell over, Arturo rolled out from under him in time to see Roly take two more arrows in the chest. Raising his pistol, Roly fired, knocking both of them down. One got back on his feet and lunged at him and Arturo fired from the ground dropping him next to the first one. Walking up to them, Roly shot both in the head.

"Shoot those two again," said Roly, pointing to the ones next to Arturo.

"Señor, you have arrows in you?"

"I've had worse, now shoot 'em again."

Finishing off the last Indian, they walked over to where Juan laid and saw an arrow sticking all the way through his neck. "They got to him first," said Roly, "he was still sleeping, and we never heard a thing. Next thing I know, they were all around me screaming and hollering and shooting at me."

"Señor, the arrows — they do not hurt you?"

Roly looked at the two sticking out of his chest. "Some, let's get 'em out so we can get Juan in the ground."

Arturo could hardly believe what he was hearing. "You want me to remove the arrows, si?"

Roly nodded. "I'll get the ones in front, but you have to do the one in back because I can't reach it."

Sitting on the tongue of the wagon, Roly grabbed the arrow in his chest and jerked it straight out without blinking. Throwing it down, he grabbed the one below his left shoulder and did the same thing. "Okay son, now get that other one out."

Arturo grabbed the shaft of the arrow, and it didn't move. It was close to the backbone and did not come out easily or quickly. With each pull, Roly remained still and didn't say a word.

"Señor, it is buried deep into your backstrap," said Arturo.

"Just keep pulling, it'll come out."

On the third try, the arrow pulled free, and Roly let out a big sigh of relief. "I owe you son, now let's get to diggin' that hole."

"Si, but the wounds are bleeding, are you okay to continue?"

Roly shrugged. "When you're this fat, those little arrows don't go in all that deep. If it was you they hit, they'd a gone right through. Besides, the good Lord ain't about to take me home just for a couple little arrows."

Lowering Juan into the hole, they covered him with a piece of canvas and a layer of rocks. Roly gave him a fitting eulogy, reciting a Bible passage that Arturo had never heard before. When he finished, they filled in the grave and put down another layer of rocks. Roly fashioned a crude cross from branches and stuck it in the ground, saying a few last words.

"What about the dead Indians?" asked Arturo.

"What about them?"

"Should we bury them?"

"You do what you want — I'm headed for the Walls."

Near the end of the second day, they met up with Dobbs heading back to camp for another load. They stopped for the night and made a good fire. "There are enough of us here now that the savages won't give us no trouble," said Roly. "Besides, I think me and Arturo killed most of them — right Arturo?"

"Si, we killed many, but not all of them. They keep on coming, like the buffalos."

"Then we'll keep on killing 'em," said Roly, "just like the buffalos."

Reaching Adobe Walls, Roly took care of the mules while Arturo unloaded the hides. The buyer noted each one in his ledger by size and quality and gave Roly a receipt.

"How many loads you got left?" said the hide buyer, closing his book.

"Maybe three or four, we're already done shootin' for the season. The buffs are already startin' to look kind of rangy. Soon as the rest of them finish drying, we'll be done for the winter season."

"You got blood on your shirt, you hurt?" asked the buyer.

"A little run in with the Comanches, they tried to ambush us."

"Let's take a look."

Roly peeled off his shirt, now stuck tightly to the wounds. "There's one in the back too."

"Kind of a bloody mess, let me wash it off so I can see it better. Are the arrows still in there?"

"No, we got them all out," said Roly.

"I got a little store-bought salve, and some linen bandages, I'll patch 'em up the best I can."

"Many thanks friend, may the Lord bless you and keep you."

Roly and Arturo spent two days resting the mules and themselves at Adobe Walls. After checking the wheels and the axles, and making some minor harness repairs, they headed back to camp. The second day they met Luther coming up the trail with a full load.

"There's a whole pile of dead, stinking Indians back there," said Luther, "you do that?"

Roly nodded. "Me and Arturo and Juan got attacked right at sunup. They snuck in on us and started shooting."

"Juan got killed right away," said Arturo, "he was a very good man."

"I saw the cross. That's bad about Juan. Did anyone else get hurt?"

"Nothin' too bad," said Roly.

"Keep a sharp eye goin' back, there's sure to be plenty more," said Luther.

"We'll do that, and you do the same — ride with God my friend."

By the time Roly reached the camp, the last two wagons were loaded, covered and ready to roll out. He handed the paperwork to Thomas and poured himself some coffee. Grabbing a handful of jerky, he filled in the brothers on the Indian attack and the death of Juan.

"Did you or Arturo get hurt?" asked Case.

"I got a couple of arrows in me is all, Arturo didn't get hurt."

"Couple of arrows in you? Are you all right?"

Roly nodded. "A man at the Walls patched me up."

The three freight wagons were lined up end to end in the morning, two full of hides and one with the camp gear. Boyd pulled up to the rear of the line with the camp wagon loaded and the canvas on the bows. When the weather turned cold in January, some of the men had switched from the canvas tents to digging crude dugouts in the creek bank. The holes they dug were little more than giant badger holes big enough to hold one or two men. They were cramped and damp and reeked of buffalo. Lined with old hides on the ground and another one for a door flap, they kept out most of the snow. Dugouts were generally warmer than the tents and provided a crude sense of security for men and rodents alike.

Del looked back at their winter camp, he was glad to be leaving. "Arturo, we never did have our skinnin' contest."

"No," said Arturo, mounting his horse. "It is probably a good thing amigo. You wouldn't want to get beat by a bunch of greasers."

The men on horseback brought up the remuda and Case gave the order to move out

Winding their way across the prairie on a blustery spring day, they reached the first campsite and set out four-man guard teams carrying the Springfields for the night watch. By the time they reached Adobe Walls, they had encountered Indians several times but had no skirmishes.

Meeting up with the buyer, they tallied up the winter season's business, selling the last of the hides and the furs. "We'll stay here until the animals are rested," said Case.

Set up against the piles of adobe bricks, a small wagon covered with canvas was being tended by two rough looking Mexican men. "Who are these two guys?" asked Tom Lee.

"Comancheros — greasers that sell and trade to whoever will buy their stuff." said Del. "They trade with the Indians a lot. Some of them have been killed or arrested for selling guns to the Comanches."

"I thought selling guns to Indians was against the law?" said Tom Lee.

"I guess nobody told the greasers that," said Del.

"Maybe they have something we can use."

"Don't be doin' any kind of business with them, they ain't any better than the Comanches themselves," said Del. "How do you think they got them guns they're shootin' at us?"

The hide buyers built a big fire that night. After chuck, they all sat back and had their smokes on a full belly and talked about the season they had.

"So what's next?" asked Boyd. "You planning a summer buffalo hunt?"

Case shook his head. "No, we don't hunt them in the summer anymore. Hot weather buffs are good for leather and meat but there ain't no good robe bulls around then, that's where the money is. There are also more damn bugs, snakes, and Indians around than there are buffs — at least down here. We got a couple of other things going on," said Case. "Thomas will take a few men north again to work with the Army. They guide for them and supply meat for the soldiers up in the Dakota Territory."

"What about you?" asked Boyd as he lit up his pipe.

"I got a deal with a cattleman named Monroe Timms, from just east of San Antonio. He's running a mixed herd of twenty-five hundred longhorn cattle up to Cheyenne. I'm guiding for him and providing him some of the trail hands," said Case.

"Why take all them bovines up there?" asked Boyd. "The military gonna use them?"

"The military may take a few, but they got plenty of buffalo and other game to eat. Mister Timms and several men in the area are looking to stake out ranches and start their own cattle outfits."

"I heard there's more Indians up there than there is buffalo," said Boyd, "that right?"

"That's the truth, they can be bad, but a lot of people are moving west and it ain't gonna stop just because a bunch of savages don't like it."

"What happens after they're delivered?"

"We'll come back to San Antonio and get ready for winter buffalo hunting," said Case. "What about you Boyd? Are you ready to get back to work?"

Boyd shrugged. "Hadn't really thought much about it. What would I be doing?"

Case looked up from rolling his cigarette, "Shit Boyd, what do you think? You're the best trail cook I ever seen."

"Back on the trail again? For how long?" Case nodded and lit up. "Three months, maybe more. I believe Timms would pay a little extra for your chuck."

"I don't know, I gotta think on it a bit."

"Well don't think too long. I told him we'd be at his ranch on the first day of May and I'd have a cook with me."

"I'll let you know tomorrow. Can you use Del and Tom Lee too?"

"Tell you what. You do this drive for me, and I'll hire them too, same as with the buffalo hunting, we got a deal?"

"Like I said, I'll let you know tomorrow."

"Fair enough. The truth is I've been meaning to talk to you for a while now. My brother and I have put in our time in learning this buffalo business and we think we're right at the start of a big opportunity. People are starting to realize that this huge supply of buffalo means money — a whole lot of money. I think that in the next few years there will be a lot more men out here killin' buffs. They're starting to use them for every kind of leather thing there is, and for robes and meat and tallow."

"With that many buffalo hunters out there, wouldn't they kill them all?" said Boyd.

"There are so many buffs I don't see how that could happen, least not for a long time."

"They can't last forever, that's for sure."

Case shrugged. "There aren't many buffalo runners doin' this right now. But since the war ended, all this empty land means new people, new towns, and a chance to make a bunch of money. The more people that come, the better for buff hunters like us."

"What would happen if the buffs did run out?"

"It's more like what will all those new people do if they did run out," said Case. "They'll have to start looking for something else. So, will the Comanches and the Kiowas and every other Indian that lives on them. Boyd, I can tell by the questions you ask and the way you work that you're a pretty smart man. You're obviously not afraid of anything or anyone. Thomas and I are looking for another partner, one that understands life on the frontier and how fast things are changing. That sound like something you might be interested in?"

"A partner? Shoot Case, I ain't got no money, except for my hide pay."

"We ain't worried about that. What we need is someone like you to run our businesses in San Antonio while we're in the field."

"Well if the buffs did run out, what would the company do?"

Case nodded his head and smiled. "Like I said, you always ask the right questions. If the buffs did go away, something else needs to be out there eatin' all that beautiful grass."

"And what would that be?" asked Boyd.

"Cattle, Boyd, longhorn cattle from Texas. There are thousands of wild cattle running free all over the range in Texas. Men like Timms have been gathering them up for a while now to start a couple of new ranching operations up north. If the buffs did go away, the cattle will be there to replace them. We plan on being part of both businesses. Are you interested?"

"I'll let you know tomorrow," said Boyd.

"We'll talk in the morning then," said Case.

Del walked over and sat down next to them, stuffing a wad of chew in his mouth. "So, Case, how do you get everyone paid way out here?"

"I was wondering that myself," said Boyd.

"Well," said Case, "we can't keep all that cash in camp, so the buyers set up an account for us somewhere, so it'll be safe till we're ready to draw it. We got one set up at a bank in San Antonio. The hide buyers generally carry just enough cash to buy supplies or replace some stock if they need to."

"So, we get paid in San Antonio?" asked Del.

Case nodded. "That's where the trip started, and that's where it ends, it's our home base. You got a problem with that?"

"Nope, that's where I'm headed anyway."

Chapter 11

The trip back to San Antonio was long and exhausting, and the weather was sticky hot with insects already plaguing the men and the stock. Only one short rainstorm had broken up the heat and dust and the endless monotony of the prairie. Several brief encounters with the Comanches had provided a little excitement but no causalities.

Reaching the Colorado River, they spotted several buffalo bedded near a large wallow. Case stopped the wagons and pulled out a Springfield and a handful of cartridges. "Boyd, we need to make some meat — you still got the itch to kill a buff?"

"Yessir, I still got it."

"Then let's go scratch it before they all run off," said Case, handing him the rifle.

Crawling slowly through the grass, they set up in a tall patch of weeds. Resting the rifle on the sticks a hundred yards from the wallow, Boyd picked a fat cow with her head down in the grass and squeezed the trigger. The sound of the bullet hitting the buffalo was clear. When the smoke cleared, they could see the cow was dead. Several other animals walked over to her and milled around while he reloaded. Before Case could say anything, Boyd fired again and dropped another cow almost on top of the first one. Case stayed quiet and let Boyd shoot, killing seven buffalo with seven bullets.

"Damn Boyd, you can shoot as good as you cook!" said Case, "just take the tongues, and a couple of pieces of hump is all. We can have some fresh tonight and dry the rest in the wagons as we go."

Reaching San Antonio, Case and Thomas left the wagons and the stock at the livery and walked straight to the bank to finish up their financial business and pay off the men. The heat had turned the blood-soaked hunters, their clothes, their gear, and even the wagons into rank, stinking messes to be avoided. Locals crossed the streets or turned away whenever they saw buffalo hunters coming just to avoid the smell.

The bank manager brought out a green metal lock box and set it on a table then walked quickly back to his office and closed the door. Case set a box of receipts and their ledger book next to it. Every hand was lined up waiting to draw his pay. The box held the company's money in gold and silver. The brothers, like most businesses, paid in coin. Nobody really trusted paper money, and only hard money was accepted by most people.

The Thomas and Case Company added up all the season's expenses first, paid the company and marked them off in the ledger. Next, they counted out half of the remaining hide money as the company's share for the season and entered it in the ledger. The shooters, skinners, wranglers, teamsters, hide men, camp rustler, and cook then received equal shares of the rest. The brothers held back a full share for Juan's family, giving it to Arturo to pass along to them. The coins were counted out into equal piles and handed to each hunter after they signed a receipt.

"Mon ami," said Baptise, "do the shooters get more than the others?"

Thomas shook his head. "You knew how the wages were paid when you took the job. Maybe others do it different, but this is the way we do it. Like I told you before, you can find another outfit if you don't like it here." Baptise signed the paper and took his cash without any more conversation.

After Case handed the last man his pay, he pulled a gold eagle out of the company cash box. "The company is giving Boyd Stamps a bonus. After all our years on the trail, we never ate as well as we did on this trip and I hope he will work for us again," said Case, handing him the coin. Everyone in the outfit nodded in agreement. When they were done, they returned the lockbox to the banker and shook every man's hand.

For Case and Thomas, the next stop was to the dry goods for a new set of clothing. Boyd, Del, and Tom Lee, now flush with buffalo cash, did the same thing. Picking a new pair of pants, two pair of thick socks, and two long sleeve shirts, the clerk, a plump middle-aged woman with brown hair pulled tightly back into a bun, wrapped them in brown paper and handed them the package. Tom Lee and Boyd also bought new red bandannas. Case and Thomas both bought a new pair of tall, black boots with thick soles and high heels.

The men walked a short ways to a Chinese laundry that had a shallow pool of water in the back. Hot water from the washroom was diverted into the small pond next to the river. Case led the men into the laundry and looked at the woman at the door. "Hot bath?"

She nodded and pointed to the back of the room.

The women working the steaming pots full of clothes watched as the filthy strangers walked through the room to the water. All five men sat their packages down and stripped naked. Throwing their old clothes together in one pile they turned to get into the water and saw a dozen female faces staring at them. The Chinese laundry ladies giggled and pointed at the strange looking men with matted beards and long stringy hair. Their weathered brown arms and faces made their pale white bodies look like ghostly apparitions.

A tiny, gray-haired Chinese lady walked over to them with a stern look. "You want hot water? Five cents each — five cents!"

"Sounds like a bargain to me," said Tom Lee. Handing her a coin, he stepped into the pool and slid into the water up to his chin. The others paid up and stepped into the water.

"How's the back feeling Tom Lee?" asked Case. "The hot water make the arrow hurt?"

Tom Lee shook his head. "It always hurts the same, but the hot water feels good on the rest of me."

The woman was still standing next to the pool. "You want clothes clean?" she asked, pointing at the pile of filthy clothes.

Case shook his head. "You keep them."

"You not keep?"

"No, you can have them for a piece of soap." The woman said something to the others, and they gathered up the bloody clothes and took them away. She dropped a rough chunk of soap into the water. "Soap five cents," said the woman.

"Of course it is," said Case. "Here's a nickel, now go away."

She pocketed the change and went back into the laundry.

"This feels so good I'm never leaving," said Del, splashing water on his face.

"Well you're gonna have to get out sometime, or you'll run out of nickels," said Boyd. "Then what would you do?"

"I'd just go and kill me some more buffs."

The brothers were partners in the ***Thomas & Case Hide & Fur Company.*** They also owned the ***San Antonio de Bexar Livery,*** a blacksmith and stable operation, and used it for their home office and for storage when they weren't working on the prairie. They lived on a small, rented ranch east of town where they pastured their remuda. The livery business sat just a short way from the old Alamo mission, now used by the army's quartermaster service and was run by a local wrangler and a full-time smith. The wagons and other equipment were repaired and readied for the next job by the two men.

Del had pitched his bedroll in the loft of the livery and agreed to help take care of the horses and work on the equipment for his keep. At night, he walked to the riverfront and picked a sporting house for the night's entertainment.

"Jesus, Del, you look like you was run over by a herd of buffs," said Thomas, as he watched Del crawl out of his bedroll one morning. "I know cutting the wolf loose every now and again is a damn good thing to do. But you keep it up every night, and that same wolf is gonna turn on you one day and bite you right in the ass."

Del shook his head. "Nah, I'm just havin' a bit of fun with a couple of the local ladies is all."

"How much money you got left? I know how those sweet smelling little women are, they'll get every last dime you got if you ain't careful."

"I still got plenty of money left, so don't you go to worryin' about old Del, he can take care of himself."

Thomas shrugged. "Suit yourself, just trying to be helpful."

Boyd and Tom Lee found a boarding house on the edge of town and spent two days and nights sleeping and eating. "I swear I still smell buffalo on me," said Tom Lee.

"You already took a bath and bought new clothes," said Boyd. "The only thing it could be is your boots."

Tom Lee held them up to his nose. "Aw heck, it is the boots," he said dropping them back on the floor. "Next stop is the dry goods store. I gotta get rid of that smell."

"I gotta say, those were good beefsteaks we had last night," said Boyd, changing the subject from the buffalo smell. "It was good to have a couple of taters and a beer with it."

"It was good all right, but I believe you could have done 'em up better," said Tom Lee.

"Maybe, but I liked that I didn't have to make them myself. So what's next? We going out and see what San Antonio's all about?"

Tom Lee shook his head. "You already know what's next for me."

"What? You really going to see Sylvie's daughter? I figured you forgot all about that by now."

"I told you I wouldn't talk about her no more, but I still couldn't forget about her."

"So that's why the smell is bothering you so much. You want me to come along?"

"Well heck no, why would I want that?"

Boyd grinned. "Just thought you might be too bashful to talk to her is all."

"I ain't too bashful, and you stay outta my business now, and don't go telling the others neither."

"I told you I'd keep your secret, you don't have to worry none about that."

"Good," said Tom Lee, pulling on his new shirt and dusting off his hat. "I'll be back when I'm back, goodbye."

Tom Lee walked back to the dry goods store where he'd bought his new clothes earlier. Walking into the store, the woman remembered him. "Didn't wear out all those new clothes already, did you?" she asked.

Tom Lee shook his head. "No M'am, I just came to buy some new boots. I can't seem to get the smell off of these old ones."

"You and your friends are buffalo hunters?" asked the clerk.

"Yes M'am, just finished up the winter season."

"Well let's get you some boots then."

All the boots in the store were the same basic style, all tall and black and made with thick hide and tall heels. He pulled one of the new pair of socks out of his pocket and slid them on. Finding a comfortable pair of boots, he asked how much.

"Five dollars and twenty-five cents."

He nodded. "That's good, I'll take them."

"What about a hat?" asked the clerk.

"I hadn't planned for a hat, this one's still good."

"Well, it's not really my business, but you look so good in those new clothes that you wouldn't want people to smell that nasty old hat you're wearing now would you?"

Pulling off the hat, he looked it over close and then put it up to his nose. "Well shoot, I guess I could use one, at least one for town business."

She led him to the hats, lined up on pegs on the front wall. Staring at the display, he reached for a gray felt one and tried it on. "It fits real good," said Tom Lee. "I'll take it."

"That's our newest style, it just came in from someplace back east, Pennsylvania I think," said the clerk. "They call it the Boss of the Plains, they say it's made out of beaver skin. I think it might be waterproof too." She held up a hand mirror for him to look at it.

He stared at the image for a minute then broke into a smile. "I gotta say it does look good — I'll take it."

"Can I get you anything else young man?"

"Uh, maybe. Do you have something sweet? Something a pretty girl might like to get for a gift?"

"Oh, I see now," said the clerk. "There's a pretty girl in your life."

"Not yet," said Tom Lee, feeling his face flush. "But maybe soon."

"How about some candy? We have different kinds, the cherry is the most popular."

"How much is it?"

"They're two for a penny." She took out a piece from the jar and handed it to him. "This is a free sample, tell me if it's what you had in mind."

The cherry candy was unlike anything he'd ever had before. Boyd's canned cherries were good, but nothing like the sweet taste flooding his mouth now. "Yes, this is very good. I would like five cents worth please."

The clerk wrapped the candy and handed it to him. "Good luck with the pretty girl."

"Thank you M'am, I'm sure I will need it."

Boyd walked to the livery and found Del and Case working on the front axle of one of the Studebakers. "Ya'll got time to talk about this cattle business?" he asked.

"Sure," said Case. "Let's get a drink and get outta this sun."

Sitting on the ground against the shady side of the barn, Case rolled a fresh smoke. "So, you made a decision Boyd?"

"I did. I'm ready to go, and I think Tom Lee is good for it, but Del here don't know about it yet. Del, Case is gonna lead a herd of beeves from here up to Cheyenne. He wants the three of us to work the drive with him. What do you think about it?"

"I don't know much about moving cattle . . . I'm not sure how much good I would be," said Del.

"We didn't know anything about buffalo hunting either," said Boyd, "but we got through it okay."

"Will you be doin' the cookin' on this deal?"

Boyd grinned, "Oh hell yes — I don't want you to get too skinny on me."

"How long will this cattle thing last?"

"We're starting out the first of May, it should take about three or four months," said Case. "If things work out like I think they will, there could be a permanent job with us."

"Well, I guess every man's gotta be somewhere doin' something, so yeah, I'll be needin' a job."

"How's your money holding out Del?" asked Boyd.

"Like I said, I'll be needin' a job."

"Del, you're a good man," said Case. "We always need good men. We'll teach you everything you need to know." He stuck out his hand to seal the deal. "Boyd, you said Tom Lee is coming too?"

"He was last night."

"Was? You think something may have changed?" asked Case.

Boyd shrugged. "He got all dressed up this morning and went to meet a girl, that's all I know."

"Let's hope he's still planning to join up. Boyd, you and Tom Lee be here in two days, and I'll get all of you fixed up with a proper cowboy outfit."

"What's wrong with what we got now?" asked Del.

"You'll find out when you get here."

Walking toward a cluster of adobe houses along the south side of the river, Tom Lee spotted the home of Sylvie Parker's daughter, Sancha. Nervously standing in front of the door, he took off his new hat, brushed back his hair, and knocked twice. After a minute or two, he knocked again, this time a little harder.

The door opened slightly and an older, Hispanic woman at him. "Hola Señor, may I help you with something?"

Tom Lee nervously played with his new hat while he stared at the ground. "Hola Señora. I am Tom Lee Daggart. I hunted buffalo with Sylvie Parker last winter. We stopped to see his daughter, Sancha, just before we left."

"Si, I remember. Please wait here, and I will be right back."

"Gracias."

After a few minutes, the door opened. "Por favor, come in. Let us sit and talk a while."

"Gracias, Señora," said Tom Lee, still nervously playing with his hat.

"Did you come with news of Sylvie, or are you here to visit with Sancha?"

"I have come for both reasons. I came to tell you that Sylvie disappeared in a fight with the Comanches up in the panhandle," said Tom Lee, trying to spare her the real truth. "We don't know for sure what happened to him."

"Gracias, it is good to know that. Did the Indios kill him?

"We don't know for sure, they may have captured him."

"Thank you — and about Sancha?"

"I have come to visit her in hopes that she might — or perhaps you might allow me to court her?"

She nodded and smiled. "I thought as much. I am Louisa, I have taken care of her since she was a child."

"You are her grandmother?"

"No. I have been her caretaker since she was brought to me as a small child."

"Forgive me Señora, but I am confused. Is she Sylvie's child?"

"No, not his real child, but a child he found on the prairie and rescued from an Indian attack. Her family had been killed when he came onto the scene. She was hardly four years of age when he found her under a wagon covered with a piece of canvas. Her face was cut, and he carried her into town and asked me if I would look after her, and I agreed."

"I did not know any of that. He said Sancha was his daughter."

"He liked to think of her that way. Whenever he visited the city, he would come by with a gift for each of us."

"It sounds as though he really cared for her."

"Yes, he was good to us. Would you like to meet Sancha now?"

He felt his face flush again, and his hands begin to shake. Nodding his head, he nervously ran his fingers through his hair over and over.

"Please wait here, I will get her."

"Muchas gracias." Tom Lee looked around the room and waited quietly while Louisa walked into a back room.

In a few minutes, Louisa came back into the main room hand in hand with Sancha. She was wearing a plain white dress with a colorful, embroidered, pattern around the neck. Her long black hair hung in braids tied with red ribbons. She looked at him from a few feet away. "Hola Señor, I am Sancha."

Tom Lee was unable to respond. He had never seen such a beautiful girl before. He stood gripping his hat tightly, his heart crashing like it never had before. Trying to compose himself, he put his hat on and started to talk, but the words wouldn't come to him. Pulling his hat back off, he tried it again. "Hola Señorita, I am Tom Lee. I am a friend of Sylvie's. We met last summer." Now that he started talking, he couldn't seem to stop. "We were on horseback, do you remember? There were three of us with Sylvie, I was the one in the middle, I . . ."

"Si Señor, I remember you, but you did not have so much beard then."

"No, no whiskers. I can shave them off if you would like."

"Señor," said Louisa, "let's sit together for a while and have some tea, do you like tea?"

Tom Lee nodded, he thought tea might help him calm down a little. "Gracias, that would be good."

They sat together at the table in the tiny kitchen for nearly an hour. Tom Lee never took his eyes off of her, and her eyes never left his. Remembering the candy still in his hand, he sat it on the table. "I am sorry, I forgot that I brought a gift for you."

Louisa unwrapped the package, looked at the candy and passed it to Sancha. "Gracias," she said, putting a piece in her mouth. In an instant, her face filled with a big smile. She offered one to Louisa and one back to Tom Lee. She couldn't quit smiling and reached out and gently touched his hand. "Muchos gracias, Mister Tom Lee, it is maravilloso!"

Tom Lee flushed again at her touch. He could only nod his head in response, but they knew what he meant.

"Would you like to come by tomorrow and have a walk with Sancha?"

He nodded. "Yes …uh …si, I will be here, uh… gracias."

"Sancha, would you like to walk with Tom Lee tomorrow?"

"Si, I would like that."

"Then we will see you, in the afternoon," said Louisa, walking him to the door. "Señor, there is one other thing though."

"What is it Señora?"

"She would like to see your face without the whiskers."

He nodded and smiled, "Si, I will be here tomorrow, in the afternoon without whiskers."

"Tom Lee, did you have a good day with Sancha?" asked Boyd.

Tom Lee nodded. "Yes, we talked for a long time. Tomorrow afternoon we are going for a walk and talk some more."

"Remember, we're going to go to the livery the day after that to talk with Case about the jobs."

"I'll be there, but I'm not so sure about leaving San Antonio."

"I thought I might hear that from you," said Boyd, "but you still need a job, just like the rest of us."

"I know. I will be there and talk with Case about it. Maybe he has a different job that I can do."

Boyd shrugged. "He's been good to us and you shouldn't let him down."

"I'll talk to him and see what he says."

Walking down the main street, Tom Lee passed by a variety of shops until he came to the familiar red and white post in front of a narrow shop with a single barber chair in the window. Several wooden chairs sat around a dusty wood stove, and a lone customer was getting his hair cut. Stepping inside, Tom Lee hung his hat on a peg and sat down.

"You here for your hair or your teeth?" asked the man behind the barber chair.

"My hair, I need to get rid of these whiskers and maybe cut off a bit of hair too."

"I can do it, there's just one to finish up," said the barber, "but it's just old Ezekiel, and he ain't got all that much hair anyhow."

"That'll be fine," said Tom Lee. Watching out the window, he was still amazed at size of the city and what all the people could be doing here. He wondered if he could make San Antonio his home.

"You're next mister." The barber, a short, pot-bellied bald man with a dirty white apron pulled up to his armpits, brushed off the seat with a towel. "Have a seat, my name is Buck. You said you wanted a shave?"

"Yessir, a clean shave, and trim down my hair a little too."

"You got it friend. What brings you to San Antonio?"

"We just finished a winter buffalo hunt up in the panhandle. Just down here to rest up and get ready to move a bunch of long-horned bovines up north."

After clipping all he could, the barber lathered him up with soap and pulled out his razor. After a few licks on the strop he went to work on his whiskers. Wiping off the last of the soap, he held up a mirror and asked him how it looked.

Tom Lee felt his newly smooth face and looked into the barber's mirror. "It looks good, and feels good too, maybe I don't need to cut any hair off."

"Friend, I think you should let me cut it off right now — all of it."

"Cut it all off? Why would you say that?"

"Nits. I don't know if you still have 'em, but by the looks of it, you're best off to get rid of that hair and get the vinegar started."

"Vinegar? You want me to put vinegar in my hair?"

"No, not in the hair son, on your bare scalp, that's why the hair needs to come off. A nit will lay eggs in your scalp then they will hatch later. I don't see any live ones right now, but if there's any eggs in there, this is the best way to take care of it."

Tom Lee could only think of what Sancha and Louisa might say if he showed up bald and smelling of vinegar. "Well how long do I have to leave it on? I don't want to stink all day long."

"You gotta dose yourself two or three times. Rub it in good and leave it on for twenty minutes each time."

"Then I'll smell bad for the rest of the day."

"Well friend, all I can say is scrub off your head with soap and water when you finish."

"Aw shoot, I thought I was pretty clean 'till now," said Tom Lee.

"That's not the only place you can get them," said the barber. "You need to check where your backside meets the saddle too."

"Anything else I should know about these little critters before I do this?"

Buck shook his head. "Just check your clothes and hat and be sure they're clean too."

"Okay, just cut it all off I guess. I can't let my girl see me if I got bugs."

After the barber finished, he handed Tom Lee the mirror. "You can see the tiny little marks on top? Those came from the lice. I can't be sure there's eggs in there now, but it's best not to take a chance."

Tom Lee nodded. "Okay, I'm off to find some vinegar and soap and water. How much do I owe you?"

"Seventy-five cents for everything," said Buck as he dropped his clippers and razor into a pail of water and closed the lid.

Walking back into the laundry, he explained what he needed to the Chinese woman. She nodded and handed him a brown pint bottle, a bar of soap and a stiff brush. She held out her hand in front of him. "Twenty-five cents for all."

Sliding into the water, he settled in and pulled the cork out of the bottle. The obnoxious smell of cheap vinegar surrounded him. As he splashed it on his head, he rubbed it in vigorously trying to ignore the odor, not sure that it smelled much better than a dead buffalo. After the third time, he lathered up his head and used the brush.

Finishing up, he reached for his new hat. Looking inside, he wondered if there were any nits hiding it. Looking it over good, he decided it was clean, but when he got home, his old hat would have to go.

Walking towards Sancha and Louisa's house, he cut across an open field and noticed a few wildflowers growing. Picking a small bouquet of pretty red and yellow flowers, he continued on to the house. When the door opened, he removed his hat and handed the flowers to Louisa. "For you Señora, I hope you like them."

"Si, they are very pretty, gracias. You look very nice today, Sancha will be pleased."

Tom Lee waited next to the table. Sancha walked in holding hands with Louisa, like she had done the day before. "Hola, Señor Tom Lee, you look very nice," said Sancha, running the back of her fingers lightly across his smooth cheek. She flashed a large smile at him. "Are you ready for our walk?"

Tom Lee just nodded, unable to get any words out even if he had to.

"Sancha, he brought some beautiful Indian Blankets for our table," said Louisa.

"They are very pretty, muchas gracias," said Sancha. "I will go change my clothes and be ready in a few moments."

After she walked away, Louisa pointed to a chair. "Please sit, there is something I need to talk to you about."

"What is it Señora?"

"Sancha is a very smart and beautiful young girl. But as you will see, she is also very outspoken and strong-willed, and does not tolerate foolish young men wanting to court her. She is much smarter than most of the men she meets. You will do well to realize this and not let her get the best of you."

Tom Lee smiled at this revelation. "Thank you for telling me this, but I'm also smart, and I think I will enjoy getting to know her."

Sancha walked back into the room wearing a long white dress and a small, plain sombrero. She picked out one of the flowers and put it in the band. "I am ready now."

Walking out the front door, they turned toward the river and Louisa came with them walking several steps behind. Sancha slipped her arm through Tom Lee's and moved closer to him. He couldn't think of anything to say, but at the moment, that was okay with both of them.

Chapter 12

Boyd, Tom Lee, and Del leaned against the horse stalls waiting for Case. "What do you think he wants to teach us?" asked Boyd.

"I guess he's gonna to show us how to get along with a bunch of bovines," said Del, stuffing a wad of tobacco in his cheek, "even though they don't look all that smart to me."

"They gotta be smarter than a buffalo," said Boyd.

Del shrugged. "From what I seen, pretty much anything is smarter than a buffalo. What do you think Tom Lee?"

Boyd interrupted, "Shit Del, he don't got no time to think about buffalos or bovines lately — all he can think about is those pretty, sweet-smellin' little girls."

"Girl," corrected Tom Lee, "just one girl. And it ain't none of anyone's business, so that's the end of it."

"The end of what?" asked Case, walking in the door.

"We're just havin' a little fun with Tom Lee about girls is all," said Boyd.

"Tom Lee, girls just mess up your mind, it's best just to stay away from them," said Case, trying to keep from laughing. "Now let's get to work, we only got a week before it's time to head north. Let's go out back and get started."

Lined up on the fence rail were three saddles. "These are your saddles; all the tack is with them."

"Case, we all got saddles, the same ones we used last winter," said Tom Lee.

"You're all riding old army saddles, they ain't no good for this work, you need a good stock saddle."

"Why's that?" asked Tom Lee.

"Because, in the buffalo business, your horse just gets you to work, you hunt on foot. In the cattle business, you do all your work on the back of your horse," said Case. "Every day and every minute you're working these cattle, you'll be doing it in the saddle."

The three men walked up to the saddles and looked them over. "The main difference is the large swell in front to help you stay in the saddle while leaning out, and the horn, for when you need to tie off your rope," said Case.

"I don't know anything about roping a cow," said Del. "I seen others do it, but I never tried it myself."

"I told Mister Timms I'd supply him at least two cowboys, one teamster, and a trail cook. If you want the job, you'll have to learn this."

"I'll learn," said Del.

"Then saddle up, and we'll get started."

For the next two days, they practiced with the rope until they understood the basics and then went to the ranch to work with the live cattle. Tom Lee and Boyd caught on to the rope quickly but Del proved to be a slow learner, missing more cattle than he caught. "Don't worry, you're gonna have a lot of time to practice on the trail. Here, use these spurs," said Case, handing each of them a new pair, "those cavalry spurs ain't made for this work."

Del held up the spurs and spun the large, pointed rowels. "These are greaser spurs, why we gotta wear them?"

"One, because I said so, and two, they take hold better than the army ones."

"How much money we gonna have to pay for all this stuff?" asked Del.

"The saddle, tack, and ropes are used, but in good condition, they're $23.00, and the spurs are on me. If you leave before the end of the drive, you pay. If you make it to the end, they're yours free and clear. That a fair deal?"

Del nodded. "I guess so. When we leaving again?"

"A couple more days. Boyd, tomorrow I want you to go over the new camp wagon and cooking gear and get everything set up the way you want it," said Case. "Then make a list of everything you need and get it filled at Flores' store."

"How many bellies are we gonna be filling total?"

"Looks like twelve or thirteen, maybe one or two more," said Case. "I'll know for sure when we get to the ranch. You and Tom

Lee check over our tents and canvas. Mister Timms' cowboys will have to supply their own gear."

"With that many hands, I'm gonna want Tom Lee for a camp rustler again," said Boyd.

Case nodded. "You can have him when you need him, but he has to get some time with the herd too."

"We'll make it happen," said Boyd. "Is he gonna be working with the horses too?"

"No. My deal is just for guiding, supplying all the camp work, the camp wagon, the hoodlum, and a couple of extra cowboys. We'll be working out of his remuda, and he'll be supplying the wranglers."

"Will we be takin' our orders from you?" asked Del.

Case nodded. "From the moment we start, I'm the Boss and what I say goes. Mr. Timms makes all the financial decisions, but I'm the one that's gotta get the herd to Cheyenne."

"We'll be bringing the Springfields?" asked Boyd. "I just want to know so I can pack them."

"It's a good idea," said Del. "If the savages don't like 'em, we best take 'em along."

"I agree," said Case. "Load them and a case of cartridges in a spot that's easy to get to. Everyone needs to bring their own rifle and revolvers too. And make sure you have good holsters for them, you'll be carrying them the whole trip."

For the next two days, they worked steady at preparing for the trip. "It must be nine hundred miles or so," said Tom Lee. "That means we'll be gone at least three months or more."

Boyd nodded and threw the last of the sacks of corn and beans into the wagon. "Don't forget coming back here, that's gonna be a long ride too,"

"Well shoot," said Tom Lee. "It'll be fall by the time we get back."

"So, what's the problem with that? You got somewhere else more important to be?"

"Maybe somewhere else I'd rather be."

Boyd suddenly understood what he was talking about. "Oh shit — it's the girl, Sancha, right?"

"Maybe so. I just don't really want to leave her alone. Besides, this arrow has been hurting bad. I think maybe I need to get it cut out once and for all."

"Case," said Boyd, "do you know a doctor around here that can take this arrow out of Tom Lee's back before we leave?"

"Maybe. Meet me here in the morning, and we'll go down and see Doc Parsons, he can probably do it. Tom Lee, you think you're gonna be good for the long trip?"

"Case, if we need to, he can ride in the wagon with me for the first couple of days," said Boyd. "He can help me until he feels better, then he can go work the cattle."

"We'll see what the Doc has to say tomorrow."

Tom Lee laid spread out on the table flat on his belly. The doctor looked over the scar where the arrow had been cauterized. "You mean the arrow's still in there? Why didn't you pull it out before you sealed it up?"

"Because it wouldn't pull out," said Tom Lee. "We tried it a couple times before it got sealed."

"Doc, you think you can get it out?" asked Boyd.

Parsons, a fat, frumpy looking old man old man without a hair on his head bent down to the examine the wound. "If you can hold him still enough, I can get anything out. But I'm here to tell you, it's gonna hurt like the holy blazes of hell — you up for that boy?"

"Just take it out, you can't hurt me more than it does now."

The old man shrugged. "I guess we'll see about that, won't we."

With Tom Lee's arms and legs pinned down by Case and Boyd, the doctor bent over and looked closely at the scar. Handing him a towel, he told him to bite down on it. Stropping a small, thin-bladed razor to a fine edge, he cut along either side of the scar then under it. Pulling off the old skin, he spread the cut open and probed with his finger for the arrow. "Don't see it yet, gonna have to go deeper." With another cut, he felt the razor hit the arrow. Cutting back the tissue around it he exposed enough to see the problem. It was tightly wedged between two ribs with the tip stuck in a rib bone."

"You gonna be able to get it out Doc?" asked Boyd.

"Like I said, you hold him still enough, I can take out pretty much anything you want."

"Just the arrow this time Doc," said Boyd. "We might find something else later."

Reaching for a pair of pliers, he clamped down on the arrow and pulled. The arrow remained stuck as tight as ever. Taking the nose of the pliers, he tapped on the arrow and gripped it and moved it side to side. After a few minutes of working on it, he clamped down again and gave it a powerful pull. As the arrow came out, he nearly fell off the stool. The bloody point was still in the grip of the pliers. He held it up for everyone to see. There was a slight bend in the tip that had been hooked into the rib bone.

"Are you done yet?" asked Tom Lee. "I'm getting tired of being held down like this."

"Just let me sew this up, and you'll be good to go."

"You got it out?"

"Hold your hand out," said the doctor. "Take a look at your prize, it's something to show your kids."

"I ain't got no kids to show it to. Heck, I ain't even got a wife for that matter."

"Not yet you ain't," said Boyd. "But it won't be long though."

Parsons splashed some alcohol on the cut and started to sew it up. Finishing up the stitches, he put some salve on it and a fresh linen bandage. Wrapping him with a long cloth, he told him he could put his shirt back on. "You can pull those stitches out in two weeks. I wouldn't go lifting anything heavy before that, and you'll be fine."

"Doc, how much do I owe for this?" asked Tom Lee.

"Two dollars to cut it out and twenty-five cents for the bandages, and here's a couple of extra to take with you and a tin of salve. Son, I gotta say, I never saw anyone take that kinda pain without making a sound," said Parsons. "You are one tough son-of-a-bitch."

Handing him the money, he thanked him and shook his hand. "Thanks. I'm lucky there was such a good doctor in town."

"Veterinarian," corrected Parsons. "I went to school to be an animal doctor — come close to graduating too."

"Well . . . uh — thank you for your help just the same."

He nodded. "Sure. Next time you get a Comanche arrow in your back, I'll be here."

Every evening Tom Lee went for a walk with Sancha with Louisa following close behind. After a week, Louisa finally allowed them to go alone. Walking arm and arm down the boardwalk of the main street, he stopped in front of the same dry-goods where he'd bought his new clothes.

"Let's go inside for a moment, there is something I want to show you."

Approaching the counter, she saw the jar with the red candy immediately. "Is this what you brought me on the first day?"

"Yes, the very same. I am hoping that you might like to have some again?"

Smiling broadly, she nodded her head. "Si, I would like that."

Walking back home, she squeezed his hand and drew close to him. "Tom Lee," she said, speaking to him informally for the first time. "Are you about to leave me?"

He nodded. "Please forgive me, I am sorry. I agreed to take the job before I got to know you. I could refuse it, but then people might think of me as someone who does not keep his word. Even if I did that, I would still need to find a job."

Walking for a while longer, Sancha stopped and turned toward him. "Tom Lee, I have a thought about this. If you leave now to take the cattle north, when will you return?"

"Case says it will be about three months to get there, so I think it could be October before we are back. So what is your thought?"

"You go on your job, and when you return, you will get a new job in San Antonio, and you will marry me. Then we will have many babies."

Tom Lee looked at the young woman next to him, his face flushed, and his heart raced. This was definitely not something he had expected to hear from her. "You want to marry me? Are you sure of this?"

"Si, is that not what you want too?

"Yes, I want to marry you. I didn't know for certain that you felt that way too."

She kissed him on the cheek. "I love you Tom Lee, and I want to be with you forever."

"I love you too Sancha, I will marry you when I return, and we will have many babies and live in San Antonio forever."

She put her arms around him and kissed him passionately on the lips for the first time. Tom Lee detected a slight cherry taste from the candy. Holding her tightly he was sure that his heart was pounding so hard she could feel it.

"Do not go and take some other women Tom Lee, you are mine, and you must come back to me."

He held her in his arms for a long time, not wanting to let her go. "There are no other women, only you."

Boyd was nearly finished packing his cooking supplies when Tom Lee walked in. He noticed several bullets on the table that had been removed from the cases. The gunpowder from the cartridges had been put into a small glass jar.

"Why are you putting that gunpowder in there? I thought you kept your secret cooking stuff in that jar?"

"Just never you mind, it's none of your business, you just go on now," said Boyd.

For a minute Tom Lee couldn't believe what he was seeing. "All those months out there hunting buffalo and we were eating gunpowder?"

"Just a little bit is all, it gives the chuck a better flavor. And don't go telling the rest of them, someone's sure to complain about it if you do."

"Okay Boyd, but you and me got a secret now," said Tom Lee, with a big grin. "If I ever want an extra biscuit or more jerky."

"Yeah, yeah, just go back to work and forget about it," said Boyd.

"There's something else I want to tell you about too."

"Now what?"

"Me and Sancha are gonna be married, just as soon as we get back from the trip."

"Married? Are you loco in the head? You just met her!"

"It don't matter, we're both ready to do it. We're gonna get married, live in San Antonio, and have a bunch of babies, that's our plan."

"Well damn, ain't that something, you're gonna get married. What you gonna to do for work after you and her get hitched."

Tom Lee shrugged. "Don't really know yet, but I'll find something."

"Well good for you and Sancha. Just don't get stuck with any more Comanche arrows before you get back home."

"Boyd, don't say nothing to the rest of them about this, okay?"

"There sure ain't nothing to be embarrassed about. Marrying a girl that pretty is a good thing."

"Just don't say nothing, okay?"

"I won't say a thing," said Boyd. "But now we each have a secret about the other one, don't we?"

After packing the last of the camp in the wagon, Boyd brought two pairs of mules into the barn and put them in a stall. He would use a fresh team every day, and the other pair would be kept with the remuda. He laid out the harness in front of the wagon and made sure everything was ready to move to the ranch in the morning.

Stashing the bows in the possum, he saw Del walk in with two rough looking Mexican men on either side of him, both with a pistol in his waistband, and two Mexican women.

"Boyd, I need a little help here, can I borrow some money till we get paid?"

"Well shit Del, now what happened?"

A black eye and several bruises stood out clearly, even in the dim light of the barn. "They jumped me Boyd, musta been a dozen of 'em at least."

"Señor," said one of the men, "he owes us for the damage he did in our cantina last night. He also cheated these two señoritas out of their money. When we told him he had to pay, he said that no stinking greaser was gonna get a single peso from him and he chose to fight about it. We locked him in the back room until he sobered up this morning. He told us if we brought him here, we could get our money."

Tom Lee looked at the bloody mess standing in front of them. "Del, why didn't you just pay them?"

"I ain't got no money left, they already got all of it."

"So, you brought them here to get us to pay?" said Boyd.

"Goddamn it Boyd, who else I got but you two? I need some help here — you know I'll pay you back."

"Well exactly how much do you owe here?"

"Twenty dollars."

"Twenty dollars! How the hell much did those girls cost?"

"A dollar for each one and a half dollar for their drinks — for each of them," said Del.

"Well what in hell is the other seventeen dollars for?"

Del shrugged. "I don't exactly remember, maybe some tequila bottles or something. Will you just pay 'em please?"

"Tom Lee, what do you think?" asked Boyd.

"Well . . . I suppose I can put in ten if you can put in the other ten."

After handing the money to the Mexicans, they looked at Del. "Estúpido hombre blanco," said one of the men as he stuffed the money in his pocket.

The two women looked at the bloody figure. "No vuelvas — nunca!"

When they left, Boyd and Tom Lee couldn't keep from bursting out laughing at their partner. "You are one pitiful looking mess. Do you need anything else before we leave town?"

Del shook his head, "I don't guess so, 'cept maybe a hat, mine's gone."

"You know what," said Tom Lee, "I got a good one from last winter, it's all yours.

Boyd pulled the wagon onto the trail with Tom Lee sitting on the canvas in the back. It was already hot and sticky as they turned into the early morning sun. Case and Del followed up with the mules and a couple of extra horses. In less than an hour, they were at the Timms Land & Cattle Company.

Boyd and Tom Lee looked at the herd grazing across the prairie. The sound of constant bawling and the sight of thousands of horns flashing and clattering in one place was unlike anything they had ever seen before. "Holy shit, we gotta take all of them to Cheyenne?" said Boyd. "How we gonna do that?"

Shaking his head, Tom Lee couldn't quit staring. "I got no idea."

After introductions, Monroe Timms, a tall, distinguished looking man with a full head of gray hair and a tight moustache walked over to Boyd. "Son, I've been hearing a lot of bragging about your chuck, where'd you learn your cookin'?"

"I learned it from my momma. We didn't have a lot, so she had to cook whatever we brought her."

"You a reb, boy? You sound like a reb to me."

Boyd flushed, stepped forward and looked directly into his eyes. "Mister Timms, I know we just met, so I'll just say this just once. I am not a reb now, and I was not a reb in the war — I was a conscript. We worked a small farm and had no slaves. Me and my brothers were forced to join the army. I don't want to talk about this again, I hope we are clear."

Timms stepped up even closer, "Son, no offense was meant here. I'm from North Carolina, I left in '59 because I hated what I saw happening. When it was clear that there would be a war, I sold my place and headed for Texas. I've been slowly building up a herd of these wild cattle ever since."

"Texas was a slave state," said Boyd. "Why didn't you go north?"

"I thought hard about it, but I'd heard that there was more open land here and all these wild cattle for the taking. The only thing I ever done in my whole life was work cattle and horses, so it sounded like the best deal. When I first moved here, my place was pretty remote, and no one bothered me too much. I provided a few cows to both sides one time or another, and the same for the Comanches when they needed meat, so they left me alone."

"How long did it take you to gather up a herd like this?" asked Tom Lee.

"About two years. The first year was some miserable, dangerous work though. Me and my three sons had to dig them out of every nasty break and thicket in Texas. Lost one of my boys that first year when one charged and killed him and his horse."

"Sorry to hear about your boy Mister Timms."

Timms stuck out his hand. "Thank you Boyd, it's good to meet you, I'm lookin' forward to eatin' some of your chuck."

Boyd nodded and shook his hand. "And I'm looking forward to cooking it for you."

Chapter 13

The cattle had been moved into a large open area near the ranch. 2,500 bulls, cows, and calves bellowed, snorted and slobbered, restlessly swinging their horns around, sensing something was about to happen. The cowboys and vaqueros surrounded them and held them together for the start of the drive. Timms' wranglers held the remuda together in a smaller pasture. Boyd was hitched and ready to go with Tom Lee next to him.

Roly pulled alongside him in the hoodlum wagon. Setting the brake, he stood up on the seat, took off his hat and gave a loud, passionate and unsolicited prayer to the outfit ending it with a deep, bellowing — amen!"

"Good to see you again Roly," said Boyd. "I wasn't sure if you was gonna make it or not, you ready?"

Spitting a long stream of tobacco juice, he dropped down onto the seat and grabbed the reins. "Me and the good Lord are always ready to roll!"

"How's your back feeling?" asked Boyd, picking up his reins.

"Back's fine. It takes more than a couple of puny little Comanche arrows to keep me from doing the Lord's work."

"Glad to hear it my friend — and good to be working with you again."

Case sat on his horse at the front of the herd as Monroe Timms rode up next to him. "Case, why is that man riding with Boyd in the wagon, why ain't he horseback?"

"Mister Timms, that's Tom Lee Daggart, he was a cavalry man till the end of the war, and with me all winter hunting buffalo. He's been carrying a Comanche arrowhead in his back for nearly a year. A couple of days ago it started to hurt him real bad, and he had it cut out. He needs two weeks before he can take the thread out, then he can ride."

"Who cut it out?"

"Doc Parsons — took some doing to get it out too."

"If Doc did it, he's suffered plenty. You think he's worth hauling around till he heals up?"

"Yessir, I personally guarantee he will be one of your top hands. If you ain't happy, I'll cover his wages myself."

"Fair enough," said Timms. "Then let's get ready to move these bovines."

Case and Timms looked back at the sea of cattle and horns behind them. It was an intimidating sight, even for someone who grew up around cattle. "It's a long way to Cheyenne Mister Timms. Did you ever move such a large herd so far before?"

"No. I've moved a lot of cattle and horses, but never that far."

"Then I think this will be something of an adventure for both of us," said Case.

The morning sky was clear, and the sun was already bearing down hard. Timms reached over and offered his hand to Case. "You ready for the adventure?"

Shaking his hand, Case nodded. "Ready when you are."

Timms looked at the riders on the flanks and gave them the signal, "Let's move out!"

The herd stood grazing as the cowboys rode up to them hollering and swinging their ropes. As they crowded and bumped up against the sides of the cattle, the herd started to take a few steps, then slowly began to move forward, gathering together in a giant, slow-moving wave. The noise was nearly unbearable, and the ground shook with a low, steady rumble. Impossibly long horns swung from side to side, banging together constantly. As they began to move, the men on the flanks put some space between them and the cattle and let them spread out slightly until they found their own space.

Several cattle began to work their way to the front. Two older steers, brought along for trail meat, pushed their way through the herd and immediately took the lead. Within a few hours, the herd was strung out for nearly a mile and moving steadily.

"Everyone keep an eye on those two lead steers," said Case. We don't want anything to happen to them."

"You're right about that. Those two are as good a pair of leaders as I ever saw," said Timms. "I think maybe we should give them names."

"Good idea, you got some in mind already?" asked Case.

"How about the black and white one we call Lincoln and the red brindle with the twisted horn we call Grant?"

"Well, they seem to work together pretty good," said Case, "I like that — Lincoln and Grant it is."

"It'll likely rub a few old gray-backs the wrong way though," said Timms with a grin.

Case shrugged. "You care?"

"Not one lick," said Timms.

Three experienced cowboys or vaqueros rode along the flanks of the herd on either side. Del rode drag with two other cowboys, to keep any stragglers in back from falling out and two more rode in front. Boyd kept the wagon well out front of the herd. Once the cattle settled in, the drag riders moved back and forth at the end of the herd to keep the stragglers from breaking away. Del settled into the middle drag position.

"We need to get them as far away from the ranch on the first day as we can, otherwise there'll be some that'll want to turn back," said Timms.

"We'll keep them moving," said Case.

Case rode ahead with Timms scouting for water for the night's camp, often covering miles of ground before finding a suitable camp spot. When they decided on a place, Case gave instructions to Boyd and Tom Lee how to find it and to remind them to keep the Springfields ready. Reaching the chosen spot, Boyd set a fire and started preparing for evening chuck.

Cooking for a cattle crew was much different than for the buffalo hunters, who had a more permanent camp and plenty of fresh meat. Moving a cattle herd every day meant the camp had to be torn down each morning and reset every night. Boyd's food was always good, but there wasn't as much time to prepare anything special. Plenty of deer and pronghorn were killed along the way, but they had to be far enough away from the herd before the cowboys would fire their rifles.

The first three days on the trail were long and hot, but mostly uneventful. Everyone found their place and the day to day work became routine. Boyd would set up every day two hours before sunup to make morning chuck and be packed up and ready to go when the herd started to move.

On the fourth day, after several hours on the trail, Case and Timms, who had been riding well in advance, came charging back to camp in a long swirl of dust, their horses heavily lathered after the ride. "Comanches! Everyone be on the watch. Boyd, get out the Springfields!"

As the men tightened up the herd, Boyd and Tom Lee loaded the big rifles and waited to see what would happen next. On a far ridge, six Comanche braves sat on their horses watching the outfit. One brave rode a little closer holding his rifle in the air while he screamed and pounded his chest. Riding closer a second time, he repeated the performance.

"Tom Lee, send one by his head and see what happens," said Case.

Laying the barrel across the wagon side, he found the Indian, took a breath and touched it off.

The Indian reacted instantly, jerking his horse to one side and racing back to the group.

"Good shot," said Case. "I think they must've got the message all right."

While they watched, two of the braves slowly began to ride toward the herd. "Want me to shoot them?" asked Tom Lee.

Case shook his head. "Just keep the rifle on them, they want to talk." As they got closer, they showed their hands and rode out to meet them. Boyd and Tom Lee covered them with the Springfields and watched.

"What do you want?" asked Case.

The older Indian spoke enough English to get his point across. "Ten cows. We are hungry, want meat — ten cows."

"No — go kill buffalo," said Case, his hand firmly gripping his pistol.

"No. No buffalo here," said the brave. "Ten cows."

Case shook his head. "No cows — buffalo!"

The Indian, now very animated, pounded on his chest and yelled at Case. "No. No buffalo here, white man kill buffalo — ten cows."

Case looked at Timms and back at the Indian. "Two cows," said Case, holding up two fingers.

"No! Ten cows," said the Indian, now screaming loudly.

"We will give you four cows," said Case, showing four fingers. "That is it — no more."

The two braves said something to each other and finally nodded. "Yes, four cows — now!"

Case motioned to the cowboys. "Cut out four old animals and run them up here."

When they brought the cattle, the two Indians immediately started pushing them up the ridge. Screaming at the top of their lungs, the other four braves came down to meet them, joining in the excitement as they disappeared over the ridge.

"You handled that well," said Timms, "you must have done this before."

"Yeah, we've bargained with the Comanche's a few times," said Case, giving the signal to move out. "I imagine we'll see plenty more of them before we're done."

Tom Lee, still unable to ride, had agreed to keep a journal for Monroe Timms. He would make notes on everything from lost cattle to Indians, injuries, and the weather. On the first page he recorded:

May 2, 1867. The Timms Cattle Company left San Antonio, Texas and started north to Cheyenne, a trip of about 900 miles or more with 2,500 mixed longhorn cattle, 40 meat steers, 83 horses, 10 mules, 11 cowboys and vaqueros, 3 wranglers, one cook and helper with camp wagon, one teamster with hoodlum wagon. Weather is hot and dry. Herd owner is Monroe Timms from San Antonio, cow boss and guide is Case – (last name unknown). All of the Timms cattle and horses carry the 3T brand. Will compile list of names of all hands for future reference.

<u>May 5.</u> Met six Comanche braves today. Some excitement when they demanded ten of our cattle. Case bargained with them for only four. Weather still hot and dry and we are crossing fields of prairie dog towns so large that a man cannot see the end of them in any direction.

His next entry was the list of names of every man on the drive. He did the best he could to include full names and any kin they might have. He still didn't know Case's last name. Timms asked if he would keep the journal until they returned to San Antonio. Riding in the wagon gave him a chance to watch and learn as the cowboys skillfully moved the herd where they wanted them. When moving the right direction on the trail, the herd needed little pressure from the cowboys to make them go. The lead animals set the pace and most of the time the herd followed without a problem.

When a single cow or a small bunch did try and break away, the nearest cowboy reacted instantly to head them off and usher them back to their rightful place in the herd. Tom Lee thought it was like watching a powerful, undisciplined sea of hair and horns just waiting for their chance to break and run for freedom. The only thing keeping them from escaping was a handful of skilled cowboys and vaqueros, expert horsemen who were fearless in the middle of thousands of flashing horns and sharp hooves.

Noting his observations in the journal, Tom Lee liked the contrast between the American cowboys, mostly former northern soldiers and freed slaves, and the Mexican vaqueros. The cowboys were fearless and coldly efficient, though sometimes rough on cattle and horses. Most were loners left without much family and few friends after the war. They found the cattle business preferable to other work like buffalo hunting or farming. Their gear was whatever they had when they signed on. Most of their pistols and rifles were leftover pieces from their military days. Hats, jackets, and boots were often just army issued clothes and equipment that were threadbare and shabby. In time, most of them understood that they needed proper saddles, chaps, spurs, and a rope to be an efficient cowboy.

The Mexican vaqueros were most often full-time professional cattle men who had been raised in the business and took pride in their appearance and in the saddles, tack, and clothes they used every day. Tom Lee admired the well-made saddles with the oversized horns and tapaderos that were common to the culture. Large sombreros, short waist coats, custom made boots, and fancy spurs were often used while they worked. They all wore soft leather leggings for protection from the trail and the cattle.

He noted that while in camp they were usually quiet, just talking among themselves. Even after two weeks on the trail, the cowboys were slow to socialize with them. He recorded in the journal that there were five Mexican vaqueros and three black cowboys. The rest of the outfit, including Case and Timms, were all white.

After two weeks on the trail, he asked Boyd to take out his stitches after chuck. "Take off your shirt and let me take a look."

"And I don't want to hear a single word about any maggots this time, you hear me Boyd?"

"Yeah, yeah, I hear you," said Boyd, peeling off the bandage. "All I see is a few dirt worms peeking outta the hole."

"Just take out the thread and quit talking."

Boyd snipped the threads and pulled out the stitches one at a time, going slowly, teasing him the whole time. "There, all out — now quit your whining."

"Boyd?"

"Now what?"

"You're sure you didn't leave any of them worms in there?"

Both men burst out laughing at the same time. "Tom Lee, you've been getting fat and lazy riding in the wagon, I think it's time for you to start doin' some real work around here."

Tom Lee shrugged. "I think I like what I'm doing right now — just aggravating you all day."

"You better be careful here, one day you might get an extra big dose of my special cooking powder in your chuck, you wouldn't want that would you?"

"So what would happen if I did?"

"The first time your horse bucked hard, your ass would explode," said Boyd, doing his best to keep a straight face.

"Well, I hope it don't mess up my new saddle," said Tom Lee, laying his head back in the grass and closing his eyes.

At morning chuck, Monroe Timms poured himself a second cup of coffee and walked over to Tom Lee. "How's the back doing son?"

"It's a bit sore, but Boyd pulled out the stitches last night. I need to start riding to loosen things up some, then I can be of some use to you."

Timms took another swallow of his coffee. "Let's talk about that for a minute. I like what you're doing in the journal — the day to day stuff. How are you with numbers?"

"I'm pretty good sir. I always liked arithmetic in school."

"Well, let me propose something to you. I hate numbers. I can count my cattle okay and those kinds of things, but I need someone to do the job while we're on the trail, someone to keep track of all the supplies, expenses, cattle counts, and stock losses and notes on anything important or interesting about the drive. Does that sound like something you might be interested in? I can put up a little extra pay if you're interested."

"Yes sir, I think I would, but I still want to learn the cowboy job before this drive is over."

Timms nodded his head. "I think we can arrange that. You keep the day to day journal and do all the bookkeeping until we get back to San Antonio and we'll make a real cowboy out of you while we're on the trail. We got a deal?"

"We do sir."

Tom Lee took out a horse the next morning and rode alongside one of the flank men for a while. Dropping back, he moved into drag next to Del. Riding side by side he tried to speak to him, but Del wasn't talking. By the time they pulled up for the night, Tom Lee's back was sore but not unbearable. Both men turned their horses into the remuda and walked toward camp. "So you ever gonna talk to me?"

"What do you want to know?" asked Del, wiping the dirt out of his eyes and off his face.

"Why so quiet back there, you mad at me or something?"

"I ain't mad at you. I'm mad at myself for taking this miserable job is all."

"You don't like cattle?"

"Cattle are okay for eatin', but I don't like working drag behind a couple a thousand pissin', shittin', dust raisin' bovines is all. Even killing buffalo ain't near as bad as this."

"You musta forgot what buffalo work was like," said Tom Lee. "All I remember was blood, guts, and smell. You ain't gonna quit are you?"

Del shook his head. "I can't quit, I need the money, or I'd already be gone."

"Maybe we'll find something better when we get to Cheyenne."

"If we make it to Cheyenne," said Del. "You ain't forgot gettin' that arrow in your back have you?"

"No, I'm just saying there are plenty of other jobs. Once we finish up this one, you'll be flush again, and then you'll have time to find a better one."

"Well it damn sure ain't gonna have anything to do with big hairy herds of meat, I can tell you that right now."

"Let's get us something to eat, I'm starving," said Tom Lee.

"I need to find some water first, then I'll be along."

After chuck, Boyd built up the fire to a roar, and the men sat down around it to smoke and tell stories. Sitting back from the fire a few feet, Case rolled a smoke and lit up. "Tom Lee, I see you riding today, how's the back doing?"

Tom Lee sat down next to him and took off his hat, rubbing his hand over the stubble. "It's sore, but I'm okay with it. Mind if I ask you a question Boss?"

"Sure, go ahead."

"I haven't seen Thomas for a long time, is he okay?"

"He left early for Dakota Territory with three hands. They're guiding and hunting for the army. We probably won't see them again until fall." Case held out the makings for a smoke to Tom Lee.

He shook his head. "Thank you but no. My momma taught me that drinking, smoking, and cussing was bad for a man's chances to get into heaven."

"She was probably right about that. I'm sure you noticed that Thomas and I are a lot different, even though we're brothers. He's always been the quiet one. He'd rather be alone on the prairie hunting than be in a city or a big group of people. We're partners in the business, but we don't often work together, and we get along better that way. It seems like maybe you got something else on your mind Tom Lee, what is it?"

"Well, I was just wondering, why don't you ever say what your last name is?"

Case sat there, smoking and thinking about the question for a minute. "You're the first person to ask me that question in a long while."

"So, what is it?"

"You do ask a lot of questions for sure. If you really want to know, ask me again after we deliver the herd, then I'll tell you everything."

Starting out in the morning was always interesting. After two weeks on the trail, the flankers had spotted most of the trouble makers in the herd. When the lead steers put a little distance between them and the main body, the next in line began to move a little faster to catch up. When the herd got up to speed, they watched closely for escapees. One morning, two mamas and a calf, bawling loudly, broke on a dead run for the brush. The swing man was quick to react. Spurring his horse hard, he got in front of the three escapees, stopped sharply and turned them back into the group. This game continued all day, every day. Groups of yearlings breaking one way and other small bunches and singles trying different routes kept the cowboys and vaqueros in motion every moment they were in the saddle.

Tom Lee continued to ride drag, between Del and one of the black cowboys. Thick dust rolled over them like a dirty wool blanket. All three men wore extra-large bandannas covering their mouth and nose and another one wrapped around their neck under their buttoned-up shirt. At any given moment, one or two of them were chasing down the stragglers that couldn't keep up.

"Dammit to hell," said Del, turning back for an old cow that had been lingering at the rear. Running her back into the herd, he fell back in next to Tom Lee. "This is some kinda fun ain't it? I got more dirt on the inside me than those cows got on the outside."

Case and Timms estimated they were averaging about twelve miles a day based on Case's experience. Reaching the Colorado River in early afternoon, he instructed the point men to hold the herd on the south side. "Pull up here and let them water," said

Case. "There's plenty of grass, and everyone needs a rest. We'll stay here an extra day before we cross."

All day and night, cowboys and vaqueros rode a circle around the herd at all times, riding watch on regular three-hour shifts. At morning chuck, the riders not on watch lounged around the camp playing dice and smoking while constantly pestering Boyd for more food. A few spent a little time in the water trying to beat the heat and dirt and drown some of the bugs. The endless army of ticks that had collected on them from the cattle created a never-ending battle for the men. "I'm damn sure tired of these little bastards tryin' to eat me," said Del one evening while he stood picking ticks off his belly and flipping them into the fire.

"Them ticks are pretty fussy about whose belly tastes the best," said Boyd. "They go right for the big fat ones first."

"That ain't so," said Roly. "I'm a whole lot fatter than him and they ain't bothering me none."

"Then I guess it must be the taste," said Boyd.

"That's just plain shit," said Del. "My belly don't taste no damn different than anyone else's."

"So who we gonna believe," asked Tom Lee with a huge grin, "you or that giant herd of ticks sucking on your belly"?"

The herd was well bedded for most of the night until the first sounds of wolves with their eerie howls and yips started to get close right at sunup. Three heifers broke for the river, and a dozen other cattle followed them. The closest cowboy was Del, and he hit the river at a hard gallop to try and get in front. When the horse felt the river bottom fall away, it tried to stop and went down in the current pitching Del headfirst into the rushing water.

In a few seconds, the horse found his footing, walked out of the river, shook himself off and trotted back to the remuda. Del was nowhere to be seen. As the rest of the camp ran to the river someone spotted him. "Look, there he is!" he said, pointing downstream.

Del was bouncing and rolling in the current, finally crawling out of the river on the other side.

"Hey — I need help here," he said, trying to stand up. "Someone come over here and get me."

"Just wade across," yelled said Tom Lee.

"Goddamnit, you know I can't swim, now come and get me!"

Riding across in belly deep water, Tom Lee threw him a loop. "Grab on. I'll pull you over."

Tom Lee spurred his horse and headed for the opposite shore.

When Del reached the fire, he stripped to his underwear to dry off. Several cowboys laughed and teased him about his first trail drive bath. "Don't talk no crap to me about this goddamnit — I coulda drowned out there!"

"Aw shoot Del," said Boyd. "We wouldn't let that happen, then one of us would have to ride middle drag, and ain't none of us want that. Besides, you smell a whole lot better now."

Del wrung out his clothes and laid them around the fire pit. "Well shit, on top of everything else, I lost my hat!"

"The one I give you?" asked Tom Lee.

"Yeah, that one. Though I gotta say, it was one itchy damn hat."

Chapter 14

At first light, Timms and Case rode up and down the river searching for a good place to cross. In areas that flattened out, they found spots with soft sand and mud, impossible to move the herd across. After two hours of riding and testing the river bed, they located a wide, level spot with a firm bottom about two feet deep and rode across to check it. When they were satisfied it was safe, they signaled for Boyd and Roly to bring the wagons over. When the wagons reached the other side without a problem, they continued ahead about half a mile and pulled up to wait for the herd.

All hands started to close in on the herd, crowding them toward the water. Lincoln and Grant never hesitated and plunged right in, swimming straight for the opposite bank where Case and Timms waited. The next wave rushed forward, trying to keep up with the leaders. Yelling and swinging their ropes, the flank men pressed the cattle toward the water. When half the herd was across, two young bulls stopped dead at the water line and swung around, trying to turn back. A thousand or more cattle, now an unstoppable force, continued toward the river and the two bulls went down, crushed along the shoreline by thousands of hooves. Within seconds, they disappeared into the boiling water. By the time the last of the animals had crossed, several more drowned cattle could be seen floating down the river.

The last man across, a young vaquero named Jesus, rode up to Case and Timms. "Cinco muerto Señors."

Tom Lee rode up next to them. "How many did we lose, Boss?"

"Looks like five head," said Case. "Take Jesus with you and drag a couple of them close ones onto the bank and cut off whatever Boyd can use for chuck. And make sure your pistols are ready.

"That could have been a whole lot worse," said Timms, turning back up the trail. "I'm sure the Comanches are already cutting up the rest of them by now. Get the crossing entered in the book, and let's get rolling." The drag men kept the back of the herd in place as the flank riders got them moving. As they started to string out everyone fell back into position.

__May 16.__ Crossed the Colorado River today. It was deep and fast, and the bosses found a fair place to cross. Everything went well until two head stopped at the river bank and tried to turn back.

The crossing cost the outfit at least 2 young bulls, 2 cows and one choice meat steer. Lincoln and Grant are proving to be excellent leaders. Took good meat from 2 dead and left the rest for the Indians and the wolves. Total herd loss as of today is 20 head. Weather is hot and dry. I will name it Del's crossing, as he was the first one to test its waters.

The outfit moved with little trouble for the next two days, finding enough water on a few small streams and natural ponds for the stock. The wolves and coyotes continually harassed the herd keeping the night shifts on high alert.

For the first time on the drive, they woke up to the sound of loose canvas snapping in the wind and heavy dark skies. "Boyd, Roly, get the canvas on the bows and everything covered," said Case, "looks like we're about to get wet." The cowboys and vaqueros mounted up and rode close alongside the cattle, knowing what would happen if the weather spooked them.

Rolling black clouds could be seen racing across the prairie heading straight for the camp. Within minutes, heavy rain lashed everything in sight. The riders managed to keep the herd together, all of them were on their feet and nervous as the rain started to pass. Just as the rain quit, a terrifying clap of thunder in the distance shook the ground then everything went dead still. For several minutes it looked like the storm was over. Then the skies opened up and began to drop hail stones the size of small river rocks. The herd bawled and thrashed as the hail pounded them unmercifully. Cattle began to break from the herd in a dozen places and part of the remuda started to follow. As the hail got worse, the stones grew larger and more dangerous and the men knew it would be a hopeless task to try and gather them until it passed. They took what shelter they could under the wagons and against the few trees in the area.

The wagon canvas was shredded, and the prairie was pounded into a muddy quagmire by thousands of panicked hooves. Ten minutes later, the rain and hail gave way to blue skies and hot sun. Crawling out from under the wagon, Case stood up and surveyed the damage. "Jesus almighty, what a mess, we even have enough horses left to go after the cattle?"

The wrangler nodded. "We're good, we were able to keep enough of them from running," said the wrangler. "I'm not sure if we have enough saddles for everyone though, a lot of them that ran were saddled."

"Well, see what you can come up with," said Case. "Any mules left? We can use them if we have to."

"We still got all the mules."

"Then saddle up what you can," said Case, "and let's get started looking."

Monroe Timms walked up next to him. "How many head of cattle you figure we lost?"

Case shrugged. "I'd guess at least five hundred or more. Looks like we lost some of the remuda too. The men did one hell of a job to hold on to that many. Boyd, you and Tom Lee get a good fire going and plan on hot chuck and hot coffee when everyone gets back here."

"You got it Boss," said Boyd.

"And set up the tents so everyone has a place to get out of the weather if it rains again. I'll take a couple of hands and see if we can get this bunch calmed down enough to bed. Everyone else head out and find our animals."

The cowboys scattered out across the prairie in pairs, looking for their stock. Throughout the day they returned to camp with cattle in small bunches, singles, and cow calf pairs. Drawing fresh horses from the remuda, they headed back out without hesitation. Dozens of head were found mired in fresh mud holes. A rope over their horns pulled by a good cow horse was generally enough to get them out. One yearling was stuck so deeply in a hole that he was left for the Indians and wolves. Often when a few head would spot the cowboy, the bunch would split apart and break into more groups, and a chase was on. Other times when the cowboys finally got a group turned back, more would start to follow along.

Riding up to a deep, muddy wash, Jesus looked down and saw three Comanche braves in the bottom butchering two dead cattle. One brave looked up, screamed loudly at him and pounded a bloody fist on his chest. Displaying his empty hands to the brave, he backed away and left them to their business.

Recovering the horses was a slow process. Most had to be roped before they could be brought back to the remuda. When Del saw a big bay mare standing alone in a small stream, he rode up and dropped a loop over her head and she barely moved from her tracks. Checking the horse, he realized she was blind. The hail had battered her head so badly that she had lost both eyes. He knew this horse was a good mount, but she was now useless. With his revolver pressed between her eyes he pulled the trigger. Tying his rope back on the saddle, he rode off in search of more animals.

Dead cattle were found scattered around the prairie, some had been trampled by the herd and others had fallen off of steep drop-offs and crippled. The hail had blinded several others, and they were put down. For two more days every available man hunted for cattle and horses. Jesus found another horse that had broken a leg in a prairie dog hole and put him down. Finding six more standing in a wash, one of them, a popular gelding known for his gentle disposition, was still saddled, the reins hung up in a cottonwood snag. Untangling the gelding he led him away, and the others fell in behind, following them back to the remuda. When they had recovered all the animals they could, Boyd made a big breakfast for everyone and extra chuck for the trail and they pushed north again.

__May 23.__ First major storm, a fierce, hard rain, blew in at early morning and flooded every creek, pond, and low spot on the prairie, which is now all mud. Before it stopped, we were pounded with hail stones big enough to seriously injure and kill several of the animals. Men found what cover they could, which was very little. The herd broke and many cattle and horses *scattered, it took three days to recapture. Lost seven horses, three with saddles. Still working on full count, at least fifty or more missing to hailstorm or Indians. Found a dozen or more unbranded wild longhorns in the herd that took up with the drive of their own accord.*

On the move again, the herd slogged through the damp prairie, making barely six miles the next day. The country still held small potholes and ponds full of water, but the sky was clear and already blistering hot. "Damn, Tom Lee," said Del, as they found themselves riding drag together again, "I really do think I'd rather be hunting buffs again, they warn't so many bugs as there is now."

"That's because it was cold most of the time. Them bugs don't like cold weather any more than we do."

Del wiped the dust off his face and rewrapped his bandanna. "The ticks from these goddamn bovines are still crawling all over me. Pulled three more off this morning."

"I still think it's because you taste so good," teased Tom Lee. "Besides, I don't know where you can get a job out here without bugs."

"So what's a man supposed to do? I don't like killin' buffs and getting' all bloody, and I don't like pushin' cattle and eatin' dirt neither."

Tom Lee shrugged. "Maybe you should be a preacher, they don't need to get bloody or dirty, and from what I can tell, they all look to have plenty to eat."

"A preacher would have to read from the Bible, and you know I can't read."

"Maybe by the time we get there you'll think of something."

"Maybe . . ."

The outfit pushed slowly north for several days, the wet prairie turning hard and dry with the usual heavy dust covering everything that moved. Returning from a scouting trip, Case rode to the back of the herd and motioned for Tom Lee to follow him. Catching up with Boyd, he told him to grab a Springfield and some cartridges. Riding a mile ahead of the wagons, they stopped and hobbled the horses. Crawling up to the edge of a dry wash, they stopped and looked over the bank.

"That's the biggest bull buff I've ever seen," said Case, pointing at a small cluster of buffalo bedded in the shade of a tall bluff.

"It is big all right, you want to kill him?" asked Tom Lee.

Case shook his head. "I want you to kill him and all the rest of them."

"Really? You want me to shoot them?"

"I know you wanted to be a shooter last winter and didn't get to — so here's your chance. You put one through the big bull's lungs, and I think you can get the rest of them to stand long enough kill them all."

Steadying the long rifle across the grass, Tom Lee fired, and the bull humped up and dropped cleanly. Handing him another cartridge, Case told him to shoot the young bull to the left. When he finished shooting, eight buffalo lay dead from eight shots.

"Well done Tom Lee, guess I should have had you doing the shooting last winter."

"I appreciate this Case, that was fun for sure. What are we going to do with them now, you want the hides?"

"No, just the tongues. I'll have Boyd cook up something different, I'm getting tired of beefsteak."

"You want some hump too?"

Case shook his head. "Just the tongues is all. If we get the craving for buff meat again, we can kill some more."

When Boyd stopped at the next night's spot, Case dropped a canvas package full of tongues on the wagon. "We're going to stop a little early tonight, cook these up for chuck. It would be a good time to bring out an extra spud for everyone along with your special beans and some extra biscuits too. If you got any of those cans of cherries, this would be the time to bring them out."

Tom Lee climbed down and tied up to the wagon. Laying the Springfield back in the wagon box, he closed the lid and loosened the cinch on his saddle. "You shoulda seen that giant buff I killed. Case said it was the biggest one he ever saw in all his years out here."

"All you took were the tongues?" asked Boyd. "We could have used some hump for jerky too."

"The boss said to just take the tongues, we can get more the next time we see them."

"Well the next time you go off chasin' buffs, you might tell him I'd like to shoot one too."

"I already did. He said you'll go next time."

"Well, thanks for that. Let's get started cooking, the herd will be here before long."

May 27. Case took me to a spot where he saw a group of buffalos. He had me shoot all eight of them. I was excited but managed to kill all eight with eight cartridges. One bull was the biggest one either of us had ever seen. Case said he had a taste for something more than beef, so we took the tongues. I hope the Indians find the dead buffs before the coyotes or wolves do. One of the vaqueros killed three armadillos while we were out. Never ate one before, but some variety for the pot would be good.

A steady rain fell as the outfit moved out in the morning. Within an hour, the clouds cleared, and steam started to rise from the backs of the cattle making a small rainbow over the herd. The ever-present coyotes followed along behind the drag men chattering back and forth, waiting for their chance at a free meal.

As they took up their drag positions, a fresh dropped calf stumbled and fell out of the herd in front of Tom Lee. The mother was lost in the herd somewhere, unable to find her baby. Del dropped a rope over its neck and drug it several hundred yards out behind the rest of the herd. Tom Lee heard a dull pop as Del put it down.

Catching up with herd, Del fell back in with Tom Lee. "Another one for the coyotes, they've been eatin' pretty well lately."

"How many is this now?" asked Tom Lee.

"Probably eight or ten so far this trip."

"Too bad there ain't no way of keeping them."

"No way could they keep up with the herd. If you try to put them in back in the herd with the mother, you'd lose both of them."

"I know, but it's still a waste," said Tom Lee, adjusting his bandanna.

The rain came and went throughout the rest of the day and for several more. The rain had turned the prairie lush and Timms and Case moved the herd across some of the thickest, greenest grass they'd ever seen.

"Case," said Timms, "this is a cattleman's dream — wouldn't it be great if the grass was like this all the way to Cheyenne?"

Case nodded, looking back at the long string of grazing cattle. "That's a mighty big thing to wish for, being so far away, but I guess we should enjoy it while we got it."

June 4. long, hot days are the norm on the trail, with an occasional rainstorm followed by more hot sun. A small bunch broke from the herd this morning. It took four hands several hours to account for all of them. Two or three of the escapees appear to be snake-bit on the head. They likely grazed over a den somewhere along the way. They're swollen but time will tell if they can keep up. Two cowboys say they need salve badly. I suspect others do also. Case says when we make Adobe Walls, there may be a peddler with some for sale.

Del rode into the remuda and changed horses for the third time that day. As he rode back to the herd, he spotted five mounted Indians several hundred yards behind them. "You see them?" asked Del.

Tom Lee nodded. "Yeah, they've been back there for a while. They must be hungry."

"They ain't no damn better than the coyotes or wolves. We do all the work, and they try to steal from us."

"They're just hungry is all," said Tom Lee. "Ain't you ever been hungry before?"

"You ain't gone and turned into a goddamned Indian lover on me, have you?" said Del, looking back over his shoulder at the Indians.

Tom Lee didn't say any more and went back to tending the cattle. The next day while working the herd through a dry canyon, a cow with a bad limp dropped out on Tom Lee's right side. "Looks like a busted leg," said Del. "You know what to do."

Roping the cow, he led it away and out of sight of the herd. Several hundred yards back he pulled off the rope and let her go. The Comanche braves rode out of the trees and looked at him. Riding back to the herd, he pulled up his bandanna and went back to work.

"Goddamnit Tom Lee, I didn't hear no shot, what did you do?"

"Don't you worry about it, everything is okay," said Tom Lee.

"Did you give her to those shit-devils? Why didn't you just kill her?"

"The cow can still walk, this way they can take it back to their camp and kill it when they're ready."

Del shook his head. "A goddamn Indian lover — I never woulda guessed it. You gotta shoot the damn things, that way the coyotes and wolves can get to 'em first."

They rode silently the rest of the day until the herd was bedded for the night. "Del, I ain't never heard you say anything about your people, where'd your family come from?"

"Jesus boy, you and your damn questions."

"I was just wondering is all. We all talked about our people before, except for you."

"Okay fine. I was born down by the Rio Grande, not sure exactly which side. My Mama was a Mexican from a farm down there somewhere. She was a little woman, very pretty and very quiet. My father was a white man, a teamster that worked out of San Antonio and a big, nasty son-of-a-bitch," said Del.

"What happened to him, is he still alive?"

Del shook his head and looked at Tom Lee. "Not since I was fourteen years old."

"What happened to him?"

"Like I said, he was big and nasty, and a terrible, mean drunk. One night he came home with a belly full of whiskey and beat my mother to death right in front of me, then laid down next to her and went to sleep."

"Jesus Del, I'm so sorry you had to go through something like that, did he get put in jail?"

"No. I took the old ten-gauge he carried on the wagon, stuck it in his snoring mouth and blew off the back of his head. Any more questions Tom Lee?"

"Uh . . . no, I guess not," said Tom Lee. "I'm sorry I asked about it Del."

"Don't be. It is what it is boy, nothin' we can do about it 'cept move on. I buried them deep in the floor of the cabin, turned the mules loose, then burned it down. I wandered around Texas for a while then went to New Mexico and worked in a silver mine and hated it, so I joined up with the army. I guess I found my callin' when I started killin' Indians."

"Case," said Del, finishing up chuck, "how far you figure it is to the Walls from here?"

"I say two days, maybe three at the most."

"You think there will be any peddlers there?"

Case nodded. "There usually are in the summer, and maybe a couple of comancheros. You in need of something in particular?"

"Socks for one, and some of that belly medicine. I think I swallowed too much dirt."

The cowboys around the fire all got a good laugh at that. "So you sayin' you don't like riding drag Del?" asked Timms.

"Mister Timms, you ever had a cowboy that said he liked ridin' back there?"

"Probably not. But you've paid your dues here, you can ride flank on the next trip."

"No sir, I ain't doin' that, nor any other position neither."

"You're quitting?" asked Timms.

"Not here and not now," said Del. "I'll do you a good job till the end of this one, but this cattle work just ain't for me."

Reaching the Canadian River, the herd crossed without incident and bedded down three miles outside Adobe Walls. Timms and Case decided to rest the herd for two days and take advantage of the fresh grass and water. Working in shifts, the hands kept the herd together, and others rode into the Walls to see what might be available. After weeks on the trail with nothing to look at but cows, any distraction would be welcomed.

Boyd and Del rode in the next morning and looked around the encampment. Two hide buyers were set up in front of a tumbled down adobe wall, with a growing rick of hides piled behind them. Three canvas tents were set up between the hides and the wall. One just advertised whiskey, another sold ammunition, guns, knives, lead, and powder and another had canned goods and dry-goods and a good supply of tobacco.

Two Mexican comancheros worked out of their wagon selling and trading a variety of items like coffee, onions, chilies, and beads.

Boyd walked into the dry-goods tent and pulled out his list. Grabbing salt pork, coffee, two large sacks of beans, and several cans of fruit, he set the supplies off to one side. After he finished filling the list, he picked out several more things that caught his eye. "You got two hundred pounds of potatoes?"

The merchant nodded. "I got some spuds. There may not be two hundred pounds though."

"That's okay, I'll take whatever you got. My boss will be in to pay for all this and he'll have a wagon to haul everything," said Boyd, walking out of the tent.

Haggling with the comancheros, he picked up a large bag of onions and another of chilies. As he turned to go to the next tent, he saw Del coming out.

"You find everything you needed?" asked Del.

Boyd nodded. "Yeah, what did you get?"

"Nothing yet. I come to find you so I can borrow a little money to pay for things."

"Oh yeah, I forgot you don't have any money," said Boyd. "You really are one pitiful example of a cowboy, you know that?"

"Yeah, yeah, I heard it all before, can I just get my socks and salve now?"

Walking into the tent, Del picked two pairs of heavy wool socks, and a tin of salve. "This stuff guaranteed to heal up my piles?" asked Del.

"I guarantee it likely won't hurt them none," said the merchant. "But I never had the need to try it myself. That'll be a dollar."

Boyd looked at Del and shook his head. "Give me two tins of the same salve, and two bottles of paregoric. What about a hat Del?"

"Yeah, I guess I need a hat too."

"Put them all on my bill," said Boyd.

The third tent was smaller, all it advertised was: **_Whiskey by the shot or the bottle_**. "What do you think Boyd? A quick stop in here? Nobody will ever know."

"You ain't got no money — remember?"

"Aw heck Boyd, you can buy us one little drink," said Del, looking back at the tent. "They also got a pretty little señorita in there too, she can't cost all that much."

"Whiskey and women is why you don't got no money in the first place — ain't it?"

When they reached the horses, a Mexican man approached them, obviously wanting to talk about something. "Señors, may we talk a moment please?"

Boyd nodded. "What is it?"

"I am looking for a large, bald-headed black man with very dark skin. I have heard his name is Sylvie. I also heard that you might know of him?"

"Sure, we know him," said Del, "but we haven't seen him since last winter's buffalo hunt. Why are you looking for him?"

"This man Sylvie, he is a horse thief. He stole two of my horses recently, and he stole from several others also."

Del shrugged, "We wouldn't have any idea where he might be now."

The Mexican shrugged. "Gracias. If you find him, you should keep your horses close."

Del and Boyd mounted up and headed back to the camp. "Well, at least we know the Indians didn't get him," said Boyd.

"He'd be better off if they'd got him that first day," said Del. "If anyone catches him with stolen horses, they'll likely leave him hangin' somewhere. If it's Case that catches him, he might be the one supplyin' the rope."

__June 27__. Crossed the Canadian River and bedded the herd close to Adobe Walls. Smaller than the Colorado, the boss found a good crossing. Lost one fresh calf here. Many of us went into the Walls to see if there were any peddlers. Several bought things like socks, salve for their piles and many bought tobacco. Del found a new hat. Much good grass here. Rumor is that old partner Sylvie did not get killed by Indians as we all thought.

On their last night at the Walls, the rain had quit, and it was a clear, cool night. A big fire had everyone comfortable and in the mood to smoke and talk. "Case, you remember last winter when we had that buff stand on that real steep hillside?" said Del.

"Yeah, I remember," said Case lighting up. "That's one you don't have to talk about, and it would be okay with me."

"What happened Del? You gotta tell the story now," said Timms.

"Well, we just finished up a nice stand, about a dozen or so buffs I'd guess, and we walked up that hill and got to cuttin' on the hides. Just as Case was bent over finishing one up, a calf all covered in blood, stood up on shaky legs, took a few steps and butted Case square in the backside — and pretty damn hard too."

"The buffalo butted into him?" asked Roly. "Then what happened?"

Del, now having fun with the story, continued. "Well, old Case, slippery from all the blood and tallow, tried to stand up on that steep hillside and the little buff butted him again and down he went again. After he slid down the hill for a few yards, he tried to stand up and dammed if that ornery little shit didn't get him again."

"Now that must have been quite a sight. I wish I coulda seen that myself," said Tom Lee.

Around the fire, everyone was now listening intently to see how the story would come out. Del nodded. "Oh, it was a sight all right. That little buff kept bumping, and Case, slicked down with blood and all, kept getting up and getting bumped down again, finally slidin' all the way down to the bottom."

"So, then what happened Del?" asked Tom Lee.

"When they reached flat ground, Case managed to get on his feet cursing that little buff like a man possessed," said Del. "Then he pulled his revolver and pointed it right at him from five feet away."

"So, he finally killed the buff?" asked Roly.

Del, now laughing so hard he was choking on the words, shook his head. "Oh hell no! The buff gave one big shudder and dropped dead right in front of him before he could even cock his pistol!"

By now everyone in camp was laughing uncontrollably. "That's funny for sure," said Tom Lee, almost in tears.

"Hell," said Del, "That ain't even the funny part . . ."

"Well goddamnit Del, get to it, what's the funny part?" asked Boyd.

"He shot him anyway!"

"He shot him anyway?" said Tom Lee, "even after he died?"

"Yeah," said Del, hardly able to get the words out, "five times!"

Even Case was laughing by now. "Well, all I got to say is that it was the best damn tongue I ever ate!"

Chapter 15

Before they moved from the Canadian River, Case filled in the crew about what they might expect next. "In the next few days, we'll be moving through a lawless chunk of country called the neutral strip, then into Colorado Territory. The Comanches are just as bad here as they have been all along the trail, but this is no-man's land, and we could run into rustlers, horse thieves, or just about any kind of killer and no-account you can think of. Keep your pistols ready and don't get caught out there alone. It's just like with the Comanches except some of these might be white men, black men or Mexicans or ex-soldiers from either side," said Case, throwing his saddle over a fresh horse. "Don't give them an inch, and don't let anyone get close to the herd or the remuda."

"How long will it take to get through this place?" asked Timms.

"Without any trouble, a couple days to get there and about the same to get through it," said Case. "Tom Lee will ride with Boyd for this stretch with a Springfield on his lap, and Jesus will do the same with Roly in the hoodlum."

"Case, when we get into the Colorado Territory, how long will it be before we cross the Arkansas River?" asked Timms. "I've heard that it can be a bad one."

"It can be. We'll hit it a few days after we get in the territory. This time of year, it'll be still be carrying a lot of water from the high country run off. It can be a tough one to cross."

"What about Indians?"

"About the same. We might run across some Arapahos or a few others from farther north. I've been hearing that most of the Kiowas around here are being rounded up and sent to government reservations somewhere. But the Comanches will be keeping close watch on us — you can count on that."

June 30. pulled out of Adobe Walls at sunup. It was a good break for everyone and good grass for the stock. Two horses missing, probably Comanches but we never saw them. Killed two meat steers for camp and Boyd made some jerky and extra good beans with backstrap and spuds for everyone. At the Walls he bought two big cans of peaches and one of cherries. We ate one of the peaches. Saw several coyotes kill a fawn, everyone is hungry.

The outfit moved northwest out of the Walls toward Colorado Territory. The first day was overcast and cool with a short rainstorm in the morning. Coming to a burned-out homestead on a small stream, they bedded the herd for the night. Three crude, weathered crosses lay on the ground near what was left of the back wall of a settler's cabin. Pieces of broken furniture and a few pages of a burned child's book lay in the ashes. Roly walked over to the graves and pushed the crosses back into the dirt and said a prayer for the dead.

That night, by their calculations, they had made nearly fifteen miles. By the time the herd was bedded, it had cooled off even more. When the rain cleared, everyone settled in around the fire.

"Sure be good if every day could be this purty," said Del.

"The good Lord has blessed us with this great day," said Roly, "and we thank you, oh Lord, for keeping us safe on this trip, and we beseech thee to watch over the outfit as we head into this wild piece of no-man's land ahead of us — amen!"

"You really believe all that God stuff?" asked Del. "It's all a bunch of hokum if you ask me."

Roly nodded. "God is real brother. Nothing happens without his blessing, and those living on this earth would do well to recognize that without him they'd all be living in hell!"

"Did you thank him for those arrows the Comanches stuck in your chest too?" asked Del.

"I thanked him for allowing me to live, and for making me strong enough to pull them out and keep moving forward."

"Well, whatever makes you happy friend."

"What makes you happy brother Del?" asked Roly.

"Right now I'd say a couple of soft, round señoritas and a big jug of whiskey would make me really happy."

"Spoken like a man in need of the Lord's guidance," said Roly. "Would you like to read from the Bible with me brother?"

"No sir I would not," said Del, shaking his head. "I can't read a lick, so I guess I'm just gonna have to die in the flames of hell."

The rest of the hands around the fire had a good laugh at this exchange. "I think he's got you there Roly," said Case.

"The Lord loves and protects everyone brother," said Roly. "Even those that don't believe."

The next two days were much the same as the last, mostly overcast with small spurts of rain. The buffalo grass was thick and the herd was strung out well and content to keep moving without much encouragement. Case saw the tracks of several shod horses along a muddy creek bank as they moved out. On the third night out of the Walls, they bedded the cattle next to a small stream close by the Texas border.

Case put extra men on the night guard and two more in the camp with the Springfields. At morning chuck, Monroe Timms grabbed Case's arm and pointed to a clump of cottonwood snags several hundred yards out. "Comanches, six or seven at least, looking right at us. What do you think they want?"

Case stared at them for a minute and raised a hand in the air. "Same as always I suppose, looking for food and whatever else they can get out of us. I'll go see what they want. Tom Lee, you ride slightly behind me and off to one side and bring the big gun."

Tom Lee grabbed the rifle, saddled up and followed him toward the Indians. Halfway there, Case stopped and put his hands in the air. Two Indians rode out to meet them. After several minutes of talking and a lot of gesturing, both sides rode back.

"What do they want?" asked Tom Lee.

"Cows and horses, like usual," said Case.

Monroe Timms rode over to them. "Mister Timms," said Case, "they want two horses and two head of cattle to let us pass without trouble."

Timms sat in the saddle watching the Indians by the trees. "Well, you know how to deal with these savages better than me. Do you think we should give them the animals?"

"Actually, I think we should give them more."

"More? Why would we do that?"

"I want to give them two cows now, and two more when we get to the Arkansas River," said Case. "I've delt with these two before, more than once. I made deals with them, and they've always kept up their end of it — but they're still Comanches."

"What about the horses?"

"I want to give them four horses when we reach the river."

"That seems like a lot to me, but I trust you to do whatever is right."

"The Comanches are horse people Mister Timms, four horses can mean a lot to a small band like this. We've been lucky so far. There's been enough cows left behind to keep their bellies full, so there wasn't any good reason to attack us. If we make this deal, they'll stay near us until we get to the Arkansas River and warn us if there is any trouble we should know about. When we get across the river, they get paid off — you good with that?"

Timms nodded. "Everything you've done so far has worked out, so go ahead and make the deal."

Case and Tom Lee rode back out and met with the braves. After ten minutes of head shaking, yelling and gesturing they came to a deal. Riding back to camp, they pulled up alongside of Timms.

"That looked like a pretty animated discussion out there," said Timms. "Everything go all right?"

Case nodded. "The big one with the red head cloth and black paint on the side of his face is called Black Dog. He felt he needed to remind us that we were crossing his land and killing his buffalo and we're only here because he is allowing us to be. I told them if they will take two cows now and two when we hit the Arkansas, they would get four horses instead of two. He also gets any animals that drop out of the herd, so we have to let them go alive. They also get whatever doesn't make it across the river — so we're all big friends now."

"Me and Del will cut out two head," said Tom Lee.

Case nodded. "Put a rope on them and stake them down out where we did the talking."

"We're on it Boss."

Case shouted instructions to the flankers and drag men and gave them the signal to move out. Grant and Lincoln got their cue and the herd began to string out. The Indians led their prizes over the ridge and out of sight.

Case put extra hands on night guard, and everyone on the wagons or in camp carried pistols and rifles with them at all times. For two days they moved steadily, occasionally catching a quick look at the Comanches riding well out ahead or off to the side of the herd.

At evening chuck, Tom Lee asked Del what he thought about working with the Indians. "You already know what I think about them shit-devils, you can never trust any of 'em. If I had my way, I'd kill ever' last one of them."

"You ever have to kill any other kinds of Indians except Comanches while you were in the Army?"

"Yeah sure," said Del. "I killed lots of Kiowas and Arapahos up north of here, probably a few Cheyennes too."

"Didn't you ever meet any good ones?"

Del shook his head. "Tom Lee, you gotta get it right in your head, there ain't no such thing as a good one, they's all just a bunch of murderin' savages."

At first light the outfit was ready to move out. Case rode the perimeter of the herd talking to every hand about what they needed to watch for. For the next several days they would be moving through one of the most dangerous places in the frontier.

Giving the signal, the outfit began to move slowly over the prairie and out of Texas. The terrain was wide open and flat, and the outfit moved steadily north without trouble. As they prepared to bed the herd the first night, the sky darkened quickly, and a steady rain started to fall. Lightning in the far distance made the cows nervous, and the herd refused to bed down. Case added several more hands to the night guard, and they did a good job of keeping them together until the storm passed.

"Tom Lee, have the flankers circle them in this big swale," said Case, pointing out a long, grassy flat. "There's enough grass here to hold them for tonight."

Seven cowboys continued to ride slowly, constantly circling them and talking to them, a few were even known to sing to them to keep themselves awake and alert and to help keep the herd calm. When the rain passed, the herd relaxed and began to lie down. Boyd was finishing up chuck when he spotted smoke coming over a hill. "Case, you see the smoke to the west?"

"I saw it. Most likely it's just our new Indian friends cooking up some of Mister Timms beef, but out here you never know," said Case, cleaning up his plate with the last biscuit.

After a long tense night, Boyd had plenty of hot coffee and a good breakfast ready to help prepare everyone for another day through the notorious strip of land. When the herd got strung out and moving smoothly, Boyd and Tom Lee spotted three men riding down off a low side hill toward Case and Timms. "Mister Timms, you should stay here, I'll have Del go with me."

"No — this is my outfit, I'm coming with you."

Riding out to meet them, Case could see they were heavily armed, rough-looking white men. One was a really large man, well over six-feet and two-hundred and fifty pounds. Wearing a Confederate slouch hat and a pair of revolvers in a sash around his waist, he was an imposing looking figure. One of the other men wore a Confederate kepi and jacket and one wore a filthy white duster and a black hat. Both carried a revolver in their waistband and a rifle on their horse. Riding straight up to Case and Timms, they stopped no more than ten feet away.

"What do you want?" asked Case, with his hand already on his Colt. Timms sat quietly, several feet to the side watching the men, with his rifle across the saddle cocked and pointing at them.

"You know where you're at mister?" said the biggest man.

"I know exactly where I'm at," said Case, not taking his eyes off of the man. "So, I'll ask you one more time, what do you want?"

"This here is my land you're on, and it's going to cost you to move your herd across it."

"No — it's not gonna cost me anything. Now get the hell out of my way, and you might not get killed today."

Timms raised his rifle, pointing it squarely at the man doing all the talking. "Mister, I'm telling you now that it would be in your best interest to listen to my partner."

The big man locked eyes with Case. "You and your bunch of greasers and nigger cowboys ain't going any farther 'till you pay up. I have a dozen men watching from the trees with rifles pointed at you, waiting for my signal to kill all of you."

"Well, shit — if that's the way it has to be," said Case, looking toward the trees.

"That's the way it is, now take your hand off your pistol and gather up all your cash."

Case raised his arms, showing him his empty hands. "Okay hold on, just don't do no shooting, I keep it right here in my bag," Opening the flap of the saddle bag he reached in and pulled out another revolver, cocking and firing as soon as it cleared the leather. The big man pitched off his horse and hit the ground with blood pouring from the side of his head.

Timms fired instantly, killing the man on the left almost before the first one hit the ground. As the third outlaw turned away and spurred his horse, Timms shot him out of the saddle.

"Good shooting Mister Timms, I was hoping you were ready for this," said Case.

Timms shrugged. "I've been dealing with people like this all my life, I figured it was probably gonna end this way. You think there are others in this gang?"

"Could be," said Case, spurring his horse toward the wagons. "But I think they might be a little more cautious about confronting us after this."

"Let's hope that's so," said Timms. "It's time to get back on the trail."

At chuck, the talk was all about their bosses killing the bandits and how quick they were to take action. A newfound respect for Timms and Case was obvious among the crew. "I'd follow those two men anywhere they wanted to lead me," said Del.

"Si, I would work for them also," said one of the older vaqueros. "They are very good men."

Case hung the bandit's revolvers and rifles from the hoodlum wagon. "The saddles were junk. If anyone wants one of these guns help yourself," said Case.

The pistols, all good Colts, were claimed quickly. Nobody took the older rifles and Roly threw them in the wagon for anyone that might want one later.

After a restless night, the outfit packed up and was ready to move out when they saw two Comanche braves riding toward the camp. Recognizing Black Dog and one of his band, Case and Tom Lee and rode out to talk with them.

After a few minutes, they rode back. "So, what did our new friends have to say?" asked Timms.

"They told us there were three other bandits in the gang that confronted us," said Case. "They caught them riding west of the herd yesterday in a hurry. Black Dog said that they knew them to be bad men that had killed Comanche women and children before. So, they killed them and took their horses — they even showed us the scalps. I told them where we killed the other three, and they're gonna get those too."

"Sounds like a profitable day's business for them."

Case nodded. "Probably good for a small band like this. Comanches are kinda like coyotes. They'll hang around as long as they think there's a chance they can get something."

"Looks like the investment of a few cows and horses is working out well," said Timms.

"So far so good, but we ain't to the Arkansas yet," said Case.

For the next two days, the outfit moved steadily across the prairie until they came to the upper stretch of the Cimmeron River. A small, murky stream, the crossing was trouble free with only the loss of one yearling that had been dragging behind with a bad foot.

On the other side of the river, they came to a well-defined wagon trail that headed southwest across the desolate landscape, Case gave the signal to stop. "Let's put 'em to bed right here for the night," said Case, giving the men the signal to circle them up.

"You think we're in Colorado Territory yet?" asked Timms.

"Tomorrow for sure," said Case. "I'd say that we can't be more than a couple of miles at most."

"Looks like there's been a lot of people through here one time or another," said Timms, pointing to the deep ruts in the trail.

Case nodded. "It's the Cimmeron route, part of the old Santa Fe Trail that goes south to Fort Union. People started using it to avoid the original trail that had to go through the mountains."

"I see a busted wagon wheel and a few empty cans scattered around, it must be a tough trip for families, especially those with kids."

"There have been thousands of people pass through here over the years," said Case. "Now that the war's over, a lot more of them will likely risk the long trail west looking for a new life than stay back east. They know things will never be the same where they came from."

The two men sat quietly on their horses watching as the cowboys, and the vaqueros expertly circled the cattle and kept them calm. The camp wagon and the hoodlum wagon were positioned together to make a windbreak while Boyd got set up and Roly and Tom Lee staked out the mules and set the tents. When the herd was calm, the hands scheduled for the first night guard walked into the remuda and caught a fresh mount for their shift.

Sitting down near the fire, several men fell asleep before they even finished chuck. Del stuffed his usual oversized wad of chew into his cheek, and others lit up their smokes. "Boss, I gotta say, 'cause it's still on my mind, you and Mister Timms did a hell of a piece of work on those outlaws back there. You ever in the war yourself?"

Case stood up, flipped his smoke in the fire and headed for his tent. "See you in the morning."

After several hours on the trail, the herd was well strung out, and everyone had settled into the routine. Two miles ahead, Boyd and Tom Lee followed Case and Timms in the camp wagon while they scouted out a place to bed the herd for the night. Roly kept the hoodlum moving close behind. Crossing a wide-open sage flat, Case and Timms rode well ahead and out of site over a small rise as the wagons followed. When Boyd reached the middle of the flat, they heard a rifle shot and looked up to see Case and Timms riding straight at them in a wild swirl of dust as fast as their horses could carry them.

Jerking the wagons to a stop, Boyd set the brake hard, jumped down and pulled open the box with the Springfields and handed one to each man along with a handful of cartridges. Case and Timms slid their horses to a stop at the back of the hoodlum, each grabbing a rifle and crawling under a wagon. Six Indians were coming at them hard, firing their rifles. Lining up his sights on the lead Indian, Timms waited until they were in range and fired. The horse went down instantly in a spectacular head over heels crash, but the rider jumped up and climbed on behind another brave.

Firing from the wagon box, Roly dropped the horse with the two riders but still didn't kill either Indian. Several other braves that were still mounted gathered up the two on foot and kept charging toward the wagons. Before they could fire again, six more screaming Indians came racing full speed from the side of the sage flat and rode directly into the attackers shooting their rifles and swinging war clubs.

"Kiowas," said Case. "The ones that attacked us are Kiowas. The others are our Comanche friends."

"Never thought I'd be so glad to see a bunch of charging, screaming Comanches before," said Timms, crawling out from under the wagon.

"Me neither," said Case.

The men watched as the Comanches killed and scalped the Kiowa, mutilating the bodies horrifically. Rounding up the loose horses, his braves screamed and pounded their chests. Black Dog rode close to the wagons and held the scalps up for everyone to see. Still creaming loudly, he rode back and grabbed the reins of the last Kiowa horse and led his band out of site.

"Well shit almighty," said Boyd. "And I thought it was us about to lose our hair!"

Timms tried rolling a fresh cigarette, but his hands shook so much he kept losing all the tobacco. "I gotta say, this one's gonna make a great story for my grandkids, but I doubt they'd even believe it."

"Here, let me roll that for you," said Roly. "All your tobacco's gonna be on the ground before you get it done."

"How is it you know how to do that Roly?" asked Tom Lee. "I thought you didn't smoke cigarettes?"
Roly shrugged. "I didn't say I never smoked them, I just said I much prefer my pipe."

They could hear the cattle bawling as the point man appeared in the sage flat with Lincoln and Grant following close behind. As the herd began to fill the sage, Case motioned to the cowboys to circle them up. "I think everyone needs a little rest right now."

"I know I do," said Timms, trying to roll a second cigarette without much success.

"Boss, did you see any water while you were scouting around up here?" asked Boyd.

Case nodded and pointed to a low rock outcropping. "There's two small springs coming out of that dark rock face on the side hill. There's a small pool below them. The cows are pretty well watered from this morning. Be sure the remuda gets what they need first then the cows can have what's left."

__July 5.__ First night in Colorado Territory. Advance riders and wagons attacked by Indians today. We first we thought our Comanche friends turned on us. The attacking party was a band of Kiowa. Just as we started shooting, Black Dog and his band charged them and killed and scalped the whole bunch. It was revolting to see the way the Comanches slaughtered them, but they likely saved us from the same fate. We should be reaching the Arkansas River soon. Very dry here, the herd needs water.

Case and Timms sat around the morning fire drinking their coffee and recounting yesterday's adventure. "Boyd, did you think we were gonna lose our hair yesterday?" asked Case.

"Naw — wasn't a bit worried, were you?"

"Not me, what about you Roly?" asked Case, "Were you worried?"

"No sir, when I saw those Kiowas bearing down on us I said a quick prayer to God and opened fire — I knew he'd keep us safe."

"Well, you're all better men than me," said Timms. "I figured we were gonna get scalped for sure. I even double checked to make sure my Colt had at least one live round left."

"What about you Tom Lee, those Kiowas scare you?" asked Boyd.

"I'm with Mister Timms on this. I think I checked my pistol before he did."

Everyone around the fire had a good laugh at this. After telling the tale once more, this time with a little touch of cowboy embellishment for good measure, Jeff, one of the black cowboys, asked them again just how many charging Kiowas there were.

"I counted ten painted up Kiowas charging right at us," said Boyd. "Ain't that about right Case?"

"Heck no, there were at least twelve, I remember because they were chasing me and Mister Timms hard — and they damn near caught us too."

"Okay," said Del. "Maybe we can get the straight story from Mister Timms. I know he's good at counting cattle so maybe he can tell us the real number of Indians."

Timms looked at them straight-faced, took off his hat and wiped off his face with his bandanna. "Well, when we first saw them there had to be at least fifteen screaming savages coming through the trees straight at us. By the time me and Case got turned and headed back to the wagons, there were even more. Truth of it is — I really didn't have much time for proper counting."

By now the crew couldn't contain their laughter. Waiting a moment for them to quiet down, Del looked at Tom Lee. "Okay, we haven't heard from you yet. How many painted savages did you count?"

Tom Lee sat quietly for a moment. "None."

"What the hell you mean none?" asked Del. "You were right there, how could you not see 'em?"

"Oh — I saw them all right, but there was way too many to count, probably at least a couple of hundred."

Chapter 16

The outfit moved steadily north across a flat, sage covered plain with less grass and water than a few weeks ago. The herd moved slower, taking longer to get their fill. The few creeks in the area were hardly enough to water the horses, with little left for the herd. A steady, hot wind blew continuously for the next several days, drying the ground out even worse.

After Case and Timms had been scouting for a few hours, they rode back to the wagons. "Tom Lee, there's a little creek about a mile from here running through some good grass, we're gonna bed down there for the night," said Case. "Tell the point man what's going on. Boyd, you and Roly go ahead and set up."

"We getting close to the river?"

Case nodded. "We're maybe five miles from the Arkansas, about a mile east of where the Purgatoire runs in. I want them kept well back from the river tonight, or they'll be off and running."

Case sipped at his morning coffee and filled everyone in on what he expected to see when they reached the Arkansas River. "I don't want to let them get as strung out like a normal day. Keep them a little tighter than usual. They've been really dry for a couple of days. When they smell water, they're gonna head straight for it."

"How does the river look Boss?" asked Del. "Is it really high?"

"It's still high. The snow from the high mountains hasn't all melted yet, but I think Mister Timms and I found a good place to cross," said Case. "There are a lot of shallow ponds and swampy areas on both sides of the river from recent floods. If we can get them to water and bed on this side of the river today, then we'll cross in the morning — but we got to keep them together."

The herd was still nervous from the storm and the lack of water. Most had trouble lying down, and those that did were up and down all night giving the night guards trouble the whole shift.

Boyd and Roly were well ahead, and the wranglers were pushing the remuda right behind them when they came to the scattering of ponds, potholes, and bogs paralleling the river several hundred yards to the south of the main branch.

"Pull her up here," said Boyd, motioning to Roly. "It's a good piece of solid, flat ground for tonight." The remuda was already watering at the ponds. As the wranglers watched the remuda, Boyd felt the ground begin to rumble. "Here they come!" shouted Roly, pointing to the herd running through dust toward the water. Every low spot that held water was instantly full of thirsty longhorns. Twenty-five hundred cattle were strung out along the south side of the river for nearly a mile. For two hours the cattle drank, grazed and returned to the water several more times. By sundown, they were bedded down.

"Did we lose any on this last leg?" asked Timms, looking up and down the river at the herd.

"Not that I can see," said Case. "And I don't think any of them got into the river yet. But tomorrow could be an exciting day."

The outfit was up and ready before sunup. The hands were noticeably a little nervous, and the mood was quieter than usual. When the wagons were packed, Case led them east for a mile to a wide stretch with low, flattened banks and solid ground on either side. Old signs showed that buffalo had used this spot many times in the past. "I crossed here yesterday," said Case. "It was pretty high, but it was a lot later in the day. I want to cross early, in case it rains and makes it worse."

Case followed the old buffalo tracks slowly into the river, firmly urging his horse forward into the cold water. The current was strong, but the bottom was solid, and the horse had no problem with footing. When he and Timms reached the opposite shore, he motioned to the wagons to move forward. Boyd slowly moved the mules into position, snapped the whip and hollered. The team moved steadily into the cold water, and the wagon rolled into the three-foot deep, rushing current. The water was just below the bed pushing hard against the running gear, causing the wagon to slip slightly downstream as it crossed.

Expertly operating the reins and talking to his team, the mules pulled the wagon cleanly up the other bank. Roly followed in the larger hoodlum wagon, and the wranglers moved the remuda across without any trouble. The men could hear the bawling and the banging horns as the herd reached the river. The point man rode directly into the water, and like usual, Lincoln and Grant followed behind, hardly even slowing down. Not all the cattle felt the same about cold rushing water. Several balked at the edge but were forced forward by the power of the ones behind them.

When the body of the herd hit the water and couldn't feel the bottom any longer, most swam without problem. Most fresh calves were swept away, and a few older cows were drowned by the others pushing them under. The flankers kept crowding the herd together and moving them forward, hollering and slapping them with ropes. Now unstoppable, 2,500 longhorn cattle pressed forward with nothing more on their mind than solid ground.

Case and Timms watched as the cattle filled the river with thousands of horns sticking above the waterline. The noise from the cattle and the horns flashing in the early morning sun made for a picture like most had never seen before. As the herd emerged from the water, they fell in behind the leaders and began to string out behind the remuda.

"Damn, Case," said Timms, watching the drag riders follow last of the herd out of the water. "That went spectacularly well, don't you think?"

Case nodded. "Yessir Mister Timms. If the truth be known, probably better than I expected."

"How far you plan to move them today?" asked Timms, watching the last of the herd disappear over the rise.

"A few miles is all, just far enough so they don't try and come back to the river. Then, if we're on decent grass, we'll take an extra day and let them feed."

Several miles north, the outfit found flat ground with good grass cut through with a narrow, wandering stream. Case motioned to circle them up and put them to bed, and the point man signaled the rest of the riders. The men began to ride slowly in a wide circle around the herd as the animals began to calm down and start to feed. One at a time, the first night guards mounted fresh horses and settled in for their shift.

While Boyd and Tom Lee prepared chuck, they spotted a band of Indians several hundred yards out from camp. "Case, you see 'em?" asked Boyd, pointing them out.

Case nodded and finished his coffee. "They didn't waste any time. It looks like it's time to pay the bill. Tom Lee, take a ride with me."

The two men rode half way to the waiting Indians. Black Dog and another Indian rode out to meet them. The meeting lasted only a few minutes and they rode back motioning for two cowboys to meet them at the edge of the herd.

"Put a rope on two cows and stake them out where we just met." Calling over to the wranglers, he told them to pick three mares and one stallion and do the same. "That way they can eat them, ride them or start their own herd if they ever want to." After their business was through, Black Dog raised his fist in the air to Case and rode off with their payment.

"They made out pretty well for a small band of Indians in the middle of nowhere, they got plenty of beef and four good horses," said Timms, watching them as they disappeared over a far ridge.

"Not to mention the horses and scalps from the outlaw's and the Kiowa's," said Case. "I think they like their hair more than the livestock."

July 9. Crossed the dreaded Arkansas River today. Lost a few weaker animals but it generally went very well. On the last big push toward Wyoming Territory. The Comanches wasted no time in collecting their cattle and horses. Though it went well, Case reminded everyone that the Comanches still needed to be watched — he said they're still Indians and you can never trust them. We have learned to scout for buffalo tracks when we look for a good river crossing.

Waking up to a hot, dry wind, Roly watched several dust devils skipping and dancing across the prairie. When one would reach the cattle, it would abruptly collapse. Within minutes several more would form and take its place. He watched the game go on for a few minutes when he spotted several pronghorns through the dust. Pointing them out to a pair of cowboys at the fire, they jumped up, grabbed their rifles and headed for the horses.

Mounting up, they headed out across the grass to claim some quick venison for a little variety in the next chuck. Heading out on a dead run, they chased them hard for two miles across the plains. When the antelope dropped over a grassy hilltop, the cowboys followed. Pulling up on the crest of the hill there was no sign of the pronghorns anywhere, just wide-open prairie, green grass, and blue sky as far as they could see. They saw a small bunch of buffalo in the distance laid up in the distance chewing their cud, wondering what the intruders were. The high peaks of the Rocky Mountains to the west were still snowcapped and a narrow sliver of a stream, nearly hidden by the grass, disappeared into the horizon.

Jeff, and Jacobo, a young Mexican vaquero sat for a few extra minutes watching several ravens floating on the air currents. "Jacobo, I think I'd like to live right here some day."

"Si, I also like this place very much. I wish I could build my casa right here."

Jeff nodded and turned back toward the herd. "Maybe someday . . ."

After giving the cattle extra time on the good grass, the outfit moved out on the last leg of the drive. "Case, how far you think it is to Cheyenne from here?" asked Timms.

"I'd say maybe three hundred miles more or less. It's not as rough as some of the country we already covered, but it can be pretty dry between here and the Platte. And I don't know the Indians as well up here."

"Are we still in Comanche country?"

"I'm sure there are plenty of them around, still some Kiowa too. I think it's gonna be a long while before they all give up and go to the res."

"What about farther north?"

"Arapaho and Cheyennes for sure," said Case, "but you never know. You can't ever let your guard down out here, no matter what they are. Every one of them will cut your throat for your hair if they get the chance."

Without an established trail or the faintest sign of the best way to head across the empty prairie, Roly cracked his whip, and the mules leaned into the harness. It was his job to keep the wagon moving in the direction the cow boss said and trust the judgment of the mules to find the best footing. After three days, it turned very dry with little more than a few trickles of water and short scruffy grass.

Boyd had just set the first oven on the coals for evening chuck when the wind came up and scattered them across the prairie. Before he could rebuild it, the skies opened up and drenched everything in camp. After pouring hard for twenty minutes, the sun came out, and the storm blew away like nothing ever happened. The downpour left enough water in the dry creek bed and the low spots to satisfy the stock for the day.

Roly climbed up on the seat of the camp wagon, removed his hat and looked up. "Thank you, Lord, for the fresh water you have provided us, and for the safe passage all these miles — amen!"

"Now if he could just give me a big jug of whiskey, and a chubby little Indian gal, I'd thank him too," said Del, pulling off his boots to dry them out.

"Brother Del, I don't think the good Lord is in the habit of providing the instruments of sin to anyone, let alone a blasphemer like yourself."

Del spit a wad of tobacco into the soggy fire pit. "Well he sure the hell oughta, life on the trail would be a whole lot more fun!"

Roly just shook his head. "Yours is not the way to heaven brother, yours is a shortcut to hell."

"Well then I'm lookin' forward to seein' all my old friends down there," said Del, "'cause it's gonna be one hell of a party!"

The outfit continued north across the dryland until late afternoon when Lincoln and Grant started to pick up the pace. The herd took the cue and started to run. As they picked up speed, the point man saw Case and Timms riding toward them.

Case was waving his hat at the rider. "Let 'em go — don't try and hold 'em back!"

When they met up, they watched the herd rush by. "What's up?" asked Del.

"Water — a long, spring fed pond about a mile or so ahead, plenty of good water. We couldn't stop them now if we wanted to, but they won't go anywhere else."

When they reached the pond, they found the wagons surrounded by cattle. Tom Lee and Boyd had already built a fire and had the ovens on the coals. Roly had already tended to the mules and was setting up the tents. For the first time in days, the herd had plenty of grass and water, and they were already starting to bed down.

After the night guard was set, Case and Timms sat by the fire drinking coffee and enjoying their smokes. "Case, I take it we must be getting close to the South Platte River by now?"

"Not more than a day or two, then maybe two or three to Cheyenne," said Case. "Mister Timms, what's your plan for delivery?"

"My oldest son, Dean, has been up there for several months already and bought a small ranch northwest of Cheyenne with a good year-around creek. He's already finished building a bunkhouse and the pens we need. His last letter said he was working on a barn. Pretty much everything around him is open range. When we're a day or two out, I'll go to town and find out where he wants them."

"Are you gonna try and run all 2500 head yourself?" asked Case.

"No. My sons Dean and David and myself are the Timms Land and Cattle Company. We're one of four investors that have bought or built small ranches in the same area. We're all close together. We formed a cattle pool association and plan to start shipping beef next spring."

"You got all the hands you need?"

"Not all of them, but I think I can make up the difference with some of the ones we have here." said Timms.

"I'm sure a lot of them will need jobs, but I wouldn't look for the Mexicans to stay. I think most of them will go back home to their families."

"What about you Case? You looking for a permanent job?"

"No sir, permanent is one thing I ain't looking for right now. Me and my brother have plans for our own outfit, in the hide and fur business."

"Buffalo hides?" said Timms. "That's a tough profession."

"It is that, but the buffs are free Mister Timms, just like your grass, and there's good money to be made."

"Well, if you ever need work, all you have to do is let me know."

"I do appreciate the offer. I believe you might do well to find a place for Boyd and Tom Lee too, if he decides to stay up here. They're two of the best hands you're ever gonna find," said Case.

Timms nodded and tossed the stub of his smoke in the fire. "I already have a proposition in mind for Boyd, but I'm not sure about Tom Lee. He's really quiet and hasn't said much about any plans he may have."

"I can tell you that Tom Lee is in love with a girl in San Antonio, and he wants to marry her when he gets back. I don't know if he would leave Texas or not. If he wants to stay down there, I may have a place for him. As for Boyd, he's definitely a loner and a little hard to figure sometimes, but he's way smarter than most and really good at anything he does. He might be willing to work for you up here if you had a place for him on your new ranch — something more than just cooking."

"My son David runs the ranch down south. I'm going back to Texas once we get things running up here. I don't like the winters this far north. I know we'll need a pool rider and a manager for the new association. You think Boyd might be interested in that?"

Case nodded. "He's good with people and animals and very independent minded, I think he'd be good at it for sure."

July 15. For several days it was dry travel, and the cattle were getting nervous. On the third night, the skies opened up and dumped more water straight down in a half-hour than I'd ever seen before. The rain quickly filled up every pothole and low spot for miles around, and it seemed to be enough to satisfy the cattle for the most part. Roly said it was divine intervention, but I think it was just mother nature. One cowboy took a horn to his thigh, nothing serious but it is the biggest, ugliest bruise I ever saw.

Having bedded the herd a few miles short of the South Platte River, the outfit was up early moving them toward the muddy looking river, often described as, "a mile wide and an inch deep." The danger in crossing the South Platte was often just finding a good firm place to cross, as it was known for soft bottoms and sticky mud.

Case and Timms rode back to the wagons and told them to be ready — the herd would be picking up the scent any time. "There's been buffs' crossing all over here, so it should be good. Just keep them together the best you can."

After the wagons and the remuda crossed, they looked back to see Lincoln and Grant already in the water with the herd right on their heels. The South Platte proved to be the easiest crossing of the trip, without any loss. Once the stock was well watered, they continued the push to the ranch. Tom Lee estimated they made more than fifteen miles that day.

Case told Timms that they were close enough to Cheyenne that he may want to head in tomorrow. "You can make the arrangements with your son and the partners to take over the herd — we'll be about a day behind you."

The hands not riding guard were finishing up morning chuck, talking excitedly about the end of the drive and what they were going to do when they got to town. As Boyd started to pack up camp, several men hollered and pointed to several riders watching them from a grassy side hill several hundred yards out.

"Indians Boss," said Del, pointing to the riders.

Case squinted into the morning sun, studying them for a minute. "Arapahos — first ones I seen in a while. Tom Lee, let's take a ride."

Riding toward the Indians, they stopped part way out and waited to see what would happen. For several minutes the Indians sat on their horses staring at them. When Case showed them his empty hands, the braves turned and rode away.

"Case, what the heck was that all about?" asked Tom Lee on the ride back.

"I have no idea, but it'd be a bad time to let our guard down. You can bet they'll be with us till we finish this trip."

Timms waited for the word from Case about the Indians. "You think it's safe to go on into Cheyenne now?"

"Mister Timms, if it were me, I'd stay with the herd until we got a bit closer. I don't know what's up with this bunch, but I know we can't trust them."

"I agree. No point on taking chances at this late date, let's move out and keep our eyes open."

As the herd moved along, the Arapahos fell in behind, just out of rifle range. Tom Lee dropped back into position behind Del, still riding drag. "Why are we lettin' those goddamn shit-devils follow us? Why don't we just go kill 'em and get it done with?"

"The Boss said to keep moving, we're getting too close to town to take a chance of anyone getting hurt now."

While they rode through the dust, they noticed an old cow not keeping up. Bawling and swinging her head from side to side, she was favoring a badly swollen leg. Tom Lee took his rope, fashioned a loop and expertly threw a loop. Slowing down, he dropped back, took out the slack and pulled, jerking the cow to the ground.

"Tom Lee, just what the hell are you doing? Tell me you ain't gonna give them goddamn savages a live cow?"

"No Del. I'm gonna show you how to get rid of Indians without anyone getting hurt." Dropping the rope, he left the cow on the ground and settled back into the drag position. When the herd had moved far enough ahead, the Indians claimed the cow and rode away. "All that's needed to get them to do what you want is feed them, that way nobody gets hurt."

Del shook his head. "I still can't believe you turned into a goddamn Indian lover. If we killed 'em, we wouldn't have to feed 'em. And the sooner they're all dead, the sooner this country will be safe for regular folks."

"What you gonna do when you get paid off?" asked Tom Lee, intentionally changing the subject.

"I'm gonna find me a sportin' house, a big bottle of whiskey, a woman and a soft bed, what about you?"

"I mean for your next job Del."

"Don't really have no plans, I guess we'll see what happens when the girls and whiskey runs out."

"You mean when the money runs out?"

"All the same I guess."

Chapter 17

When the herd was a day out of Cheyenne, Timms prepared to head for town. "Mister Timms, I'd feel better if you take Del with you, you never know when there might be trouble," said Case. "He's had a lot of experience with all kinds of Indians."

Timms nodded. "That'd be good. Plus, I think he'd like to breathe some clean air for a change. No need to move too fast. I'll be back with extra hands to help move them to the ranch. Swing west a couple of miles, away from town. Once we cross the rails, it's about five miles farther."

Reaching Cheyenne without trouble, Timms and Dell turned west without stopping and reached the ranch an hour later. A long, squat log house sat back off the trail against a small pond ringed with cottonwoods. A hundred yards behind the cabin was a new clapboard bunkhouse with a tin roof, several pens and corrals, and a nearly finished barn. Walking through the cabin door Timms hollered out for his son, "Dean — you in here somewhere?"

"No goddamnit, I'm out here," said a voice from outside. "What in hell took you so long?"

The men embraced and walked into the cabin and sat down at the table. "Dean, this is Del, one of our top hands — Del, this is my baby boy, Dean."

When the introductions were over, Dean Timms pulled out a bottle of whiskey and poured each of them a long shot. "Here's to cowboys, cows, and railroads!" said Dean, holding his glass out for a toast. Pouring each of them one more, they quickly downed it. He corked the bottle, and they headed for the door.

"Son, I gotta say, you must have been blessed with good rain, the grass looks great."

"Yessir, we did. We got rain, we got grass, and we got water — all we need now is cattle!"

"How many hands can you get together?" asked Monroe, pulling off his boots and leaning back in the chair. "We'll could use a few more to help get them to the ranch."

"There's four or five hands here now, that should be enough. How many head did you loose on the trail?"

"Not sure yet, maybe a hundred or so — plus a few horses."

"That's better than I expected. Indians get the horses?" asked Dean.

"They got a few, and the weather got some too."

"And you didn't lose any men?"

"Nope. Nobody got hurt bad, but we did have a few exciting moments with some Comanches and Kiowas though."

"You're gonna love that story," said Del. "It gets better each time he tells it."

"I can hardly wait to hear it," said Dean. "I'm sure that nobody in your outfit would stretch the truth now, would they?"

Timms shook his head and grinned. "They'll all swear to it, that is if they want to get paid."

When the Wyoming cowboys reached the herd, they found places between the flankers and fell into the routine. By midafternoon the outfit hit the new rails, and the wagons and remuda crossed without problem. For the first time in hundreds of miles on the trail, Lincoln and Grant hesitated at the steel rails, looking confused. One of the cowboys pushed through the herd to the back of the pair and hollered at them, swatting them with his rope. The two steers remained with their front feet firmly planted at the edge of the gravel bed, prepared not to move a single inch.

The scene remained a standoff — Lincoln and Grant against the steel rails. When the rest of the herd reached the river, one old bull, a truly giant beast with enormous horns pushed his way past the two steers and easily crossed the tracks with several others following him. Realizing their place as leaders had just been challenged, Lincoln and Grant quickly bolted across the tracks and overtook the old bull, regaining their rightful place at the head of the pack. The rest of the herd crossed the rails without problem.

Case and Timms watched for the last time as the herd started to string out across the prairie. Reaching the ranch, Lincoln and Grant led the cattle directly to the water for the last time. Timms leaned against the cabin watching the herd file into the ranch.

"Damn, I do have to say, that is one fine sight — twenty-five hundred beautiful Texas longhorns eating the Timms Cattle Company's grass."

"A beautiful sight for sure," said Dean.

Case walked up to the cabin and took off his hat, wiping his face with his bandanna. "Mister Timms, that was a hell of a trip, and I gotta say, I'm glad it's over."

"Let's go inside. Dean get that bottle of yours, I think we all need a drink. There is one thing I've been meaning to tell you about though."

"What's that?" asked Case, throwing back the whiskey.

"After all we've been through over the last few months, I think it's time for you to call me Monroe," said Timms. "There are two Mister Timms here now, you don't want to get them confused."

"You got it," said Case, holding out his glass for a toast. "Here's to Monroe and Dean Timms, new cattle kings of the Wyoming Territory!"

After several more toasts, Dean threw the empty bottle in the fireplace. "Let's make sure the remuda is settled in the big pasture. The cattle will be good where they're at for now. Tomorrow we'll get everything squared up.

"I like the sound of that," said Monroe. "I want to sleep in a real bed tonight. Dean, you took care of that for me, right?"

"Yessir, I sure did. I made a great big soft bed for both of us and even bought a couple of new blankets for them. I also put a new pitcher pump inside the cabin, so we don't have to go outside for water and built a brand new privy for your saddle sore old butt."

"You did good son. You got a woman yet?"

"No god-dang it — you know I ain't got no women! I ain't had a lick of time for any of that — I've been busy building a ranch!"

"Well you better get on it. You and your brother are gonna need a couple of sons to run this operation before you get too old!"

"Yeah, yeah, it'll happen when it happens," said Dean. "First I gotta finish the ranch."

Monroe shook his head. "That's what you been saying for two years — it needs to happen soon."

"Okay, I got it, now let's change the subject. We need to get started if we're gonna feed all these guys tonight."

"Well then, pick out a good-looking steer and butcher him for chuck," said Monroe. "Whatever we don't eat, we'll make into jerky."

Boyd and Tom Lee made one last meal for the whole outfit. Steaks, beans, biscuits, and the last of the spuds — fried and boiled. He also opened the last big can of peaches he'd kept hidden since Adobe Walls. Dean came up with a bag of apples, several loaves of heavy dark bread, fresh cornbread, and a pile of pork sausage. Setting out four new bottles of whiskey on the tailgate of the wagon, he told everyone to pass them around.

"Boyd, I gotta say — that was one hell of a hell of a meal. My father said you were quite a cook. That old twisted horn steer

tasted every bit as good as any fancy meal I ever had in the city —
even after months on the trail."

"Crooked left horn? What color was he?" asked Boyd.

"I think kind of a red or brown brindle, why?"

"You killed Lincoln!"

"Lincoln? What in hell are you talking about?" said Dean.

"He was one of the herd leaders. Him and Grant led the drive
the whole way."

"Grant? You saying that steers named Lincoln and Grant led
the herd all the way from Texas?

"Best damn leaders I ever seen," said Boyd.

Dean shrugged. "Well shit, then all I gotta say is Mister
Lincoln was mighty fine eating, maybe we'll eat old General
Grant next."

The men lounged around the fire telling trail stories and
passing around the first whiskey they had tasted since San
Antonio. They told the story of the attacking Kiowas, now
adjusted to the latest version of more Indians than they could
count. Monroe Timms proved to be a good storyteller, causing the
crew to laugh out loud at the incident of Del falling into the
Colorado River. Whenever the conversation slowed down,
someone would shout out — "Goddamnit, you know I can't swim
— now come and get me!" Every time it got a laugh, Del would
take a big pull from the whiskey bottle. The white bandits, Black
Dog and his band of hungry Comanches and everything else they
could recall was repeated over and over again. A few hands finally

gave up and headed for the new bunkhouse. Several others passed out cold right where they sat, including Del, and slept off the whiskey all night on the hard dirt.

Monroe and Dean Timms, Case, Tom Lee, and Boyd threw a last log on the fire and talked about the future and what they might do. Poking at the fire with a stick, Tom Lee started to talk about his plans. "Well, by now you all know that I'm heading back to San Antonio to marry my girl, Sancha. It appears that someone couldn't keep a secret about it," said Tom Lee, looking straight at Boyd. "As soon as we're finished up here, I'm heading back."

Monroe rolled one last cigarette, drew it in deeply and exhaled slowly before he spoke. "Because of you men, and that includes Dean and our unconscious friend Del, we have done something I didn't know was even possible, moving a large, mixed herd of wild Texas cattle, and a good start to a big remuda, to a ranch in the newly formed Wyoming Territory. We are one of the first outfits to do such a thing. With the new transcontinental railroad getting' so close to completion, we'll be able to sell and ship our cattle almost anywhere. I think this is gonna be the start of a big cattle business up in this country."

Standing up, Monroe held up his glass and made a toast. "To the absolute finest group of men I have ever met or had the pleasure to work with. And especially to my cow boss, Case, who led the way through hundreds of miles of everything this wild-ass country could throw at us without losing a man. Wherever we go, whatever we do, we can always carry our heads high knowing we rode with the best and accomplished something very few men have ever done!"

Everyone downed their drink and gave a cheer for the sentiment. "One more toast, then I gotta get a little sleep," said Dean. "To my father for realizing his goal and for the life he made for his family."

As they finished up the round, Roly spoke up. "Just one more thing, I want to say how thankful I am for the job and to Case and Mister Timms in particular. And I have to give thanks to Father God, for keeping us all safe on our long, difficult journey, both on the trail and in our lives — amen!"

"Thank you everyone, I need to head for that soft new bed myself," said Monroe. "I want to sit down with every one of you in the morning and talk about possibly working for us from here on. Then we'll go to town and get everyone paid off. I'll see you all in the morning."

Case was up at first light looking across the ranch, watching the herd grazing. Finishing his morning coffee, he dumped the grounds, rolled a smoke and lingered over the sight for a few more minutes. They had delivered twenty-five hundred wild, longhorn cattle from San Antonio, Texas to Cheyenne, Wyoming Territory. It was something he would never forget, but he wasn't sure if he would do it again.

Dean walked out of the cabin and leaned against the wall next to Case without speaking. Of average height and very muscular,

Case thought he looked softer and smaller in the early morning sun. "Dean, everything okay this morning? You're awfully quiet."

He kept his eyes down and shook his head. "Case, my father is dead — he died in his sleep."

Case stood quietly wondering what to say. "Dean, I'm so sorry to hear that. After all he'd been through, building up the outfit and on the trail for all these months."

"He was a hell of a good man Case. He was a friend to everyone he ever came in contact with. He helped Indians, soldiers from both sides, farmers, and fellow ranchers. I used to think he gave away more cattle to hungry people than he ever sold," said Dean, wiping at his tears. "When the pox took mother, it nearly killed him, but he still had the ranch to run and three small boys to raise. I believe it made him even stronger and more determined to be successful."

"I'd say he did a pretty good job on those things," said Case. "He's left a wonderful legacy for you and your brother."

Dean nodded, still looking down. "Did you know that when he first decided to round-up Texas Longhorns a few years back, people thought he was crazy to go chasing after them? Even when my brother Daniel was killed, he never gave up. Then, when he announced that he was moving them to Cheyenne to start a new ranch, they laughed at him in public. Hell Case, there were a lot of local cowboys that wouldn't hire on because they said the trip north was too dangerous. That's how we ended up with so many vaqueros, they weren't afraid of the trip."

"Dean, I know how hard this must be, but what can we do to help you right now?"

"I need to go to town and send a telegraph to my brother."

Case nodded. "Maybe you should have someone ride along with you? Del can go with you."

"No, thanks just the same, but I have to do this by myself. I need the time alone to think of what to say."

"I understand. Do you have a spot where you'd like to bury him?" asked Case. "We can get it ready for you while you're gone."

"Thank you. I think on top of that little flat-topped grassy knob west of the pond would be a good spot. You can see the whole ranch from there. He would've liked that. I'm heading out...I should be back in a few hours. Leave him in the bed for now, and we'll move him when I get back."

Case called the outfit together and broke the news to them. Giving them directions on the location of the grave, everyone volunteered to dig or do whatever else was needed. Case picked two Texas hands and two Wyoming hands to prepare the grave.

The wranglers moved through the pasture holding the remuda. After checking the fences and the feed, they let themselves out just as Case rode up. "Everything okay?" asked Case.

"Looks good Boss. It's very sad about Mister Timms, after all he went through to get those cattle up here."

"It is for sure. But everyone should be proud to have been a part of this drive, it's something they'll remember forever. I need everyone to hang around another day or two until Dean Timms buries his father. Then he can finish up business — you okay with that?"

The wranglers both nodded. "Sure, I think everyone else will be good with it too. What can we do while we're still here?"

"Thanks. Let's get a head count on the remuda and look them over good. If any of them have any problems, run them into one of the small pens so we can check them out."

"We'll take care of it, no problem."

Tying up to the wagon, Case dismounted and motioned for Tom Lee, Del, Boyd, and Roly to come over, then sat down on the tailgate. "I know last night was the end of your commitment as far as the delivery goes, but I need you to do one more chuck for tonight and one in the morning. After Mister Timms is laid to rest tomorrow, I'll pay you for the extra time myself, then you can get on with your plans."

"Don't worry about it Boss," said Boyd. "We'll take care of everything, and nobody's paying anything extra."

Case shook everyone's hand. "Thanks everyone, and Roly, you know we'll want you to say something at the service."

"Already been thinking on it Boss, I'll have some real good words for him."

Dean Timms walked into the Cheyenne telegraph office and waited for the operator to come out of the back room. After looking out the window for a moment, he turned back to see a stout woman, several inches taller than him, about thirty years old with fair skin and ruddy complexion. Her red hair was pulled back into a tight bun and covered with a colorful scarf.

"Good morning sir, how can I help you?" asked the woman.

"Uh . . . I need to see the telegraph operator please."

"You are looking at the telegraph operator sir, do you wish to send a telegram?"

Timms removed his hat and nodded his head. She spoke with a slight accent that he wasn't familiar with. "I am sorry M'am, I never met a woman in this kind of business before."

"Do you want to send a telegram now?"

"Yes I do, to my brother in San Antonio, Texas."

She handed him a piece of paper and a pencil. "Just write the name of the recipient, where to send it and your message on this sheet, pay me, and I'll have it sent in no time."

"Recipient?"

"Yes, it means the person you want to get the message."

"How much will this cost?" asked Timms.

"It all depends on how many words you send. For example, a ten word message will cost you three dollars and seventy-five cents."

Timm's hands shook slightly as he wrote the brief message:

David Timms, Timms Ranch, San Antonio, Texas.

Our beloved father died in his sleep, one day after

he arrived.

Your brother Dean

"This is more than ten words," said Timms, handing her the paper. "Just tell me how much more I owe, and I will pay it."

The woman behind the counter read the message. "Mister Timms, I'm sorry for your loss. I'll get this right out, and there will be no charge to you."

"I can pay, it's no problem."

"When it's this kind of message, I don't charge."

"Thank you very much," said Dean, still holding his hat and the pencil. "M'am, may I ask your name?"

"Anny Werner."

With his hat still in his hand, he couldn't take his eyes off of her. "My name is Dean Timms."

She nodded. "I gathered as much. It's nice to meet you Dean, despite the sad circumstances."

"Thank you Anny. May I ask you a personal question before I leave?"

"You may ask, but whether I choose to answer is another thing altogether."

"Are you married?" asked Dean, surprising himself by what he just said.

Breaking a smile for the first time, she shook her head. "No Mister Timms, I am not married, nor do I have a boyfriend."

"Thank you," said Timms, putting his hat back on. Walking toward the door, he stopped and turned back to the counter. "Anny, may I call on you some time in the future? I mean after I get my business sorted out and the ranch running properly?"

"Yes, I would like that," said Anny. "But please don't wait too long, and Dean . . ."

"Yes?"

"My pencil?"

Handing her the pencil, he left the telegraph office and walked toward the funeral parlor. Speaking so bluntly to a woman he had never met before was something he would normally not even think about doing. This woman just caught his attention like none had ever done before. He couldn't help but think how ironic it was that his father's death may have caused him to meet a woman.

The Undertaker, a round, bald man wearing a black long coat that dusted the floor made his way through two rows of coffins, meeting him at the counter. "Good morning friend, I am John J. Packer, Undertaker, coffin maker, grave digger, and proprietor. Is there something I can help you with today?"

Timms nodded. "My father passed last night. I'm in need of a coffin. I intend on burying him at my ranch in the morning. How much for a coffin and how much for you to deliver it to the ranch?"

"I'm very sorry to hear of your father's passing — Mister?"

"Dean Timms. My ranch is about five miles west and north of town. Bear Creek road will take you right by it."

The Undertaker nodded. "Would you like something special? I have some wonderful mahogany wood that makes a truly beautiful top. I can also put in a viewing window and install brass handles that I recently got from New York City. Are you a Christian sir? I can put on a nice cross if you would like, all for a little extra of course."

"Mister Packer, my father was a plain, straight-forward man. He wouldn't have wanted anything fancy. The plainest coffin you have will be fine. Now how much do I owe you?"

"That will be seven-dollars for the coffin and a dollar and a dollar for delivery."

"You will have that to the ranch yet today?"

"It will be late this afternoon."

Timms pulled a ten-dollar coin from his pocket. "You can keep the extra two dollars if you get it there yet this morning."

"I'll leave right away sir."

Timms handed him the money and headed for the door. "Then I'll see you at the ranch — oh, there is one more thing . . ."

"Sir . . .?"

"Where can I order a stone for the grave?"

"There is one stone cutter here, and he is on the very east edge of town. However, I can order it for you if you want."

"No thank you, I will wait and talk to him after the burial."

The grave was ready when he returned. Stripping his horse, he turned it into the pasture and walked back to the cabin. "Case, I appreciate your helping with everything. The coffin should be here soon, and we can set him in the barn overnight if anyone would like to see him."

"We'll take care of him as soon as it gets here. I also want you to have this. I think you and your brother might want to hang it up somewhere to remind you of him." Case handed him the Springfield that his father used when the Kiowas attacked. It was rough looking piece and had a heavy rawhide patch on the stock. "This is the rifle he used to shoot the Kiowa brave's horse out from under him — it was a really spectacular shot."

Dean took the rifle and nodded. "Thank you, my brother and I will treasure it."

"That's a very special rifle. It has killed hundreds of buffalo, deer, pronghorns, and whatnot, as well as a fair pile of Indians."

Dean shouldered the rifle and looked through the sights. "I'll hang it up right away."

"Mister Timms, this also belongs to you now," said Tom Lee, handing him the logbook he'd been keeping on the trail. "This is a record of every day we were on the trail, your father asked me to keep it for him. It has everything from cattle counts, Indian confrontations, daily weather, and river crossings."

Timms flipped through the pages feeling his eyes fill with tears. "I don't know what to say, thank you. My family will be able to look back and see what an adventure filled life he had. I suppose everyone is anxious to get paid," said Timms, changing the subject.

"Whenever you're ready to sit down is good for me," said Case.

After morning chuck, Roly brushed out a single black mule and hitched him to the empty camp wagon, wiping down all the harness and polishing the brass. Backing it up to the barn, Dean dropped the tailgate, pulled open the door and walked inside. Looking at his father lying in the coffin one last time, he straightened his bandanna and brushed his hair back. "Thank you father, we owe you everything." Nodding to Boyd and Tom Lee, they placed the lid on top and nailed it shut. Six men then shouldered the coffin, walked it to the wagon and slid it inside.

Tying a lead rope to the mule's bridle, Roly began to walk him toward the hill. An early rain had moved out and settled into a gentle breeze and the grass glistened in the morning sun. Stopping the wagon just short of the gravesite, he set the brake and climbed down. Dean had chosen Boyd, Tom Lee, and Del to carry the coffin as well as one of Monroe's Texas cowboys, a Mexican vaquero, and his most trusted Wyoming cowboy. The men shouldered the coffin again and walked toward the grave.

"Dean, the cattle are feeding all around us here, do you want me to have them moved out?" asked Case.

"No," said Dean, looking at the cattle spread around the site. "This is perfect, my father would love it. There would be no ranch without them."

The men walked the coffin slowly through the grass to the grave site. The rest of the crew stood quietly with their hats in hand as they passed by. Lowering the coffin onto the timbers across the grave, the six pallbearers moved back into the group. Roly stepped alongside the coffin and opened his Bible.

"Mister Timms asked me to say a few words for his father on this sad day. I was going to choose some appropriate words myself, but he asked for a special Bible passage that his father loved. It is much better than anything I could ever say myself. Before I read it, I just want to give my personal thanks to the Timms family for the opportunity to work for them and to tell them how much his father was loved by everyone on the drive. He was a true man among men and a pioneer that will never be forgotten. I will now read the twenty-third psalm, Monroe's favorite passage."

"The Lord is my shepherd, I shall not want. He maketh me to lie down in green pastures: he leadeth me beside the still waters. He restoreth my soul: he leadeth me in the paths of righteousness for his name's sake." Roly stopped for a moment and wiped his eyes with his bandanna. "Forgive me for that. *Yea, though I walk through the valley of the shadow of death, I will fear no evil, for thou art with me; thy rod and thy staff they comfort me. Thou preparest a table before me in the presence of*

mine enemies: thou anointest my head with oil; my cup runneth over. " He stopped once more to wipe away the tears. Apologizing to everyone again, nobody made a sound while he took a minute to compose himself. *"Surely goodness and mercy shall follow me all the days of my life: and I will dwell in the house of the Lord forever — amen."*

Every man was silent when he finished speaking, and many were fighting back their own tears after the emotional reading. Dean Timms stood up, walked over and embraced him. "Thank you Roly, that was beautiful, I know that my father loved it."

"We can take care of everything else Mister Timms," said Case. "Maybe you'd like to go back to the cabin now."

Timms nodded and turned to go back to the cabin when he spotted a woman at the back of the crowd. Walking up to Anny Werner, he removed his hat. "Miss Werner, I'm surprised to see you here, what brings you so far from town today?" asked Dean.

"I received this telegram for you this morning. I thought I would bring it out to you."

"Thank you for that, I imagine it's from my brother," said Dean.

"It is. I also brought these flowers from my garden. I thought they might look good on the grave." Handing him the telegram and the flowers she slid her arm through his and walked with him.

When they reached the cabin, he invited her in. Filling a jar with water, he put the flowers in and sat it on the table. "I will place them on the grave later, thank you. Would you like some water? It's good fresh spring water."

"No thank you Dean, I'm fine."

Reading the telegram, he folded it and put it in his pocket. "Thank you for bringing it. David will be busy for a while taking over the business down there, so he won't be here any time in the near future. We'll each have to run our operations alone now."

She gently touched him on the hand. "The telegram wasn't the only reason I came, but I think you know that."

Dean looked closely at her face. A plain but very strong woman smiled back at him. He couldn't remember seeing such clear, riveting eyes before. "I do, but I have to confess, I've never had a relationship with a woman before. I feel very attracted to you Anny, but I'm not really sure what to do now."

"I'm attracted to you also, but I was afraid I was being too forward with you. We can take as much time as you would like to get to know each other."

"I would like that very much, and you are definitely not too forward. I need to get my men paid today. Then I need to get the herd branded, and the new men hired. Maybe then we can talk some more, if that's all right with you?"

"That will be fine, whenever you are ready just come and see me at the office."

Chapter 18

Sitting at a long plank table set up in front of the cabin, Dean Timms and Case were ready to finish up the business of the Timms Cattle Company drive. The men stepped up to the table one at a time for their pay. The regular working hands were paid $45 dollars a month for three months on the trail. Case entered each one in the ledger by name and amount. Boyd received $55 dollars a month for cooking, and Tom Lee got $50 a month, the extra money was for keeping the logbook. Everyone started the drive with their own horse and chose one more from the remuda as a bonus.

Dean Timms thanked each man, personally shaking each one's hands as he handed them their pay. Del was the last man in line. "My father told me you're a good hand, but you never wanted to see a longhorn cow ever again. You still feel that way? I can find work for you here."

"Mister Timms, I seen all the bovine asses and ate all of the prairie dust I ever want to. Cattle work just ain't for me, but I thank you anyway."

"So, what do you think your gonna do now?" asked Tom Lee.

"I'm gonna go to town, get a jug and find me a soft little gal. After that, I guess I'll look for a job that don't have no big, stinkin' animals in it."

"Well, good luck Del," said Timms. "I wish you well."

"Thank you Mister Timms. Would you consider doin' me a favor and holdin' onto part of my money for a few days?"

"Please, just call me Dean. Sure, no trouble, I have a good, strong safe. Just come by when you want it."

Tom Lee looked at Boyd with a grin. "I do believe old Del might have learned a lesson about not carrying all his money into the sporting houses," said Tom Lee.

Del shook his head. "I ain't gonna get in trouble no more. I can control my whiskey drinkin' just fine."

"Sure you can," said Boyd with a grin.

After Timms paid off Boyd and Tom Lee, he looked at Case straight-faced. "I suppose you're wanting to get paid too?"

"Well, it would be nice to get a little money in my pocket," said Case, breaking a smile for the first time in a long while. "Even a cow boss has to eat every now and then."

Timms paid him $120 a month wages to get them to Cheyenne and a two-hundred dollar bonus for the company. Dean shook his hand and thanked him. "You're absolutely sure I can't talk you into working for me?"

"I'm sure. My brother Thomas will be in town soon. We're looking at a couple of deals for the fall and gearing up for the winter buff season. But if there's ever a time I need a job, you'll be the one I come to."

"Tom Lee, you're for sure gonna go back to San Antonio and get married?" asked Timms.

Tom Lee nodded. "I'm probably leaving tomorrow. I've been away too long already."

"I can have my brother David put you on down at his place, he'd be a good man to work for," said Timms.

"Thank you for the offer, but I think that me and Case may have something worked out for the future in his livery business in San Antonio," said Tom Lee.

"Well shoot, I'm not doing too good here. Boyd, what are you gonna do now?"

"Truth is Mister Timms, I was kinda hoping you might offer me a job."

"What is it you think you might want to do?"

"Anything but cookin' will probably be good."

"Then I got a proposition for you," said Timms. "Me and the other three ranchers that own the herd are gonna run things as one large cattle pool. We're calling it the Southeast Wyoming Cattleman's Association. We need someone right now to work as the pool rider. You'll keep an eye on the herd and be in charge of all the cowboys. You can watch out for potential trouble until we get all the rest of the hands hired, that'll give you a chance to learn the range. When we finish the counting and branding, you'll become the association manager. It pays ninety a month. All four ranches share equally in the cattle work and expenses, you'd be the boss of all the day to day operation — what do you think?"

"I ain't opposed to that Mister Timms, long as one of my duties ain't cooking."

"No cooking involved," said Timms, offering his hand. "So, we got us a deal?"

Boyd nodded and took his hand. "We got us a deal."

"Great! Go ahead grab a spot in the bunkhouse. Tomorrow the new association is having our first meeting here, and we can get things started. We're gonna need to hire the last of the hands and get moving on the branding, we want you involved in all of that. In fact, anyone here that needs a place to stay for a few days can bunk up right here if they want."

Del tied up in front of a butcher shop and took a walk along the main street of Cheyenne. The railroad had reached town from the east, and it had already grown to several thousand people. Tents and clapboard buildings and a few cabins lined the main street. Stepping through the door of the first saloon he came to, he took a minute to let his eyes adjust. Through the smoke and dim light, he could see a dozen men at the tables and several more bellied up to the bar. The low ceilings and dirty windows made it feel more like a cave than a room. Stepping up to the rail, the barkeep asked what he wanted.

"Whiskey, a full bottle of good whiskey and it best not be watered," said Del.

"We only got one kind of whiskey, and it ain't watered down. You get it the same as we get it."

Slapping the money on the bar, he picked up the bottle and glass. "Where's all the women in this place?" asked Del, looking around through the haze.

"Have a seat mister, they'll find you."

Del sat down and poured himself half a glass, chugging it down quickly. By the time he poured the second one, there was a woman on each side of him.

"Well it's about time," said Del, downing the drink. "Where you two fine ladies been hiden'?"

"We were just waiting for you honey, how about we all go upstairs and talk?"

Now on his third glass, he downed it and shook his head. "M'am, I ain't plannin' on doin' no talkin' at all, I'm plannin' on stretching out yer cooches — what do you think of that, ladies?"

"That's big talk mister," said the one on his left. "You got any real money or you just talkin shit? It ain't free you know."

"I got enough money to stretch yer cooches a dozen times with plenty left over."

The one doing the talking, a heavy, pale woman with a pockmarked face and enormous breasts spilling out the top her dress took him by the hand and led him up the stairs. The second woman, much smaller, younger and prettier with a wild nest of straw-colored hair followed them up.

In the room, the women sat on the bed on either side of him. Del sat the whiskey on the table, tossed his hat across the bed and reached around each of them, grabbing for their breasts. Both women slapped his hand away at the same time. "No money, no honey mister," said the pretty one. You're a ranch cowboy, you know how it works."

"No M'am, I ain't no cowboy, least not no more I ain't," said Del, trying to get another pull from the bottle and take his boots off at the same time. "Goddamnit to hell, help me get my boots off, and I'll get your money. How much is this gonna cost me anyhow?"

The women looked at each other and nodded. "Ten dollars for each of us."

The whiskey rush now starting to take hold of him, Del fell back in the bed, still holding onto the bottle with a death grip. "That's just goddamn bullshit, and you know it! Ain't a cooch in the whole goddamn world worth no ten dollars and I ain't payin'! I'll give you three dollars each and you stay 'till the whiskey's gone."

Trying to sit up, he pulled the cork from the bottle and took another swallow, dropping the cork. "Aw shit almighty, I lost my cork — goddamnit I gotta find my cork."

"Look here cowboy, I found the cork for you," said the young one, now standing in front of him. Pulling down the top of her dress, the cork was firmly trapped between her breasts. Reaching out, she grabbed his head and pulled him toward her breasts, pushing them against his face. You can have me and the cork for ten dollars."

"But it's my cork — it came with my whiskey," said Del, trying to control his spinning head.

"Well it's mine now, and it'll cost ten dollars to get it back."

Del, now too drunk to argue just nodded. He pulled two ten dollar coins out of his pocket and threw them on the bed. "Okay ladies, climb aboard!"

Waking up the next morning on the ground in back of the saloon, the last thing he could remember was arguing with the women about money. He still had his boots, but that was all he had except for his shirt and trousers. His hat and bandanna were both missing, and he couldn't remember where he tied his horse.

Stumbling across the main street, he heard someone holler out. "Where the heck you been Del? I found your horse this morning, but I couldn't find you."

Del looked up to see Tom Lee sitting on his horse looking at him with a huge grin. "Least you didn't lose your boots."

"No, just my hat and my bandanna."

"How much money did you have with you?" asked Tom Lee.

"Thirty dollars."

"How much did you lose?"

"Thirty dollars."

"Well come on, I took your horse to the livery."

"Tom Lee . . ."

"What?"

"I ain't got no money to pay for it."

"Delbert Beale, you are one sorry cowboy for sure."

"I ain't a cowboy."

"That's for certain — a real cowboy has a horse."

Boyd sat at the table with Dean Timms and the three other ranchers in the new association. One, a middle-aged farmer from northern Illinois named Clifford Platt, had lost his only son, a union captain, early in the war. The moment the war ended he sold out, pulled up stakes and headed west for a fresh start. His wife, Marie, was a small, fair, fragile looking woman who rarely spoke.

A rigid, distinguished older man with a mustache curled at the ends, and the improbable name of Basquiat Dere sat next to Platt. He had moved his wife Drenna and their two daughters to the frontier and bought the ranch next to Timms. To Boyd's ear, his accent was clearly deep south, and his dress and manners convinced him he was likely a wealthy plantation owner or was before the war.

The third man, Wilf Rikard, was a tall, muscular, mixed blood man. Strikingly handsome by anyone's measure, he had a pretty Indian wife and a young son that clung tightly to his mother's leg. He'd been a scout for the Western Army, a buffalo hunter and had started a small farm with a few cattle several years earlier, one of the first in the area.

The thread that brought them together was the new transcontinental railroad now under construction. All four ranchers understood early on how the new intercontinental railroad was going to change everyone's life. They would be able sell their live cattle to anyone they wanted. The immense amount of open rangeland in the territory provided unlimited grass and was free for anyone that was tough enough to take it. All they had to do was collect their cattle when they were ready to ship.

Boyd listened carefully but didn't have much to say about their grand plan. He liked all the men in the new association, but he knew running a large cattle operation would not be as easy as they said. Indians, thieves, wolves, and weather would all have something to say about their success. He needed the job, so he toasted to the new business along with the others.

Tom Lee's gear was packed and sitting on his bunk. All he could think of was San Antonio and Sancha — that, and the long ride to get there.

Case walked into the bunkhouse and sat down across from him. "Tom Lee, you really planning on heading out right away?"

"Tomorrow morning, what about you?"

"I'm meeting Thomas here in two days, then we'll be heading back to Texas," said Case. "Tom Lee, I don't want to see you make the trip alone, it's too dangerous for one person."

Tom Lee shrugged. "I ain't got no reason to stay here, so I just as well get started."

"How about this. You wait with me for Thomas, and we'll all head back together. He has a couple of his hands with him too. Roly is gonna drive the hoodlum, and we're taking one extra set of mules and a few extra horses. That way we can carry our camp and supplies with us, and it'll be a more comfortable trip. We can shoot a couple of buffs as we go. It's a whole lot safer than one man traveling alone."

Tom Lee thought about the offer for a moment then nodded his head. "Makes sense Case, I'll be ready when you are."

As Case stood up to leave, Boyd walked in. "I just remembered something Case. Something you told me when we signed on to the drive, you remember what I'm talking about?"

Case looked confused. "Not really, what are you talking about?"

"I remember what it was," said Tom Lee. "Exactly who are you and Thomas? You promised to tell us your last name and where you're from."

Case sat back down. "Yeah, I guess I owe you that. But I need to keep it between us — you'll understand why when I explain."

Both men nodded their head.

"We're originally from New Orleans. Our family name is Ashurst. I am Henry Ashurst, and my brother is Anthony. Before the war, we ran a large family cotton company right on the river."

"So, how'd you end up on the frontier hunting buffalo?" asked Boyd.

"Before the Union captured the city in '62 we were one of the largest suppliers of cotton to the south. Thomas and I weren't soldiers, we ran the company. Our father was a major and a fervent supporter of the Confederacy. After the Union took over the city, they put a short, fat general named Baker in charge — everyone called him the Beast. He caused more damage to the city of New Orleans than the war ever did."

"Did he arrest you and your brother for something?" asked Tom Lee.

"No. He just marched in one day and took over our cotton business in the name of the Union Army and ran us off our property. He even took the farm and home for his officers — our mother is buried there. He captured our father, and two other Confederate officers gave them a quick, phony trial and found them guilty of treason against the union. Then they were taken away by three soldiers. Two days later we found them dead along the river bank. They'd been tied up, put on their knees and shot in the back of the head."

"I'm sorry to hear that — and they say the Confederates were murderers," said Boyd. "So, you left for the frontier after that?"

"Thomas and I had nothing left but two horses and the clothes we had on. We planned on leaving but decided to make things right before we left. So, we tracked down the three killers, took them to the river and killed them with a bullet in the head, just like they did to our father and the other two men. If we could have found the general, we would have killed him too. Now we're both wanted outlaws — two men on the run. That's why we both have long hair, long beards, and big hats. That's why we spend as much time away from civilization as we can."

"I can see why you came to the frontier, but why buffalo hunting?" asked Tom Lee.

"The farther away we are from people, the safer it is for us. We hope we'll be forgotten after a couple of years," said Case.

"Well, thank you for that," said Boyd. "I appreciate you telling us, you know we'll keep your secret. But those were acts committed during wartime; I don't think you have much to worry about now."

"Maybe not, but we'll stay out here just the same."

"I got one more question if you don't mind."

"What is it.?

"Did your family run the cotton business with slaves?" asked Boyd.

Case nodded. "We did. Everyone had slaves; it was just part of everyday life in Texas. Our folks were born there and had been in the business for years. Most of our slaves had been with us since we were little kids. We contracted with the farmers for their raw product and processed it at our plant. The farmers couldn't grow the cotton without slaves, and they couldn't get it to our gins without them. When the raw cotton reached us, we needed our slaves to gin it, bale it, and to move it onto the boats. It's very labor intense work. Processed bales can weigh as much as five hundred pounds. As the cotton business got more efficient, the farmers were able to grow more, and we all had to add more slaves."

"What happened to the slaves when the Union took over?"

"The northern states didn't allow slavery, so they were free," said Case. "The Army took over the business thinking they could keep things running as usual. The problem was they had nobody to work the fields or the gins because white civilians wouldn't do that kind of work. So the general made a new rule that said the former slaves were now a different classification of citizen. He said the Union needed the cotton, so for the rest of the war they had to go back to work for the army doing the same thing."

"Don't hardly seem right," said Tom Lee. "All that killing over people owning slaves and the Union Army ain't one bit better than the South."

"That's what turned me and Thomas into buffalo hunters," said Case. "Boyd, if you don't want to work for us after what I just told you, I'll understand."

Boyd looked at him and shook his head. "You can't scare me off. I'd be proud to work for you no matter if you were North or South."

"Tom Lee," asked Case, "What do you think about it?"

"There ain't no North or South anymore, and I plan on forgetting everything I ever heard about it."

Del hung around the Timms ranch for a few days, helping out with the sorting and branding. Every time he thought of going back to town, several of the cowboys working with him took great delight in reminding him of his last trip.

"You headed to town Del? I heard that Big Mae's got something special for you this time!" said one cowboy poking at the branding fire. "I heard that if you bring her all yer money and an extra jug of whiskey, she'll let you have a little peek at the goods this time!"

Del did his best to ignore the comment.

"You gotta be careful with Big Mae," said another cowboy from horseback. "Everbody knows those big 'ol titties of hers can suffocate a man to death in no time flat!"

"I told you I ain't goin' nowhere near that woman again," said Del, stuffing a fresh chaw in his cheek. "Besides, I don't mind a little meat on the bone, but she's way too big for me."

"Well hell, Dell," said the first cowboy, "them fat gals need love too."

"Not from me they don't," said Del, shaking his head.

Del saw Case and Boyd standing next to the wagon with a clean-shaven, white-haired stranger. They motioned for him to come over. When he reached them, the stranger offered his hand to him."

"You must be Del?"

Del shook his hand. "Yessir, Delbert Beale."

"My name is Wesley Tompkins. I'm the U.S. Marshal for the new Wyoming Territory, and I'm looking to hire a couple of deputies to work it with me. Case here tells me that you might be the man for the job. He says you know the country, hate Indians and outlaws and ain't afraid of a fight. Does it sound like something you might be interested in?"

"Well, maybe. But I ain't never carried a badge before, is that a problem?"

"It don't matter none, if you're as honest and fearless as Case and Boyd say you are, then you should do good in the job."

"Then I'm interested Marshal."

"Just call me Wes. I'm glad to hear it Del, that makes three of us so far. I still need one more good man. I'm working out of the Cheyenne Sherriff's office for a while. If you want to meet us there in the morning, we'll talk about the details."

"Then I'll see you in the morning Wes, and thanks," said Del, shaking his hand again. "And thank you Case, I much appreciate the introduction.

"Actually, it was Boyd's doing. He'll be working with most of the local officials and lawmen around here. When he met Wes, he thought about you and took it from there."

"Boyd, I owe you big and if I can do anything for you . . ."

Boyd shook his hand. "Maybe someday, glad I could help. Good luck to you Del."

The second meeting of the new Cattleman's Association gathered at the Timms cabin. Two young women, close in age, maybe twenty-years-old, came to the meeting with their father, Basquiat Dere. As they walked into the cabin, everyone suddenly stood up and removed their hats. "Gentlemen, these are my daughters, Isabel and Flora," said Dere. "They are partners in my operation, and they will be involved in all my ranch business. If for any reason you can't find me, either one will be able to make the necessary decisions."

As Del watched them walk to the table, Basquiat and Isabel passed by, never looking at him. Flora stopped and stared at him from three feet away. "And just who are you?" she said, sounding very official.

Quickly removing his hat, he was surprised at the question. "I'm Boyd Stamps. I'm the pool rider and manager for the new association."

"Really? I didn't know we had a manager yet."

Boyd was clearly flustered with the conversation. He had little experience with women so direct. "Well we do, and it's me — and that's why I'm here."

"So, you're a southerner I take it?" said Flora, looking him up and down.

"I was from the South, but now I'm a cowboy in the Wyoming Territory."

A slim, attractive woman with long brown hair pulled back in a loose ponytail and an oversized cowboy hat, she wore a man's shirt and pants. She had an intensity about her that Boyd had never seen in a woman before. "It's uh . . . very nice to meet you," said Boyd.

"Mister Stamps, we'll talk again," said Flora, as she turned toward the table. "Of that I have no doubt."

The group spent several hours working on the business, and in the end came up with a brand that would represent any cattle belonging to an association member. They would call it the Southeast Four. The new irons would burn an S/4 on all the cattle and horses owned by the association.

The next order of business was hiring cowboys and wranglers. Two of the ranchers had bunkhouses with enough room for all of the men. Each of them hired a cook and Timms and Dere split up the remuda because they each had good barns with a forge.

For the next two weeks work was a frenzy of branding, cutting, sorting and building more pens. The wranglers were kept busy working on the remuda and Boyd spent most of the days in the saddle, learning the open range and chasing down any strays that still needed branding. Twice he saw Indians in the distance but had no trouble. He found several good spots for future line shacks and recorded all the locations of good water.

The association members met at the cabin every Saturday morning to discuss the progress. Basquiat and Flora came every week, but they seldom saw Isabel any more. "She likes to do lady things in the house more than she likes riding horses outdoors," explained Basquiat. "But she still knows the ranching business."

The group had settled into a routine for the regular meetings. They hung their hats on pegs recently set by the door, and each found a favorite spot at the table. Somehow, Flora's regular seat ended up next to Boyd's. He liked the idea of sitting by her, even though she mostly ignored him while she was there.

Chapter 19

Del rode into the Timms ranch shortly after a Saturday association meeting and tied up to the rail. Walking toward the bunkhouse, he reached it just as Boyd was coming out the door. "Hello Del, how's the lawman business working out?"

"Not so bad, I get a bunk, a horse and all my gear 'cept my guns, plus they pay me. Looks like I'll be workin' outta the new office over in Laramie."

"Well, if it don't work out you can always come and work the cows for us," said Boyd with a grin. "I know how much you love cows."

"That ain't never gonna happen — I'd shoot myself first."

"So, what brings you out here if you ain't looking for a job?"

"I wanted to show you this, I thought you should know," said Del, handing him a poster.

It had a bold headline on the top:

$ 250 DOLLAR REWARD $

For the capture of rustler, horse thief and robber:

<u>Sylvester (Sylvie) Parker</u>

Black man, very dark color, 40 years old, 5'- 9", heavyset, beard.

Deliver to **Cheyenne Vigilance Committee**, alive if possible.

Boyd read the poster. Looking at Del he shook his head. "What is this vigilance committee anyway? Are they the law in Cheyenne?"

Del shook his head. "They're a bunch of local men, mostly local ranchers and businessmen. There's a couple from the railroad in it too. They're all tired of the rustlers and thieves workin' in the area. Cheyenne ain't hardly a big town yet, but it's growin' fast and there are only a couple of us marshals in the whole territory. So, the locals decided to do something about it themselves. They raise money privately and use it to hunt down the bad ones. If they can't find 'em, they put on a reward to get others to go after them."

"This sure can't be legal."

Del shrugged. "Welcome to the Territory — this is how it works when there ain't no law around. That's why the government hired Wes as the new territorial marshal and why they're hiring more deputies."

"What'll they do if they catch him?"

"They'll hang him — that's what they do to all of 'em."

"Well, I hate to see that, but he made his own choices," said Boyd. "I guess he'll have to live with the consequences."

"Or die with them," said Del. "Just thought you outta know, in case you run into him somewhere along the line."

"Thanks. I remember Tom Lee telling me how Sylvie saved him when they were down in Brownsville. It's a shame to see him go this way."

"Yeah it is. I was there when that happened, he was a good man back then," said Del. "So is Tom Lee already on his way to Texas?"

"He left about two weeks ago, with Case and Thomas. Roly and several others were with them. I guess he's gonna run Case and Thomas's business in San Antonio. He was pretty excited to get going, all he can talk about is getting married to Sancha. He was ready to go alone until Case talked him out of it."

"Them women can get a guy all twisted up inside, that's for sure. What about you Boyd? I caught a bit of a rumor that you're keepin' time with that fancy lookin' rancher's daughter? Any truth to that?"

Boyd's face flushed quickly, and he nodded his head without speaking. "We're only friends. I don't think she'd really want to be with someone like me. She's busy running her father's ranch anyway."

"Your gonna have to stop thinkin' like that Boyd. Like I told you before, if you want her for a bed warmer, you're gonna have to go after her — 'cause them women like to be chased a bit before givin' in. But a pretty thing like that ain't gonna wait around forever. Besides, some of those high-falutin' women are just teasers. If you don't get a good hold on 'em quick, they'll keep you around until they get bored and find some other man."

"Yeah, yeah," said Boyd. "I know what you're saying, it just ain't all that easy, okay?"

"Well, good luck with that. All I'm sayin' is that there's way more men out here than there are women, 'specially pretty ones like her."

"You can go back to work now Del, I'm sure there's a rustler somewhere you need to catch," said Boyd.

"Well if you do get that little gal, let me know. I want an invite to the wedding," said Del, untying his horse.

"Del, do you think we should inform the sheriff in San Antonio about Sylvie?"

"Wes already sent him a telegram. He's gonna keep an eye out for Tom Lee and Case and let them know what's goin' on when they get back."

Dean tied off his horse and walked into the telegraph office. Anny Werner had her back to the counter when he walked in. Turning around, her face lit up. "Mister Timms, how nice of you come by, I hope your business is well?"

"It's good, thank you. But please, it's just Dean."

"Of course."

"I was concerned that you may have thought I was ignoring you or forgotten our past conversation. I hope you are still interested in what we spoke of before?"

"I wasn't concerned Dean. I knew how busy you must have been, I'm glad you were able to find time to come to town. Forgive me if this is too forward, but would you consider having supper at my home some time? I'm a very good cook."

Dean nodded. "You're not forward at all. I would like that, but it could set a few people to gossiping around town."

"If you don't mind the gossip, neither do I."

"Then just tell me when and where," said Dean, nervously twirling his hat, "and I'll be there."

"Tonight would be good if that's okay. Do you know Murray's boarding house?"

"Yes, I've been there before."

"In back of the building there is a small cottage, I rent it by the month. It is much quieter than the big house, and I can cook for myself and read without being disturbed," said Anny. "Can you be there at seven o'clock?"

"I will be there at seven tonight, thank you."

"Wonderful. Do you like fried chicken by the way?"

"I do, but I don't get it all that often out here. Mostly just deer and elk or beef. Sometimes we have buffalo."

"I keep several hens for fresh eggs. One of them will make us a good meal tonight."

Dean nodded and put his hat back on. "That sounds wonderful, I will see you tonight."

Brushing off his hat, Dean Timms looked at his reflection in the window glass. He hoped he was presentable to a proper lady like Anny. The ride to town went quickly, and he found himself standing at her door with his hat in hand. Gathering up his courage he knocked on the door and waited nervously.

The door swung open, and Anny invited him in. "Right on time Dean, the meal will be done soon. Can I take your hat?"

He handed it to her. "I'm sorry, I should have left my spurs off, I don't want to scratch anything."

"No, no, it's fine, come and have a seat and we can talk while supper is cooking. Would you like coffee?"

"Yes, thank you, that would be nice," said Dean, looking around the small cottage. "You have a lot of books."

"I love reading," said Anny. "I hope to write my own book one day."

"What would you write your book about?"

"Adventure in the frontier, you know, the country of the West, cowboys and Indians and buffalo, that kind of thing. I think people back east would like to read about it."

"I guess they might. I was never much of a reader myself. I just wanted to be outside and ride horses. That's pretty much what I do on the ranch now."

After finishing the meal, they talked about Dean's past growing up in Texas. "Did you have slaves on your Texas ranch?" asked Anny.

Dean nodded. "All the cattle work was done by white and Mexican men. My father had two black women in the house for cooking and cleaning. They were sisters that he bought many years before, right after our mother died."

"And what happened to them when the war ended?"

"Father had already given them their papers when the war first started. He didn't want them to be hurt if something happened to him. These two sisters, Rosa and Jenny, raised me and my brothers; our father was gone a lot. They stayed with us after the war doing the same thing as free blacks by choice."

"Are they still on the ranch?" asked Anny, pouring each of them a second cup of coffee.

"Rosa died about a month after the surrender and Jenn died shortly after that," said Dean. "They were part of our family, a really important part. How about you Anny? Where are you from?"

"Are you sure you have enough time Dean? This could take a few minutes."

"If you have the coffee, I have the time."

"Okay then. I was born in the state of Vermont. We never had slavery there, that's why I'm curious about it. My father had a farm outside of a town named Bradford. It's a very small place, and most people have never heard of it."

"I know of Vermont from the books in school," said Dean, "but I've never been there before."

"It's a beautiful area, but not a great place for someone curious about the world."

"So how did you come to be in Cheyenne?" asked Dean. "Anny — I hope I'm not being too nosy."

"Of course not. It's good for us to get to know each other. I married a union soldier that was part of a group getting ready to join the war. We were together about a year when he left. He was severely wounded in a place called Balls Bluff. He lost his left leg above the knee and several fingers on his left hand."

"I'm sorry. It must have been awful for both of you. Was he able to work again?"

Anny shook her head. "He never worked again. He was a different person when he returned. He was a skilled wheelwright before the war, when he came back, he never touched a tool again. About a month after he returned, he went out to his shop and shot himself."

"Anny, I'm so sorry, I didn't mean to bring out all those bad memories."

"It's nothing to be concerned about. I made my peace with it a long time ago. I needed a job, so when I saw a poster that said Western Union was looking for telegraphers, I applied."

"Was it hard to learn the code?" asked Dean.

"No, it's fairly simple. They didn't want a woman for the job, but since they weren't getting enough applicants, they took me."

"So, they sent you out here?" asked Dean.

"Not at first, but I kept asking about transferring out West. I knew that the closer the new transcontinental railroad got to completion, the more telegraph operators they would need. It seemed obvious to me that all the opportunity lay in the West. I think they finally got tired of me asking, so they sent me to the end of the line to get rid of me. They actually did me a huge favor by sending me out here."

"I have to say, I never heard of a single woman who would choose to come all the way to a wild place like the this for a job like that," said Dean. "You are a high-spirited lady for sure."

"That's the thing Dean, I didn't really come here for a job, I came here for an adventure. I came here for a new life, and this was the only way I could see to get here."

Timms wasn't sure how to take this unusual woman from Vermont, but he was sure that he wanted to get to know her better. "Anny, do you like horses?"

"Yes I do, but I'm not a real experienced rider. The horses where I grew up were mostly work animals."

"Would you like to go riding with me someday?"

"I would like that very much, when would you like to do it?"

"We can plan on the day after tomorrow. That's Sunday, if it doesn't interfere with your church services."

"I have no church Dean, do you?"

"No M'am never had one. I'll be here early with a horse for you. I would like to start by showing you our operation and a few pretty spots I know of."

"I'll be ready when you get here."

"Oh, I just remembered something, I don't have a lady's saddle, but I'll try and find one before I get here."

"That's not necessary Dean. I've never used one before, no need in starting now."

Dean walked to the door and picked up his hat. "Then I will see you two days."

Anny leaned forward and kissed him on the cheek. "Thank you, Dean, I'm looking forward to our day together."

Chapter 20

Boyd rode slowly through the trees, coming out at the clearing where the fresh-cut logs were piled for the new line shack. Two of Timms' men were busy peeling the bark off a log and preparing to put it up on the back wall. Some of the cattle were scattered out across the fading grass and standing in the creek, others were strung out through the trees.

It was obvious that there weren't many warm days left, most of the aspens had already dropped their leaves, and the creek was frosted over in the morning. "Looking good," said Boyd. "We got a new stove coming, should be here in a day or two. You got plenty of logs to finish with?"

The cowboy, an older hand named Jess, nodded. "We're in good shape Boss. More than enough for the cabin and the pens and there's plenty left over for firewood too."

"Looks big enough to keep a few cowboys warm on the bad days," said Boyd. "Let me know when you're ready to stock it and bring out the extra horses."

As he rode along the creek, he crossed the tracks of two unshod horses less than a mile from the new cabin. He rode back to the site to tell the men what he saw. "Yeah," said Jess, "We seen a pair of braves twice already, look like Arapahos to me."

"Just wanted to be sure that you're wearing your pistols."

"No problem, our rifles are close by too."

Boyd nodded. "Just keep a good watch, they can't be trusted. If they're hanging around here, you're likely to find a few dead cows."

"We'll keep a steady watch Boss."

"Good enough. I'm heading back to the ranch. Let me know if you need anything." Riding through the sage, the wind picked up, and he pulled his hat down tighter. He liked the sting of the cooler days, but knew that winter was close and there was a lot of work to do before the snow hit.

Dean Timms ran a good outfit and proved to be as good a boss as his father was. This was the second line shack built since the herd was delivered to the ranch. All the hands had been hired, the barn was finished, and the necessary feed and supplies had been stocked. Boyd still needed to set up an accounting system for the new association, find and brand the last of the calves, and build a few more pens connected to the barn.

Throwing a few sticks of wood in the bunkhouse stove, Boyd hung up his hat and coat, pulled off his boots and lay back in the bunk. An hour later, one of the cowboys shook him awake. "Boss, there's someone here to see you."

Sitting up he looked around and saw Flora standing at the foot of the bunk. "Boyd, I need to talk to you, wake up."

"Flora, what are you doing? A woman in the bunkhouse is bad luck, I told you that before."

"Oh twiddle, there ain't a cowboy in here that don't like looking at me — and I told you that before too."

"Okay, what's so important that you have to come in here?"

"I want to go riding is what. Let's go."

"Flora, I've been in the saddle all day, I need to rest a while."

"Come on, let's get going," said Flora, ignoring his protests and tugging on his sleeve.

Boyd pulled his boots and coat back on without saying anything. Putting his hat on, he walked outside with her.

One of the cowboys lying back in his bunk laughed at the idea of this petite little woman ordering the Boyd around. "She is a pretty one, but I don't believe I'd let her talk to me like that!"

"I guess she must do something special for him, otherwise he wouldn't be acting that way," said another cowboy, laughing at what they just witnessed.

The first cowboy shook his head. "Nah, he's just blind in love is all, he don't know what's in store for him down the line."

"Yeah, I guess we all gotta learn sometime."

The freshly painted sign over the door said *U. S. Marshal*. Wedged between a new dry goods store and a string of canvas tents, it was one of only a few clapboard buildings on the main street of Laramie. Wes and Del walked into the office and looked around. At twenty feet wide by thirty feet long, it had a single window next to the door, covered with bars and a well-worn desk, two chairs and a small table. A stove was in the middle of the room with a fresh supply of firewood stocked in a large box next to it.

"Looks like they got everything finished," said Wes." What do you think?"

"Looks good Boss, it's even got a brand-new stove — I like that." Behind the desk was a cot covered with a mattress and an oversized Indian blanket. The stark looking room still smelled of fresh-sawn lumber. Walking over to the stove, he started a fire, threw in a few sticks of wood then sat down behind the desk. "This'll work just fine," he said, "just fine."

In the back corner was a ten-foot square cage built with flat, iron bars running vertically and horizontally up the sides and across the top. "A job, a bed, and meals," he said, "no more big stinken' animals for me anymore."

"The keys to the cell are in the drawer," said Wes, "along with a few other supplies you might need."

"I think I'll start by hanging up this poster of Sylvie Parker next to the door," said Del. "As I get more, I'll hang them up too."

"Del, you know that you're the only law around here right now. They're working on finding a town sheriff, but until then I expect you will be handling some local disputes as well as chasing rustlers and thieves. The new circuit judge for the territory comes by every other Friday," said Wes. "The telegraph office will bring over any telegrams for you immediately and the cafe across the street will feed you and any prisoner you might be holding. Use the livery at the end of the street for the horses. Any questions before I head back to Cheyenne?"

"Shouldn't be too much trouble in a small town like this."

"For now anyway," said Wes. "When they finish connecting up the railroads, that'll change forever." Wes walked out the door and untied his horse. "Just wire me if you have any questions or problems."

Walking back inside, he sat down behind the desk, pushed back the chair and put his feet on the desk. Opening the drawer, he found pens, pencils and paper and several forms that would be needed for business with the café and the livery. He also pulled out a book of laws and instructions that explained his duties. His first job would be to find someone, maybe one of the women teaching in the new school to help with the paperwork since he had failed to tell Wes that he never learned to read or write.

Case and Thomas called a halt for the day along a tiny trickle of a creek. Roly backed the wagon up against a line of bushes to help break the wind. The trip back to San Antonio had proven to be long and tiring. An incident with the Comanches a day south of Adobe Walls cost them one mule, but otherwise there were few conflicts. The weather turned out to be the worst part of the trip south. It had rained or snowed nearly every day, and the wind had blown relentlessly since they left.

"Shoot Tom Lee," said Roly, cracking the whip across the mules. "I ain't been warm since we left Cheyenne, how about you? You doing okay?"

Tom Lee nodded. "I'm okay."

"Thinking about that little gal all day long keeps you warm does it?"

Tom Lee didn't answer, but he was right, Sancha was what kept him going. "Roly, what is it you're gonna do when you get back to San Antonio?"

"I ain't sure yet. Case asked me if I wanted to stay on and work for him and Thomas. I told him I would think about it. Just one bad thing about it though . . ."

"What would that be?" asked Tom Lee.

"I might have to work for you!" said Roly, laughing out loud. "Heck boy — I don't think I could tolerate you all that much!"

"Well shoot old man," said Tom Lee with a straight face, "if I'm gonna be your boss then maybe I'll just fire your sorry old butt right now and save us both a lot of trouble later."

"You'd never do that boy; you need me to help get you right with the Lord!"

"That's just one more reason to get rid of you right now!" said Tom Lee, lying back on the pile of wagon canvas. "I think you oughta be treating me a little better old man. You can start by not hitting so many holes. I'd like to get a little sleep back here."

Roly snapped his whip and moved the team to the right, aiming for the biggest rut he could find. "Sure Boss, whatever you say."

Holding on to the side-rail with one hand, Tom Lee grabbed for the seat with the other one just as the wagon crossed the rut nearly bouncing him off the wagon. "How's that Boss? Better?"

"Maybe you're right," said Tom Lee. "Maybe I should start praying all right — for a new teamster!"

After the sun dropped out of sight, a slight, dull flicker of light could be seen far to the south. "What you thinking Case," asked Roly, "is that San Antonio down there?"

"Yeah, that's home for sure. Maybe ten miles or so, an easy trip tomorrow." The men huddled around the fire and finished a meal of antelope stew and beans. The wind stirred the campfire and swirled the ashes around the cowboys. "Well, I'll be the first one to say it, I'm tired of the rain and the snow and the goddamn cold, hard ground," said Case, taking a deep drag on his cigarette.

"Brother," said Thomas, trying to roll his own smoke. "You ain't getting old and feeble on me are you?"

Case shook his head. "I ain't old or feeble, but I'd surely like to separate my ass from that saddle for a while and sleep in a soft bed by a warm stove."

"Tomorrow brother. We'll have it all tomorrow."

"That's good — me and my piles appreciate it."

"Don't get too used to it though," said Thomas, finally getting his cigarette lit. "We gotta get ready for the buffs, and we're already running late this year."

Chapter 21

Riding into town, they followed the muddy main road to the livery. Swinging open the gate to the big pen, the men ran the wagons and all the stock inside. After giving instructions to the wrangler, everyone walked through the barn and into the blacksmith shop, the warmest place in the building.

Case pulled out a fresh bottle of whiskey, took a long pull and handed it off to the next man. "I just want to thank everyone for sticking with us on the drive. We're gonna take a few days then start getting ready for the winter buff season. We're planning on shortening up the trip this year, probably from November first to March first depending on the quality of hides we're seeing. Also, Tom Lee has agreed to work for us as the company's business manager and will be based here in San Antonio. He will take care of all the day to day operations for the hide company and the livery. When we're gone, he runs everything."

"That's if you can keep him away from his little sweetheart long enough to get any work done," said Roly, poking at him with his elbow.

Tom Lee flushed at the comment. "Old man, you need to worry less about me and more about yourself. You get any fatter, and you're gonna need to bring some extra mules along just to haul you around!" The cowboys all had a good laugh at that, including Roly.

Tom Lee walked into the same barber shop he used after the buffalo season. "How's those lice doin'?" asked the old man, sweeping the floor around the chair.

"You got a good memory sir. The vinegar seemed to work for the lice problem, unless you find some new ones today."

"Well, have a seat, and we'll see what's there. You want me to take off all the hair and whiskers like last time?"

Tom Lee nodded. "That would be fine."

Within minutes the summer's hair and beard was scattered around the chair. "Want a shave too?"

"Yes, please."

"If I remember correctly, you had a pretty girl waiting, that still the case?" said the barber, lathering him up."

"Yessir, it is. Did you find any lice?"

"Nope, just one ol' dead tick is all, and it don't look like he done any damage."

Tom Lee handed him the money and thanked him. Stepping outside he headed for the Chinese laundry and a hot bath. After the bath, he put on his freshly brushed clothes and hat. He had one last stop to make before he got to Sancha's house.

Standing nervously at the front door with his hat and a package of candy in one hand, he knocked on the door. Not getting an answer, he tried again.

"Señor, no one is there right now."

Tom Lee turned to see a middle-aged woman walking up behind him. "Who are you Señora?"

"I am Maria Rodríguez, a friend of the family. Louisa passed away three days ago. I think Sancha is at the cemetery right now, that is why I have flowers with me. Would you like to walk there with me?"

Tom Lee nodded, and they started to walk to the church. "Señora how is Sancha? I have been gone and didn't know about Louisa's passing."

"I think she is well. She spoke of missing her promised one, would that be you?"

"It is. I have been working cattle up north and we just got home. Do you know what caused her death?"

"Sancha said she just didn't wake up. They had a wonderful velorio yesterday. Many friends and church members came to the house and paid their respects. Today is the service and burial. I know you will be a great comfort to Sancha right now."

Several dozen people were seated in the front of the small adobe chapel. Sancha hugged the priest and turned to be seated. Spotting Tom Lee, she ran to him and into his arms. They hugged for a long time, and she kissed him again and again, sobbing and shaking. She led him to a seat and motioned for the priest to begin.

Still sobbing, she put her head on his shoulder. "I was scared you were never coming back, and then I would be all alone."

"I will never leave you alone again, I promise. I have taken a job that will allow us to be married and live in San Antonio."

Sancha buried her head deeper into his shoulder. "I love you Tom Lee. I will make you a good wife and give you good babies, just never leave me." The priest finished the service and walked over to Sancha. "Father Garza, this is Tom Lee, we are going to be married." Sancha told him that they would need his services again for their wedding.

"When would you like to marry?" asked the priest.

She looked up at Tom Lee then back at the priest. "Next Sunday father, we would like to be married next Sunday."

"If that is okay with your young man, then we can do it Sunday," said the priest.

Tom Lee stood still holding his hat and the package of candy he'd forgotten about. "Yes sir, it is good with me."

"Very good, now let's go to the cemetery and finish the service."

After the final words were spoken, family and friends filed past the grave and sprinkled a handful of dirt onto the coffin.

"She was everything to me," said Sancha, as they sat alone in the chapel. "After Sylvie rescued me, he brought me to Louisa to care for me, I was about three or four then. She had no children, and her husband had died several months earlier. She agreed to take me in and raise me as her own."

"How often did you see Sylvie after that?" asked Tom Lee.

"Not more than once every year or two, he always brought each of us a small gift and some money for Louisa."

"Do you remember the time when you were rescued?"

"No, but Sylvie told me that he came on a campsite with two burned wagons and everyone had been killed by Indians. He found me hidden in a canvas under a wagon wheel. I had this cut on my face," said Sancha, touching the scar. "I don't know what caused the cut, but he covered it and rode with me in his arms back to San Antonio. That is why I am so afraid when I am left alone."

"You no longer have to concern yourself with that. I will take care of you. In a few days I will start my new job. We will be married Sunday as you told the father."

"Tom Lee, I am sorry for talking so quickly about the marriage, I should have spoken with you first."

"There is nothing to be sorry for, I am happy you did it. What will you do until Sunday?"

"I will speak to the father again. The members of the church will make the arrangements. Several friends have also offered to help. Where will you stay until then?"

"I now work for the Thomas and Case Hide and Fur Company. They also own the San Antonio de Bexar Livery, on the east end of town. That will be the headquarters for the company and where I will have my office. I can stay there until the wedding."

Sancha began to cry softly, and Tom Lee pulled her close, stroking her hair and kissing her again and again. They held each other for a long time, not wanting to let go of the moment.

Tom Lee walked around the small space that Case had been using as an office. Two water barrels with planks across the top had served as an office desk for the Case & Thomas Company. All the records and paperwork were kept in cardboard folders stored in several wooden boxes stacked behind the desk.

"What do you think Tom Lee?" asked Case. "Can you make this place into a real business office?"

The room was in a corner of an ancient timber frame barn that had been expanded over time to include more stalls and a blacksmith forge. "The room is big enough, but we need a proper desk and a good safe for a start," said Tom Lee, walking around the space. "It's also cold. We need to finish the inside walls and get a good stove. A few shelves for supplies would be good too."

Case nodded as he talked. "I already have a good safe; I just need to move it here. I'll find a good desk or have one made when we build the shelves."

"Then I think this room will work well," said Tom Lee. "Case, I will need to keep a bunk here for a few days if that is okay with you. I will be getting married on Sunday. I would like you and Thomas to come if you can."

"Well congratulations Tom Lee, I'm glad it worked out for you and your girl. Thomas and I will be there, and I'm sure Roly would like to come too."

"Thank you, I would like very much for you to meet my new wife. For now, I will start sorting through the old paperwork and get things in order here. When will you head out for buff season?"

"Thomas is leaving Monday to connect with the Army up north. We need to be loaded and rolling about ten days later," said Case. "Tomorrow you and me and Thomas will go to the bank and set up the accounts and get your name on the business."

"Case, I can't tell you how much I appreciate your trust in me, but I've never had a job like this before."

"Neither have we. We're not bookkeepers, we're hunters, our life is on the prairie. We decided that if this business was going to be successful, we needed someone that could run the everyday business of the hide company and the livery while we were gone. You were the first choice for both of us."

Tom Lee offered his hand. "I'm proud to be part of your company, Case, and I won't let you down."

"I know you won't," said Case, shaking his hand firmly. "Tomorrow it will be part your company too. Me and Thomas will pay you ninety-dollars a month and give you ten-percent ownership of the company. That way you will share in the profits at the end of each year. One more thing, David Timms brought this telegram by the livery, it's for you."

"A telegram? I wasn't aware that anyone even knew I was here." Opening it up, he read it to Case. "It's from the U.S. Marshal in Cheyenne. It says that Sylvie is a wanted man in the Wyoming Territory, there's a reward on his head too."

"Well, I can't say I'm surprised," said Case. "What's he wanted for?"

"Stealing horses, rustling, and robbing miners," said Tom Lee.

"Pretty much everything but murder. How much is the reward?

"It says the Cheyenne Vigilance Committee will pay two-hundred and fifty dollars."

"I'll be sure and keep that in mind if I run into him out there," said Case. "I could use the money."

Tom Lee woke up Sunday morning to someone pounding on the office door. "Wake up boy," said Roly at the top of his voice. "Today's the day . . . I can't hardly believe it, but that pretty little girl's actually gonna marry you!"

"Yeah, okay, let me get my trousers on!"

"Just as well leave them off," said Roly, laughing at his own joke. "Your just gonna be taking 'em off again anyway!" Tom Lee opened the door and Roly quickly pushed his way in. "Wake up boy — I got a present for you."

"Fatman, what are you talking about a present? What are you doing here? The sun ain't even up yet."

"Boy, stand up and shut up before I sit on you. This here is a guayabera, a Mexican wedding shirt — put it on."

"Oh bull, I ain't never seen no shirt like that before."

"That's 'cause you ain't never been to a Mexican wedding before!"

Looking over the shirt, he was surprised how well-made it was and how well it fit. "I ain't never been to any wedding before — so you better not be poking fun old man."

"Boy, you worry too much, this is the right shirt, I got it from a Mexican friend of mine as a wedding present for you."

"Well, okay then, I guess, thank you for the shirt."

"If you ain't never been to any wedding before," said Roly, "then I got a lot to teach you boy. You stick with the old Fatman, and I'll show you everything you need to know about weddings and women."

"Well, thank you for the shirt and all, but I don't need anything else from you. Now get outta here and leave me be."

"Okay boy, but if you have any questions about the mysteries of a woman . . ."

"Go away!"

"Okay, I'm going, but I will be saying a prayer for you at the wedding, don't try and stop me neither!"

"If I let you say a prayer will you go away?"

"I'll see you at the church," said Roly, as he walked through the door.

Tom Lee was surprised to see so many people at the church. He didn't realize Sancha and Louisa had so many friends. Walking up to Father Garza, he nervously put his hand out. "Buenos Días, Padre."

"Buenos Días, young man, are you ready to take a bride today?"

"Yessir, I am," said Tom Lee. "She is all I have been able to think of since I first met her — we are both ready."

The priest motioned him into to his small office at the back of the chapel. "Come sit with me for a few minutes so we can visit."

Following the priest into the room, Tom Lee sat down across from him. "Young man, how much do you know about Sancha?"

"I know what Louisa told me about how she came to be in her house. I know what Sancha told me about her time with Louisa."

"That is all good, but I just wanted to tell you a little about Sancha herself. I have known her since she first came to be with Louisa, and I baptized her shortly after that. She is perhaps the smartest young woman I have ever known. She could read and write in English and Spanish by the time she was ten years-old and understands numbers much better than anyone I know."

Tom Lee nodded. "Louisa told me some things about how quickly she learned."

"She is very quick to learn, but she can be impatient with people and her words are often very sharp. She has little time for those that that don't quickly understand things."

"I have seen little of that so far, Padre, but thank you for the talk."

"I say this to help you better understand her, but I also want you to know that many men in this town have tried to get close to her. Not all of them were good men. I tell you this to make you aware that there are those that might attempt to harm her or you."

"Again, thank you for telling me that, but I will be able to care for my wife without any problems."

The priest nodded. "It was just something I felt I had to say, I hope you understand."

"I understand Padre. When will we begin the service?"

"The guests will begin to arrive in about an hour. When they are all seated, we can get started. One more thing, are you a religious man?"

"No sir, I have no religion. I never had any growing up and know little of it."

The priest nodded and leaned close to him, "I ask because it is customary when marrying a Catholic girl in a Catholic church, that you and your children will become members of the church also."

"Father, since I know nothing of the church, I will have to speak with Sancha first," said Tom Lee. "I will let her make the decisions in this matter."

"Very well, but I will expect an answer very soon. You should prepare for the wedding now."

Roly stood out front of the chapel next to Tom Lee. The morning had been cold and cloudy, with light rain all morning. "Look there boy," said Roly, pointing to a break in the clouds showing some blue sky. "That's a sign boy, the Lord is pleased — he's giving you his blessing!"

"Really? What would he say if it continued to rain — that he wasn't happy with me?"

Roly shrugged. "If it kept raining, the Lord would say he was washing away all your sins."

"Who said I had any sins to wash away?"

"We all have sins boy, and only the good Lord himself can forgive you for them."

"Says you anyway."

The priest motioned for him to come to the altar. Spotting Case, Thomas, Roly, and David Timms in the crowd helped calm him down. When the crowd got quiet, he saw Sancha at the back of the chapel in a long, beautiful white dress, the nerves came rushing back, and his hands began to shake. She was being accompanied to the altar by the assistant priest. He felt himself get warm and badly in need of a drink of water.

Staring into the eyes of the most beautiful girl he'd ever seen was all he could think about as they stood in front of the priest. When the priest was speaking, he had to touch Tom Lee on the arm to get him to respond. The next thing he remembered was Sancha kissing him and Roly giving them a blessing.

After the service, the newlywed couple greeted the guests and his friends and thanked the priest.

"I wasn't sure you were going to make it through the service, Tom Lee," said Father Garza, taking a sip of wine. "You were looking very nervous up there, particularly during the lasso ceremony."

"Lasso?" said Tom Lee, "What is a lasso ceremony?"

Sancha, standing with her arm in Tom Lee's, kissed him on the cheek. "I will tell you all about it tonight. For now, let's have some food and thank all of our guests."

A church friend delivered them to the house in his carriage. Walking inside, they were surprised to see decorations and gifts on the table. "I did not know they were going to do this, this is so wonderful," said Sancha, looking at the small collection of gifts.

Embracing Tom Lee, she kissed him passionately. "I love you, thank you for coming back for me, you make my life wonderful."

They stood locked together for several minutes. "I could not be more happy than I am right now," said Tom Lee. "I never want things to change."

Sancha walked into the bedroom, stopping at the door and looking back at him. "If you will wait a few minutes, I will get ready for you."

A few minutes would be fine, thought Tom Lee. He had never been with a woman and wasn't really sure what to do next.

Sancha called for him to come into the bedroom, and the only thought that came to him was that he should take off his boots. Pulling them off, he walked to the door and looked inside. Sancha stood by the edge of the bed with her long, beautiful black hair flowing down over her shoulders.

She wore a long, white nightdress, her slim figure silhouetted against the lantern light. Tom Lee was frozen in his tracks. He had never seen anything so beautiful in his life. "Husband, do you not want to be with me?" asked Sancha.

After a minute of staring at her, he found his words again and nodded. "Yes, wife, there is nothing I have ever wanted more than to be with you right at this moment."

Sancha walked over and took his hand. "Come husband, we will get into bed together."

"Sancha, I love you, but I need to tell you that I have never been with a woman before."

"Tom Lee," I love you too, but I have never been with a man before — come to bed, and we will learn together."

In the morning they woke up and embraced each other and made love again. "Husband, it is time to get started, I will make us something to eat while you get dressed."

Tom Lee swung his legs over the bed and stood up. "What do you mean time to get started? What exactly are we starting?"

"Our life of course, we are starting our life together."

Tom Lee thought about this for a moment. "So what is the first thing we do — after we eat, that is?"

"I will want to go to your work to see what it is that you do all day long."

"Okay," said Tom Lee. "But I don't have to go to work until tomorrow. Maybe we should stay here and organize things."

"Things are very well organized already. We will go into town to your work and then to the dry goods for cloth. Come and eat so we can get started."

Case, Roly, and the buffalo hunters were mounted up and ready to head out for the winter hunt. Tom Lee and Case discussed some last-minute business and shook hands.

Tom Lee climbed up on the wagon to shake hands with Roly. "Well Fatman, don't let any of those Comanches stick any more arrows in you, I won't be there to pull them out."

"Don't you worry boy, the good Lord is riding with me!"

Swinging open the gate, Tom Lee watched them ride out. "Husband, do you wish you were going too?" asked Sancha.

"Wife, I have only one wish, and that is to be with you."

"Then we have started our life well."

Chapter 22

Boyd pulled off his coat and hat and walked straight to the stove in the middle of the bunkhouse. Sitting down alongside it, he pulled off his boots and slid them close to the heat. Lancy, an old

Texas hand, moved his chair next to him. "Shit Boss, just what in heck you doing out there on a day like this anyway?"

"Chopping the ice off of the horse troughs," said Boyd, clearly not happy about something.

"Well shit, I shoulda thought to do that."

Boyd nodded and continued to rub his hands together. "Yeah, you should have! Everyone here listen up! One of you will take a turn at chopping the ice off the water troughs every hour! You can work out what order you go, but you will damn sure get it done or tomorrow you can all hit the trail — anyone here don't understand that?" All the cowboys understood what he was saying, and they also understood that when he was unhappy, they knew they had better listen.

When Boyd left the bunkhouse, one of the Wyoming cowboys moved his chair by the stove. "The boss has sure been grouchy lately."

"He may be pissed about the ice," said another one from his bunk, "but I think it's that fancy rancher girl that's got his number. Any way you look at it, we better not let it get froze over again."

The first real blizzard of the winter had dumped nearly 18 inches of snow and dropped the temperature to zero for several days in a row. Both line shacks had cowboys laid up in them for the duration of the storm. As soon as the weather broke, all hands would be out looking for cattle. They could only hope the loss wouldn't be too great.

The Saturday stock association meeting had been cancelled last week because of the snow. Today the weather had let up enough for everyone to get to the ranch. Filing into the house, everyone peeled off their heavy clothes and hung up their hats. The stove had been freshly stoked, and the coffee was already brewing.

"Anyone want a nip of whiskey in their coffee this morning?" asked Dean. "It'll help warm you up."

Everyone automatically held out their cups, including Boyd and Flora. Pouring each of them a good shot, he also poured one for the newcomer to the group. "Everybody," said Dean, "This is my friend Anny Werner. She is the telegrapher in Cheyenne, and her little house was too cold for this weather, so she is staying here until it warms up."

Everyone said hello and sipped at their coffee. Anny looked over the faces at the table. "I recognize some of you. You have been in the office before."

"Good to see you again Miss Werner," said Flora Dere. "I remember meeting you, it's so seldom we see a woman in that kind of job. Do you enjoy the work?"

"I do, but it's not all that challenging. The transcontinental railroad will be finished soon, and there will be more opportunities coming available. My hope is to be a writer someday, but this will keep me going for now."

"Just what is it that you plan on writing about?" asked Flora. "Aren't most successful writers men?"

"I plan on writing about the people of the western frontier and the mountains and animals," said Anny. "And yes, I guess most successful writers are men, but that does not mean a woman couldn't do it."

"Anny already has a good start," said Dean. "She is working with the logbook that Tom Lee kept while moving the cattle up here. I do think people in the East will enjoy reading about life on a cattle drive."

"Well," said Flora, "I certainly don't see anything about the cattle business that would make an interesting book. Are we finally ready for association business?"

When the group concluded its work, Dean and Anny walked them to the door. When the last person was gone, Anny hugged Dean. "Thank you for including me in the meeting, it was nice to meet your business associates and friends."

"Mostly just business partners, we don't have much social contact," said Dean. "Did you like them?"

"Well, all but one."

Dean looked surprised. "If you don't mind my asking, who was it that you didn't like?"

"We said we would always be honest with each other. The truth is, I don't like Flora one little bit."

"She seemed very friendly to you."

"She was just checking me out. She wanted to see if maybe I was going to be some kind of competition for her position in the group."

Dean shrugged. "I guess I don't notice things like that."

"It's not uncommon. I know a lot of women like that. I think your man Boyd will have his hands full trying to tame that one."

"Well, that's his business — I hope things work out for him."

Anny slid her arm into his. "Dean, I just want you to know, I'm very happy that we have become so close, are you?"

Dean wrapped his arms around her and pulled her close, kissing her on the lips for the first time. "Anny, this is the happiest I have ever been. I love you, and I want you to be my wife and share our lives together."

"I love you too Dean. I will marry you and we will have a wonderful life on this beautiful ranch. We can raise kids and cattle and horses, and I can write all about it."

Acknowledgements

Like always, I owe so many people a huge thanks for their work as test readers. They help me keep things straight when I wander off into places I shouldn't go. They keep me out of trouble by pointing out things like when you give a character a name in the second chapter, he should still have the same name in the 15th chapter – who knew! I still have to remember that corporals do not call sergeants "sir". I hope I don't forget anyone here, but if I did, feel free to call and yell at me!

Bob Baker: Longtime friend and reader, always ready to take on my latest project no matter how good or bad it might be and give me great feedback.

Wes Marshall: My old high school classmate from Rochelle, Illinois that I caught up with at our last reunion. A wonderfully detailed reader with a great eye for fine details.

Gary and Lynetta Haynes: My husband and wife dynamic duo who are each able to catch different details from their different perspectives.

Greg Wood: My four-wheeling buddy and always ready to take on my projects no matter how many times it takes me to get it right.

Steve Butler: My fishing buddy and reader of the West, see you on the steelhead river this spring!

Phil Singleton: My old classmate, reader and supporter of all my work, we need to get together one of these days – dinner is on me!

Bruce Flourquist: Friend and supporter and a great help on things about the mountains and plains. We also need to get together one of these days, I'm sure I owe you at least a couple of dinners by now.

Sheldon Jones: Friend, neighbor and writer that is always willing to find time to read my work, you always have thoughtful feedback.

Tim O'Byrne: My friend and editor of Working Ranch Magazine, for more years than I can remember and expert on all things cowboy and cow related – thank you for all your support!

Liane Laroque: My editor who is constantly keeping me on the right track no matter how bad I try to crash and burn.

Blackmulepress.com